LEX and LU

J. SANTIAGO

RIVER GROVE
BOOKS

Published by River Grove Books
Austin, TX
www.rivergrovebooks.com

Distributed by River Grove Books

For ordering information or special discounts for bulk purchases, please contact River Grove Books at PO Box 91869, Austin, TX 78709, 512.891.6100.

Design and composition by Greenleaf Book Group
Cover design by Greenleaf Book Group
Cover credit: ©iStockphoto.com/Courtney Keating

Cataloging-in-Publication data
Santiago, J. (Jennifer)
  Lex and Lu / J. Santiago.—First edition.
    pages ; cm
  Issued also as an ebook.
  1. First loves—Fiction. 2. Man-woman relationships—Fiction. 3. Intellectuals—Fiction. 4. Soccer players—Fiction. 5. Betrayal—Fiction. 6. Love stories. I. Title.

PS3619.A675 L49 2014
813/.6   2014941291

Print ISBN: 978-1-938416-88-0
eBook ISBN: 978-1-938416-89-7

First Edition

For my brother Stephen, who has always believed in me.

For Xander, Nico, and Lucas.

PART 1

1

"That is one beautiful man," Sky said with a sigh as Lu took the seat on the barstool next to her.

Lu smiled indulgently at her friend. "Who this time?" she asked setting her cell phone on the bar so that she could see any activity.

Sky moved her head slightly, nodding toward one of the dozens of flat screens surrounding them. Lu looked up with little interest.

Sky laughed, but didn't take her eyes from the screen. "You know how much fun I have looking."

"Soccer this time, huh?" Lu teased. "You didn't drag me out so that you could ogle men on TV, did you?"

Sky ripped her eyes from the screen. "Of course not. I made you come out so that you could be a normal, twenty-six-year-old, single woman."

"Normal? So all I have to do to be normal is come to a bar and watch TV?"

"No, Louisa May Knight. We have to order drinks, maybe do a couple of shots too, and flirt with actual real-life men. You do know what men are, right? 'Cause I'm not quite sure I've ever actually seen you take an interest in one."

"Don't start. My mother and sister have this conversation down to a science." Lu tried to control her frustration. "I don't need you on my case too."

Sky, as usual, bulldozed over Lu's annoyance, raised her hand to signal the bartender, and had two shots of Patron sitting in front of them before Lu could protest. "You do know how to do a shot of tequila, right?"

"Ugh, Sky, what is with you tonight? Why are you suddenly so hell-bent on pushing me? I feel like you've channeled Willa."

Sky threw back her head and laughed, which drew attention because Sky had one of those throaty, sexy laughs that men can't resist. "Willa would love that. Now, drink your damn shot."

Rolling her eyes, Lu imitated Sky, without looking directly at her. After licking her hand, she took the saltshaker from Sky, shook it, licked again, threw back her shot, and shoved a lemon wedge into her mouth. Wincing, she directed her gaze at Sky.

"That was horrible," she said. "Why do you feel that it's necessary for me to go out? I'm in the middle of my comps. What is the point of all of this?" Lu asked.

"You never have any fun."

"How do you know? I have a great time with Nina. So it might not be normal, irresponsible fun, but I've never been that person. Ask Will."

Sky rolled her eyes this time. "Do you not think Willa and I haven't talked this subject to death? Why do you think I made you come out with me tonight? You're too young to be this serious."

Lu chuckled. "Will didn't tell you that I've always been this serious? My mom started calling me an old soul when I was two. I tried irresponsibility when I was a teenager and it got me more responsibility. It's not all it's cracked up to be."

"Oh, woe is me. Just shut up and relax tonight. That's all I'm asking." Sky winked at her. "How 'bout a drink?"

"Fine. What are we drinking?"

"I'm thinking we should stick to tequila. Margarita?"

Resigned to her fate, Lu agreed. There was little reason for her to try to fight the tornado that was Sky. The irony was not lost on Lu. In an attempt to escape her fun-loving sister, Lu became best friends with Willa incarnate. Right now, she wasn't sure who was worse—Willa or Sky. But whoever penned the phrase "Opposites attract" pegged every meaningful relationship Lu had ever had—even the one she had spent the last eight years attempting to forget. Margaritas delivered, Sky lifted her glass for a "cheers!" moment.

With the clink of their glasses, Lu and Sky surveyed the bar. "Not many options here tonight," Sky muttered, disappointed.

"Well, if there are any good options, I'm sure you'll find them," Lu said with a laugh. She had a difficult time keeping track of the revolving door that was Sky's love life. "And bad options too," Lu said, winking at her friend.

"Very funny. An eight on the joke scale," Sky replied. "And if you check your phone one more time, I'm going to take it from you."

Lu shrugged guiltily. "Sorry. No more, I promise."

"Look, it's 11:00. If you haven't heard anything by now, you won't. Right?"

"Absolutely. I'm done."

Sky's gaze shifted back to the TV. "Hey, isn't that the guy you grew up with?" she asked, pointing at the screen.

Lu closed her eyes briefly and took a deep breath, steeling herself for what she was about to see. She turned slightly and watched the action on the TV. The cameraman chose that moment to get a close-up of him, and Lu's stomach dropped. "Yup," she said, "that's Lex."

Sky whistled low. "Wow! Did he look like that when you knew him?"

Lu studied him on-screen. "I don't think so. He's all grown up now, filled out." She watched for another second. The sweat rolled down his face, his short hair no help in absorbing it. She couldn't help a small smile. "One thing that hasn't changed—he's always sweated like that. It was nasty when we were little and it's still gross."

"I wouldn't mind helping him work up a sweat," Sky murmured with a wink as Lu turned away.

"I suppose there are thousands of women that feel the same way," she replied.

"Oh, yeah. That man gets what he wants, when he wants. No question."

Lu shifted uncomfortably in her seat. "So, what's next? We hanging here?"

Sky's gaze drifted back to the TV. Annoyed, Lu waved her hand in front of Sky's face. "Sky, let's finish these drinks and either call it a night or go somewhere else."

Sky pushed Lu's arm out of the way. "Wait a sec! I'm trying to read this."

"Read what?" Lu asked, getting more frustrated.

"The announcers just said that right before the game, he found out that his father had died. No one was sure if he was going to play tonight, but he did."

"What are you talking about?" Lu asked, panic rising in her chest. Everything around her faded out. She stood up and yanked on Sky's hand, trying to get her attention.

"What are you talking about?" she demanded.

Startled by Lu's tone, Sky stopped watching the game. "The ticker at the bottom of the screen said that Lex Pellitteri's father died earlier today," Sky explained.

Shocked, Lu stared unseeingly at Sky until her cell phone lit up and buzzed with a text message.

Lu picked up the phone. It was from Willa.

Willa: Mr. P. was in accident today. Will call later. Hang tight and don't even think about coming home.

Lu: I know he's dead. I'll be there as soon as I can.

Willa: DON'T!

Lu: I'm coming home.

Willa: ALONE???????

Lu paused. She wasn't sure how to answer that. She didn't want to cause any trouble, but there was no way she was staying away this time. She'd stayed away for too long. And Mr. P. was the one person who had supported her. It would be OK if she went alone. No one would begrudge her that.

Lu: Yes.

Willa: OK. Text me when you leave.

Lu picked up her purse. "I've got to go."

Sky grabbed her arm. "What the fuck is going on, Lu?"

"I need a favor."

"Only if you tell me what the hell is going on."

"You're blackmailing me—*now*?" she asked, incredulous.

"Hell, yes. What's going on and what do you need?"

"I have to go home. Mr. Pellitteri is really special to me. I have to go home, but I need you to take care of everything here. Can you do that for me?"

Sky was completely taken aback by Lu's show of emotion. Ordinarily, Lu never lost her composure, never showed any sign of anything affecting her. But now her big, cornflower-blue eyes were luminous with unshed tears. Her hands, one of which was still held by Sky, was shaking.

"Of course. But I don't understand."

Lu heaved a big sigh. "Lex is the guy. And I have to go home."

Sky needed no other explanation.

⁀

Amber slid the French door open. She tried to make noise so that Jo wouldn't be startled. Long ago, they had stopped knocking on each other's doors. But after a day like today, startling her friend wouldn't have been good. She made her way into the kitchen, the house as familiar as her own. In the third drawer over from the sink, she found the wine opener. Pulling two glasses from the rack above the minibar between the kitchen and the dining room, she made her way back to the island and proceeded to open the wine.

In a haze of disbelief, Amber sat heavily upon the bar stool that faced the kitchen. She'd lost count of the times she had sat at this counter drinking wine, laughing, sometimes crying over the past seventeen years. If she couldn't believe Mike was gone, how was Jo feeling?

She heard Jo's footsteps before seeing her face.

"Hey, Dr. J.," she called out, hoping to elicit a smile from Jo. The kids had long ago tagged her with that nickname.

It may have worked for a split second, but the smile was fleeting. Dr. Josephine Pellitteri rounded the corner in all her weary glory. Even at 57, with two adult children and the sudden loss of her husband, Jo's beauty was still apparent. Her black hair had one or two grays, while everyone else had been hiding it for years with a rainbow of colors from the hair salon. She looked tired to Amber as she entered the room.

"Hello, my friend," she said with a weary smile.

"Somehow, 'How are you?' doesn't seem appropriate."

Jo crossed the kitchen and picked up the waiting glass of wine. "Cakebread?" she said, her eyebrows creeping up into the shadow of her bangs.

"Yes, always have a bottle for special occasions," Amber said, while slowly turning the glass in her hand. "I figure we have about five minutes before the rest of them show," she reminded gently.

"That long?" Jo responded. The weary smile still in place.

"Four and a half. Have you heard from the boys?"

Jo sat on the edge of the stool. With a chuckle, she said, "I think you can probably answer that question for yourself."

"Peter will be here as soon as he can, and Lex's agent didn't know when he would arrive?" she offered, sure of her response.

"Nail on the head." Jo paused to take a sip of her wine. "He played tonight."

"We all cope in different ways."

"I couldn't help it. I watched. And you'd never know. He scored and there he was, 'swag' and all." She put her hand quotes around the word *swag*.

"He wouldn't be Lex without the swag," Amber replied knowingly.

"Cocky son of a bitch."

Amber couldn't help it. She laughed. "Always has been."

Returning to her wine, she braved the next subject: "How are you?"

Jo stared into her glass. "To be honest, I haven't had much time to process that he's gone. I mean this morning we bickered about when we would go see Lex again. Then he leaves here in a bit of a fit for his ride. As soon as I park at the hospital for surgery this morning, I'm ushered into the chief of surgery's office. They tell me what happened, but all I hear is blah, blah, blah. I want to know who was on in the ER when he came in, but it didn't matter. He was dead at the scene, so my walk— more like huff—down there was futile. And then it's identify the body, notify the boys, his brothers, you guys. It's all sort of happening to some- one else." At her pause there was a hesitant knock on the door.

The other four women walked in, each with a bottle, looking as if they were the ones who had lost their husband.

Jo glanced at Amber, picked up her wine, and led the way out to the patio. Everyone followed somberly, as if they were on their way to the gallows. Quickly, Jo's protective wall reasserted itself and she looked around at the women who had been her pillars for fifteen years. No one said anything for some time as they got glasses and poured their drinks.

Amber raised her glass when everyone else's was full and said, "To Mike!" Robotically, they all clinked glasses, each secretly thankful that this toast wasn't to one of their husbands. "To Mike!" echoed off the walls of the empty house and surrounded them.

"Fuck," Stacey said as she set down her glass. "What happened, Jo?"

Amber shot daggers at her and opened her mouth to tell her to stop being so insensitive, but Jo's hand on her arm stopped her.

"Might as well say it once so we don't have to rehash it later." She paused—to catch her breath, really. Telling the boys earlier that day had been the most difficult thing she had ever done. Somehow she knew this wouldn't be as bad. "He was on his morning ride. And, to tell you the truth, they're not sure what happened specifically. But he died of TBI—sorry, traumatic brain injury. He was dead on impact." She didn't offer more details and no one asked.

An unnatural silence followed. There typically weren't any quiet periods among the group. Jo watched with a sick fascination as all of her friends, with the exception of Amber, avoided her eyes. She imagined she would see reflections of pity, sympathy, and relief in all of them. She knew her gaze would probably mirror that if she were on the other side. They drank in silence.

The appearance of Willa broke the quiet, which was par for the course with her. Jo sat watching as Willa walked over to her, crouched down in front of her chair, and pulled her into an embrace. "I'm so sorry, Dr. J.," she murmured. "I will always miss him."

Jo grabbed ahold of Willa and hugged her fiercely. "Thank you," she said.

Willa pulled away and stood. "Anyone need a refill?" she offered. Knowing that none of the ladies would turn down more wine, Willa moved toward the sliding glass doors, turned slightly and said, "Mom, what's a good chaser?"

Amber looked curiously at her oldest daughter. Meeting Willa's gaze, she stood and walked toward her. "I'm not sure what we've got. Let's check it out."

Even in her exhausted state, Jo knew Willa needed to talk to her mom. She'd seen that move countless times over the years, although when the kids were younger the excuses had been different. There was the nail polish that they couldn't find or the brush that had too much hair stuck in it. In her house, Jo had heard about the cleat that was missing or the toilet that hadn't been flushed. Excuses all, to get their mother or father alone to ask for a sleepover, or to borrow the car, or for money.

Conversation had picked up around her, but she wasn't in it. Her mind had moved on to the things she needed to take care of over the next few days. When Amber and Willa reappeared with wine, Jo started to decline. Willa poured her a glass anyway. "You'll need this," Willa explained.

"What can we help with?" Cami inquired.

"I am sure there will be things, but at the moment, I don't know specifically," Jo answered, still absorbed with making her internal list. Distracted, she missed the byplay going on around her, so she was surprised when Stacy, Cami, LeeAnn, and Natalie began to make excuses to head out.

"I'll get with you when she's had a chance to make the arrangements," interceded Amber.

Standing, Jo embraced them all—Stacy, Cami, LeeAnn, and Natalie. More alert now, she said good-bye to her friends. Over the years, they had been there for all of the growing pains that families experience. And normally, you didn't go through anything that one of the other women had not already been through. You could always rely on someone's willingness to discuss her own struggles. It had become another family unit that wrapped around each of their own and made the struggles easier to bear. They knew each other pretty well. Which is why Jo didn't hesitate to sit down at the table, pick up her wine, and pin Willa with the death stare that she was famous for.

"What the hell's going on, Willa?"

Willa looked to her mother. Somehow, she felt Amber could deliver the news more effectively.

"Willa just got a text from Lu." Amber paused, gently picked up her wine, and took another fortifying sip. "She's on her way home."

Jo leaned back in her chair and closed her eyes. She wasn't surprised, not really. Maybe it was time. In her mind she saw her family fracturing even more but there was little she could do about a decision that had been made earlier. Partly horrified, partly relieved, she looked at Amber and Willa.

"Is she coming alone?" Jo asked, fearful of the answer.

"Yes," Willa replied.

"Thank fucking God!" she murmured. Maybe she wasn't ready to set things straight.

Exhausted after a hard game and a sleepless night, Lex rolled over and shut off the alarm clock on his iPod before the blast of music coming from it shattered the early morning quiet. Eighteen hours of knowing that his dad was dead hadn't lessened his sense of disbelief. His father had died while he in the midst of his pregame warm-up. His manager had handed him the phone as he walked off the pitch so that his mother could tell him before his game. Normally they would have waited, but with information flying all over the globe at warp speed, they were afraid that a reporter would ask him about it in postgame interviews. And the last thing they wanted was for Lex to be blindsided by that kind of news.

He wasn't sure whose idea it had been. But knowing his mother as he did, he was pretty sure she had forced his agent to have his club make the arrangements since Lex never checked his phone once he entered the stadium. He also knew his mother figured he'd play in his game. She'd spent the majority of Lex's life making sure he could play soccer, so his walking onto the field a couple of hours after learning that his father had died wouldn't have shocked her.

Playing in a critical game was exactly the kind of therapy he needed. Sex would have been good too, but he'd been avoiding that for a bit. No messy entanglements allowed this season. And that would have made his father proud. Lex managed a fleeting smile, thinking of the last conversation he'd had with his dad about that subject. They'd been out at a pub down the street from his club's stadium when his father mentioned Lex's lack of a groupie—as he referred to all of the women Lex had been with since he was 18.

"Bit of a dry spell?" he'd said, winking at Lex.

Lex graciously acknowledged the dig. "No sir. Just trying to focus in on playing soccer."

His dad grinned. "Yes, I've been wondering when you were going to get serious about the sport."

He laughed. One of the things he loved about his dad was his ability to look at things from Lex's perspective. "Ya know how it is, Pops. Even when things are supposed to be uncomplicated with women, they don't ever stay that way."

"If you'd stop binging on groupies, maybe things wouldn't get complicated."

"No, Pops. That's what keeps it from getting complicated," he replied with a wink.

"Seriously, Lex," he said, suddenly changing the mood, "any plans to find a nice girl and settle down?"

Lex eyed his father. "How 1950s of you. Where's this coming from?"

"I look around you and I know you are successful. You're driven and ambitious. But don't you feel like something is missing? Don't you want to share this with someone?"

"That's what I have you, Mom, and Pete for," he answered. "Ready for another?" He pointed at his dad's empty glass and waved to the bartender, hoping to change the subject.

"Lex, I'm serious. I don't want you to be alone. I have seen your capacity to love someone—outside of your family."

Suddenly, completely uncomfortable with the direction of the conversation, Lex ordered another round of drinks. Turning back to his father, he said, "I was a kid and didn't know any better." And with that, he left his father sitting at the bar while he went off to flirt with a groupie.

Thinking back on that conversation, the irony was not lost on Lex. He hadn't been home in almost eight years. When he'd left he'd been caught up in the middle of an emotional nightmare. And now the prodigal son was returning home in the midst of another emotional nightmare. What the fuck? Glancing at the clock, he realized he needed to get moving to make his flight. When his phone rang, he knew without looking that it was his brother.

"What up?" he said without preamble.

"Are you packed? Or does your agent take care of that too after wiping your ass?"

Lex laughed. Leave it to Pete to lighten the mood. "I am trying to get out of bed. Was just thinking about a conversation I had with Dad last time he was here."

"Ah, yeah, I've had a few of those moments today."

"What are you doing up at this hour?"

"I decided to come home right after I heard. I could have broken up the drive, but when I thought about Mom being here alone, I just felt like I needed to come."

"Good man. I take it you got my itinerary?"

"Yes sir, Lex. We will send a car to pick up his majesty."

"You're such a dickhead," Lex said, laughing.

"Seriously, I got all of the information. Shouldn't you get your ass out of bed and in the shower?"

"Yeah, yeah, I'm moving." Lex paused before asking, "How's she doing?"

"Really, you need to ask? She's fucking amazing. Was sitting up with Dr. A. and Willa when I got home. Pretty much everything has been arranged."

"Shit, I haven't thought about Willa Knight in a long time. How was that for you?"

"Ha. All good. Aside from providing a wake-up call, I wanted to give you a heads-up."

"About what?" Lex heard the intake of breath on the line, and from across the Atlantic he could tell that what his brother was about to say was going to bother him.

"Lu's coming home. She'll be here by the time you land tomorrow. With everything going on and, ya know, proximity, I don't think you'll be able to avoid her."

"Who says I want to avoid her?"

Pete sputtered. "I just assumed. . . . I mean, you haven't been home since you left. I thought that was why."

"Nah. I'm done avoiding Louisa May. We'll have a conversation, clear the air, and then everyone will be able to relax. Don't worry, Pete. I'm not looking to make this any more difficult than it already is."

"Roger that. All right, I'll see you at the airport. Be safe."

"Over and out, bro."

Lex gently placed his phone on the bedside table and fell back on his pillow. Twenty-four hours earlier his life had been proceeding according to plan. Now, he was faced with the death of his father and the prospect of going toe-to-toe with the girl who had broken his heart.

2

Lu grabbed her coffee mug and sneaked out the back door, across the worn path, and to the Pellitteris' sprawling back deck. She knew that Dr. J. would be sitting in her chair, book in hand, drinking her coffee. When they were younger, any sneaking in and out had to be handled before 6:00 a.m. because Dr. J. would be up, in the same position even then. Wrapped up in a gigantic UPenn fleece, she shuffled up the stairs, across the deck, taking in the powerhouse that was Josephine Pellitteri. Although this time there was no book perched in her lap, taking up all of her concentration. She was gazing out into the early morning light, obviously lost in thought.

"Hey, Dr. J.," Lu ventured.

Jo looked up and the weary smile she'd sported over the last twenty-four hours appeared on her tired face. She started to rise, but Lu beat her to it and stooped down to hug her. Lu tried to hold back, but once in Dr. J.'s arms, her composure crumbled. Attempting to stop the tears, Lu heaved a sigh that ended with a dry sob. Jo, also trying to hold her emotions in check, managed to caress Lu's back, comforting her as she had when Lu was a child.

"It's OK, Lu," she somehow managed, although she was far from OK.

Both, slightly embarrassed, pulled back. Lu stood and moved a chair closer so that she was facing Jo. "I'm so sorry. And sad. I'm so sad that he's gone," she said, wiping away the tears which seemed to have a mind of their own.

Jo reached out and rubbed Lu's clasped hands. "I know. You and Mike always had a special relationship. Especially over the last few years. You gave him so much joy."

"I couldn't stay away. I don't want this to be any harder for you, but I couldn't not be here to say good-bye."

"And to set things straight?" Jo said before she could stop herself. But once she said it she knew that it needed to be said. They had to have this conversation before her son arrived. Pinning Lu with the death stare she decided to move forward. "Is that why you came, Louisa May?"

Lu, startled, but only slightly, took in the double whammy. As kids they had all joked that the death stare paired with the full name meant serious trouble. Without meaning to, Lu smiled. "Dr. J.—you're pulling out the double whammy on me at 6:00 a.m.?" she asked.

Jo laughed. "I suppose I am."

"You know it still works. Even as a twenty-six-year-old, with my own set of responsibilities, I fold under the double whammy." Lu got up, uncomfortable being in such close proximity. Without meaning to, she paced, rubbing her wrist, a habit left over from childhood. Again, Jo found herself smiling. So interwoven were their families that this gesture was as familiar to her as when she saw Lex's ritual after scoring or when Pete rubbed his ear.

"When it comes to Lex, I haven't really thought very far. Maybe that's surprising, but it's more about being here to celebrate Mr. P. I shouldn't have come alone. For the first time in eight years, I am shirking my responsibilities, but I couldn't do that to you. I just don't know. I don't know what it will feel like when I see him." She stopped pacing and returned to her chair. "We were so young. But I still miss him. Not that soul-searing emptiness I experienced when he left—and let's be honest, for a couple of years after. But we were so close for so long, I wonder what it will be like when we see each other again."

"Lu, you know that's not what I'm talking about," Jo responded, more annoyed than anyone should be so early in the morning.

Lu, suddenly angry over being backed into a corner, responded with raised ire. "What about you, Dr. J.? This is as much your secret as it is mine. How much longer are you willing to keep this from your son?" she challenged.

"Do you know that he never forgave me?" Jo said, looking directly at Lu but somehow looking beyond her, into the past. "He died yesterday, and he had never really gotten over it." Jo paused and Lu let the silence descend over them, each lost in the memories of that fateful decision.

Lex had already left for the U-20 World Cup training camp when the shit hit the fan. And even though it didn't seem that long ago, they didn't have smartphones as they did now. Lu often wondered if there would have been a different outcome if she and Lex had been able to communicate with each other. Could they have text messaged their way to a different outcome than the one their parents chartered for them. No day had passed that she had not regretted the outcome of the decision, but she could barely stomach the collateral damage to all of the people they loved.

"I'm at a loss here, Dr. J. I know what the right thing to do is. I have always known that. But I'm not going to be losing Lex this time. Chances are you will. And can you handle that without Mr. P. here?" Quiet settled between them again.

"I need some more coffee. Would you like some?" Jo asked.

Knowing this was far from over, Lu stood. "I'll go," she offered, needing to move. She picked up both mugs and went into the house. Again, she was overcome with memories of the times she had spent there. She had been walking in and out of this house at will since she was six. And although she and Lex didn't have an auspicious beginning, they were soon inseparable.

Her mom and dad had begun building their house next to the Pel-litteris' when Lu was five. So when they moved in after almost a year of construction, eight-year-old Lex and six-year-old Pete were a little upset that their construction site/playground was no longer available.

They already knew all the ways into the house and were not shy about expressing their displeasure over their neighbors being girls. When Dr. J. showed up at their door with a store-bought cake (she never baked), a vintage bottle of wine, and her two sullen children, Lu and Willa were left with the task of entertaining them while their mothers drank wine—a scenario that would play itself out, over and over, throughout the next ten years.

It was at this meeting that Lex had dubbed Louisa May Knight "Lu," a nickname that she would never escape. After being introduced, Lex and Pete followed the girls upstairs into their very pink and purple playroom.

"Why do you have such funny names?" Lex asked.

"You have a funny name too," Louisa shot back. "And they're not weird. We were named after famous authors."

"That's weird," smirked Lex.

"My mom's an English professor," Willa offered. "We're named after Louisa May Alcott and Willa Cather."

"Well, those are old-lady names. I'm just gonna call you Will and Lu," Lex announced.

"You have a stupid name," Lu returned.

Willa pushed her slightly and whispered loudly, "You're not supposed to say 'stupid.'"

"Well it is. Why is your name Lex?"

He moved his head toward Pete, "'Cause he couldn't say 'Alex' when he was little. He could only ever get out 'Lex.' Doesn't matter. It's just a name. And no one else has it."

"Well, no one has the names Louisa and Willa either."

"Trust me," Lex retorted, "some old ladies have those names."

Willa couldn't help herself. She laughed. But Lu didn't think it was funny at all.

"Don't you ever smile?" Lex asked her.

"My mom says she has an old soul and she's much too serious for a six-year-old," Willa informed them.

"Looks like your mom is right," Lex concurred.

Lu, who may have had an old soul, also had a quick temper. Without letting anyone see what she was doing, she went over to their easel, which was set in the back of the room, and picked up a bottle of blue paint. She walked behind Lex, stood on her tiptoes, and poured the paint over his head and onto his favorite soccer jersey.

Willa and Pete cracked up. Lex, sputtering more from surprise than anything else, turned and ran downstairs. Willa, Pete, and Lu followed, racing down the steps. To Amber and Jo, who were almost done with the wine, it sounded like a herd of elephants was coming toward them.

"Uh, oh," murmured Amber.

"Mom," Lex said, "look at my jersey!"

"What happened?"

Lex opened his mouth to tell his mom what the little jerk had done. But before he could say anything, he caught sight of her. She stood with her hands on her hips, looking mad, but with tears unshed in her big, blue eyes. And he couldn't do it. "I was messing around by the easel and the paint fell over."

Pete and Willa's eyes got wide and Lu turned and ran up the stairs.

"Alexander James Pellitteri. You need to march upstairs and clean up the mess right now. Then get home and into your room." Jo's voice rang out in the kitchen. No one really wanted to mess with Dr. J.

Amber, who had been watching her children, knew that there was something wrong with the story. Those paints were always secured, tops tightened. But before she could get to the bottom of it, Lex, Pete, and Willa ran back upstairs.

"Wow," Willa said. "Why didn't you tell?"

"Ah, I probably deserved it," he said with a devilish smile.

There wasn't much to clean up and Lu had hidden herself away so she didn't have to face Lex. But he had sealed their fate that evening. Lu, who had been saved from a spanking and probably a very public apology, swore to never do anything bad to Lex Pellitteri. And Lex discovered that he was a sucker for big blue eyes.

Lu pulled herself back to the present. Grabbing the two mugs, she headed back out to the deck. Sitting down across from Jo again, she handed her a mug. Jo took a sip gratefully.

Neither of them spoke for a few minutes, savoring their last few moments of perfect harmony. Then Jo reached out and grabbed Lu's hand.

"Louisa May, I think it's time."

Lu met her gaze. And although she had been prepared for this moment, she still felt stripped bare. She knew Jo wasn't done with what she had to say, so she held her tongue.

"I want you to go home," Jo told her.

Anger hit Lu like a punch to the gut. "I am not leaving. I need to be here. You can't keep deciding my fate for me." All the resentment that had built up over the last eight years rose up like bile in her throat.

Jo took Lu's other hand and caressed them both, again comforting her as she had done many times over the years. "You misunderstand me, Lu. I want you to go home and get my grandchild. I think it's time that Lex meet his daughter."

3

"What are you going to do, Lu?" Willa asked. Walking over to where Lu was sitting on her bed, Willa gently rubbed her back. "Whatever you want to do, you know I've got your back. No pun intended."

"Ugh, Will. I don't know." Lu stood up, disengaging herself from Willa's contact. She didn't want to be touched. She needed space to think. "I haven't thought this far ahead. Why does everyone assume I have a plan all carved out for this funeral?"

"Shit, Lu, you always have a plan. You were born with a miniature FranklinCovey planner in your hand."

"Yes. I have a plan for school and a plan for Nina. But I never planned on Lex Pellitteri. And see what happened?"

Willa couldn't help it. She laughed. "You're actually cracking jokes?"

"No, Will!" Lu snapped, exasperated. "I don't think any part of this is funny."

"Sorry. Have you talked to mom about it?" Willa asked.

"No. I haven't had a chance. And I certainly didn't expect for Dr. J. to tell me that it was time to tell Lex. I thought she was going to order me to go home—tell me that I wasn't welcome. And instead she orders me to go get Nina. I thought I was doing the right thing coming alone. I don't want to spring his daughter on him. Doesn't he deserve an explanation? And what if he doesn't want her? There's no guarantee that he is going to want his eight-year-old-daughter that he didn't even know existed."

"You don't want him to hate you," Willa observed. "You want to break it to him and give him a chance to get used to it. But, Lu, he's going to want his daughter. And he's going to hate you. And his mother. And our mother. And maybe even Pete."

"Right, I know that. And knowing that, should I tell him he has a daughter right after he's lost his father? Because while he might be excited about having a child—and that's probably the wrong word— he'll find out that everyone who loves him has deceived him for the last eight years. How can I do that to him?"

Willa made a fist with one hand and put it against the palm of her other. "Rock," she said, shaking her fist. "Hard place!"

Lu wanted to engage in a full-fledged temper tantrum. She wanted to fall on the floor, cry, and beat her fists and kick her feet. She wanted to have a throw-down that would make Nina proud. Frustrated and sad and scared, she walked to the window of her old bedroom. It faced the front of the house and provided a good view of the street. Out this window she would crawl, onto the flat part of the roof, to sit and think, to escape her room. It was on the roof that she had told Lex she was pregnant. There, they had made a plan for their future. There, she had retreated when their parents stepped in and changed the plan.

Turning away from the window, she sat heavily upon her bed. "So what's the plan for the next few days?"

"Dad gets back soon. He caught the first flight he could from Australia. Takes a while to get back from down under."

Lu acknowledged that with a nod. "And the arrangements for Mr. P.?"

"Oh, sorry. The viewing is tomorrow. One from 10:00 to 2:00 and then another from 6:00 to 8:00. Memorial service on Friday at 10:00. No burial. They are cremating him. And I think it's a closed casket."

"Do you know if Lex is staying after that? Is he staying for the weekend? Does he have to get back?"

"Sorry, sweetie. I don't know his plans." Willa knew Lu was trying to work out what to do. She wanted to be able to help her by talking it through, but often, Lu planned on her own and shared her thoughts after she had formulated them.

"What about after the funeral? People going back to the house?"

"Oh, I *do* know something of Lex's plans," Willa said excitedly. "They were going to read the will on Saturday. Something about Lex having to get back before Monday."

"So I have three days?" Lu murmured without looking for a response. She turned away from Willa, walking back to the window. "Three days." Leaning her head against the pane, she let the tears flow. She cried for the children they had been, for the decisions that had been made, for the loss of Mr. P. She cried because she had never been away from Nina for more than the length of a school day. And she cried because she suddenly realized that the dream she had buried for the last eight years, the one where she and Lex figured everything out and became a family with their daughter, that dream was never going to come true.

⌒

Pete watched as Lex made his way from the Jetway of the plane into the small Sarasota airport. Of course Lex was not alone as he walked toward him. He guided a beautiful woman, his hand resting in the small of her back, around a row of airport chairs, toward the baggage claim. He looked completely engaged, leaning down so that he could hear what she was saying. With a wink and a mischievous smile in Pete's direction, Lex was merely killing time, Pete knew. Following at a safe distance, Pete let his brother do his thing. Which he had to admit was pretty impressive.

Although he had lived in England for the last six years, Lex didn't have that pallid look of those in his adopted country. He had inherited his mother's olive complexion, which served him well. He definitely looked European, though. Something about the cut of his clothes, jeans and a T-shirt hinted at a sophistication that couldn't be mistaken for American. When his companion's luggage arrived, Lex made sure she was all squared away and pushed her out the door with a haste that Pete was sure the woman would find offensive. But Lex being Lex, she just beamed at him as she left the airport. Task complete, Lex found his brother and drew him into a guys hug. The one where they clasp hands first and then one-arm each other. It was all either one of them could handle.

"Bro, thanks for picking me up. Caroline was going to have a limo pick me up, but I said that my brother would be honored to do it."

"Was that after she wiped your ass?" Pete retorted, so pleased to have Lex with him.

Eyes sparkling, Lex bent low to Pete's ear and said, "No, right after she sucked my dick."

Pete couldn't help it; he cackled in the baggage-claim area. "I'm sure she would love to hear you say something like that."

Lex smiled, then shook his head. "She'd kick my ass. So please don't tell her that I even joked about that."

"You're a prick."

"Yes, I know. But all of your good-natured humor brought out the wicked in me," Lex replied with a smirk.

"Like that's hard to do."

"True," Lex said. "Let's go."

"Where's your luggage?" Pete asked.

Lex nodded his head toward the empty conveyer belt where a lone bag continued to circle. "Right there."

"We could have been out of here ten minutes ago if you weren't flirting with that girl."

"Woman, that was all woman. And she kept me from thinking about the reason why I am here. Totally worth the ten minutes."

"Point taken!" Pete said.

Gathering up the luggage, they strolled through the sliding glass doors toward Pete's car.

"So you drove straight here last night? That's a hell of a drive." Lex said.

"Yeah, I know. But I just needed to get here. Somehow it didn't seem real to me. And I thought if I was here, I would know he was gone. Hard to explain."

"Does it seem real now? 'Cause I'm struggling with that." All hints of his smile fled. "I just can't quite get there."

"Maybe after we see that body?"

Lex stopped in midstride. "We're going to see the body? And why are your referring to dad as the 'body'?"

Pete stopped and turned back to look at him. "He's gone. All that's left of him is his body."

"Is this your idea of a good bedside manner? Is this what they teach you in med school?" Lex replied, annoyed.

"Look, I need to see him. You don't have to come with me, but it just doesn't seem possible to me. I need proof." Pete continued walking to his car.

Overwhelmed, Lex scrubbed his hands over his face, picked up his bag, and followed his brother to the car. Pete opened the trunk for him and he put stuff away, still reluctant to continue this conversation with his brother. Pete got in the car, but Lex hesitated, leaning on the trunk, trying to figure out if he wanted to see his father's body. It seemed like too much—coming home after such a long time and going straight to the morgue. He didn't think he could do it. But he knew it was what his brother needed. And Lex always looked out for his brother.

Opening the door and folding his large frame into the front seat of Pete's Nissan 300X, he leaned his head back and breathed deeply. "Is that bar still there, on 301, or is it 41?"

"Which bar?"

"The BiHi Hut?"

"Yeah," Pete smiled. "How do you know about that place? You weren't old enough to go there when you left."

"Ha. Like that stopped me. I need a drink if we're going to do this thing."

Pete looked at his brother. "You'll come with me?"

"Fuck!" Lex said. And, closing his door with too much force, he looked over as his brother started the car. "Get me a Scotch and I'll go with you to see Dad."

4

They returned from the morgue to their empty house. Depositing his bag in the room over the garage, Lex quickly changed into his training gear, pulled on his running shoes, and grabbed his iPod. Heading back downstairs, he found his brother and told him he'd be out for a while. Although he was exhausted as hell, he needed to get a workout in. A hard game, a sleepless night, a transatlantic flight, and a viewing of his father's body—oh, and a Scotch in between—had his body craving a good, hard run. He wished like hell he had a game so he could forget for a while.

Turning out of the driveway, he set a hard pace through his childhood neighborhood. He ran by all the old haunts, memories assailing him from every direction. When they were young, the kids counted the ratios. There were sixteen of them and only twelve adults. Lex felt confident that if they'd ever had to mutiny, the kids would win because they had the majority. They'd joked about that all the time, even though, deep down, none of them wanted to take on their mothers. He wondered how many of them would show up for his father's memorial service. He didn't relish being the first family to lose someone. And while he figured most of them would be there, he had to admit that the loss of one of their parents wouldn't have brought him traipsing across the Atlantic. Made him feel like the prick his brother had dubbed him as at the airport.

It wasn't that he didn't respect and love the group of parents who had molded him as a youth; it was just that his path had taken him away long before the rest of them. At fourteen, he had started in the Olympic Development Program. By sixteen, he was missing school to travel to training camps for youth world cups. And by eighteen, he'd left for good—not returning until this visit. Maybe if things had been different, if Lu had followed through with their plan, he would have visited more. He would probably be playing here in the States. He wouldn't have stayed away.

At eighteen, everything had seemed possible to him. He knew their plan would work. He had no doubts that an eighteen-year-old, hell-bent on playing soccer at the highest level and his sixteen-year-old girlfriend could have handled raising a child while they were an ocean apart. Wasn't there some saying about the foolishness of the youth? Looking back now, with the perspective of an adult, he knew that what they envisioned would have never worked. He wouldn't be Lex Pellitteri, world-class soccer player. And truth be told, he probably would have resented Lu for that. So maybe she did the right thing. Maybe having an abortion and telling him to move on was exactly the way it was supposed to be.

At some point, in the middle of his eight-mile run, he forgave Louisa May Knight and silently thanked her for her foresight. He wished the peace he was feeling had come sooner and wondered if he had allowed himself to come home at any point over the last eight years, if he would have reached this conclusion earlier. The dread that had settled over him since his brother's phone call earlier in the day lifted. Picking up his pace for the last half mile, Lex made his way into the garage to grab his soccer ball.

Leaving dinner early to get the house prepared, Amber walked the familiar path between their two houses. She had stocked the bar earlier, but she wanted to make sure they had everything. She desperately wanted Chris to get back from his trip, but he'd been delayed in Miami and wouldn't be back until the next morning. Even after a couple of glasses of wine at dinner, Amber was strung tight. As much as she loved Jo, she wanted to beat her when Jo had revealed her conversation with Lu. She wasn't supporting Jo on this one. Whatever Lu wanted to do, however, she would support. She was fighting for her daughter this time.

It had almost broken Lu. That fateful decision had almost broken Lu's spirit—until they put Nina in her arms. Then she rose up like the phoenix in all its glory. And when it came to raising Nina, no one was allowed to interfere. Amber didn't think Lu did it to be spiteful; she wanted to be true to herself as a parent. So for Jo to order her to bring her daughter to meet Lex—her unsuspecting father—Lu wouldn't have it. Amber was fairly certain that however this all went down, her daughter was directing this tragedy.

Amber tried to shake off the feeling of impending doom when she spotted Lex. Watching him for a moment, the past played out in front of her like a movie. Lex never went anywhere without his soccer ball. When they met him at eight, he already had that fire in his veins. You just knew he would defy the odds and reach his goal. Every night, right before they got called in to eat, Lex would stand in that exact spot and practice. Just him and his ball. Amber had no idea what the moves were called or what he was doing—she was the mother of girls. But over the years, it became a thing of beauty to watch. Like a ballerina executing a series of spins, Lex maneuvered and manipulated the ball. As an eight-year-old, it looked nothing like what he could do now as a twenty-seven-year old. But even a non-sports fan couldn't help but be impressed. She smiled as she realized she knew his routine—what he would do next. It hadn't changed in nineteen years.

She couldn't stay away. Knowing he was coming to the end, she sat on the bottom step, waiting for him to finish and approach the deck. He did the last move, where he flipped the ball up off the back of his foot and it sailed over the top of his head, where he trapped it with his foot. Then he flipped it back up into his hand and began moving toward her.

"Shit, Dr. A., how long have you been sitting here?" Lex said, obviously startled.

She laughed. "Since about halfway through. It's the same?" she asked even though she knew the answer.

He grinned. "Yup. You remember?" he said, a little surprised.

Returning his smile, she said, "I watched you do that every day since you were eight. If I had any coordination, I could probably do it. The choreography is embedded in my brain."

"Dr. A., I really want to hug you, but I'm sweaty as hell."

"If I remember your ball tricks, do you think I'd forget how much you sweat?"

He threw his head back and laughed. "No, I don't suppose you could forget that."

"How many times did I have to get on you for trying to hug the girls after practice?"

"More times than I can count. It was just too fun making them run away screaming."

"And you were always about eliciting a response," she said, smiling at him fondly.

"How was dinner?" he said, suddenly remembering the occasion.

"It was fine. Your uncle is here, so we thought we'd entertain him. He had some stuff to talk to your mom about, so I made myself scarce for a bit. I'm not sure how good of an idea it is, but your mother needed a distraction, so the gang is coming over."

"That's fine. I figured as much. Should be interesting to see everyone."

Amber couldn't help herself. "Everyone?" she asked.

Lex intentionally misunderstood her question. "Yeah. I guess it'd be nice if I saw my mom before chaos rules, huh?"

Properly put in her place, Amber backed off. "Yes. It would. She's going to be a little bit still. Probably time for you to shower so you can give her a hug," she joked, putting things right between them.

"And you too. Once I'm cleaned up, I owe you a hug. Thanks for taking care of her the last two days while Pete and I made our way here."

"She'd have done the same."

"I know," he said. "But still."

"Go shower. I'm going to go make sure we have everything we need."

Lex started up the remainder of the stairs. But stopped and turned back. "Good to see you, Dr. A." And with that he went into the house to get ready to face his mother.

⁓

Lu felt a little like a stalker. She watched him come out of the garage, mesmerized by his grace. He danced with the ball into his spot and performed a routine worthy of the stage. He'd gotten better, more fluid and sure. Floored by his persistence and determination, she couldn't look away. So she watched, struck still, while he practiced. She missed her mother walking in the house and leaving to head to the Pellitteri's. She missed it until Lex finished and headed into the house. She noticed her mother then. She took in the conversation. It worried her that she lost herself in Lex—that easily, just like when she was sixteen.

"Lu, we need to head over," Willa called, shattering the spell.

Steeling herself, she walked upstairs.

"I don't think I can go over there, Will," she stated, sitting heavily upon Willa's bed.

Willa finished messing with her hair and turned to her sister. "You can and you will. You're not going to be able to avoid him tomorrow. Might as well get it over with tonight."

Heaving a huge sigh, Lu fell on the bed. "I don't want to go."

"You're acting like Nina. You realize that, right?"

Lu smiled. "But I'm a bit more dramatic, wouldn't you say?"

"If it will make you feel better, I'm sure Nina would be proud of your two-day pout. Now, why don't you make me proud—get your ass up off the bed, put on something cute, and get control of this situation."

"You know I hate you right now, right?"

"Yeah, yeah."

"Fuck! Can we at least come up with a code so I can let you know when I'm ready to go?"

"Don't we already have one?" Willa said, smiling at the memory.

Lu returned her smile. "Yes, but somehow I don't think 'Can I borrow your pink pants?' is going to work."

"Probably not. Why don't we just agree to stay for an hour? We have to clear out of here anyway tonight. So let's just agree to one hour. Everyone will understand. I don't think this is meant to be a throwdown anyway."

Lu sat up, nodded her head, and held out her pinky to Willa. "Pinky promise—one hour."

Rolling her eyes, Willa wrapped her pinky around Lu's. "One hour."

5

The Supper Clubs often ended at the Pellitteris' house because the kitchen was a wide-open, inviting space that seemed to draw people to it. An L-shaped breakfast bar provided a break between the kitchen and the family room, which had an amazing barrel ceiling. The back of the room opened out onto the patio through a series of sliding glass doors that slid into the walls like old-fashioned pocket doors. The sprawling back deck and pool area made the space seem far larger than it truly was but also provided plenty of area for all of the families to congregate.

Even though she'd been to the house this morning, when Lu entered she was struck again by the loss of Mr. P. That, coupled with the prospect of seeing Lex, had her stomach churning. Willa immediately pushed a glass of wine into her hand. "Drink this," she ordered. Lu complied, feeling a little like Alice in Wonderland. Everyone around her was familiar, shades of her childhood coming at her in various colors. She looked around cautiously, thinking she wasn't quite ready to see him.

A pair of arms encircled her waist and she almost jumped out of her skin. "It's just me," Pete said.

Smiling sincerely, Lu turned and embraced him. "I'm so sorry," she whispered as she hugged him harder. "So sorry."

He pulled back and looked at her. "I know. But I appreciate it. How are you?"

"I'm OK," she answered honestly.

"Don't worry; he's talking to my mom. You're safe for a bit."

He saw her visibly relax.

"How are you?" she inquired, feeling remorseful for letting him see her worries rather than letting them go so that she could be there for him.

"That is a very difficult question to answer. Too many emotions to wrap my head around one." Drawing her aside, into the bar between the kitchen and dining room, they leaned back on the counter that housed the ice bucket and the open and empty bottles of wine. Because of their location, there wasn't much hope for a private discussion, which neither of them really had the stomach for. Heads together, they chatted about any inane subject they could think of in an attempt to avoid discussions of death, reunions, and uncertainty. And that was the sight that greeted Lex when he came out of the den with his mother.

His mom had spent the last thirty minutes giving him the rundown of the events over the next couple of days. Although she attempted to cover her annoyance with his schedule, tension had run through the entire conversation. Annoyed and overwhelmingly tired, Lex wanted everyone out of the house. He had managed to hide from everyone up until this point, but he had aunts, uncles, and old friends waiting to greet him and his mother. He opened the door for his mother and held it for her, allowing her to set the pace through the small gathering of people. He could see how tired she was, and while being with her family provided a soothing balm, she wasn't up for a long night. Situated at the front of the house, across from the dining room, his father's den afforded him an unobstructed view of the proceedings.

As they prepared to leave the sanctity of the den, he bent toward his mother's ear. "How long can you go?" Glancing at her watch, she looked vaguely surprised. "Tomorrow is going to be a long day. Maybe an hour? I think Amber will be ushering my family out of here in a bit, so we should be able to make that happen."

"We'll make it happen," he assured her.

From his vantage point in the doorway of the den, Lex had an open view of kitchen and hallway. Without meaning to, he surveyed the rooms looking for Lu. He didn't see her at first. Disappointed, he decided that both he and his mother needed a drink. "Want some wine?"

Grateful eyes met his. "Absolutely. Pinot noir, please."

Attempting to take the most obscure way to the bar—not through the kitchen but backtracking through the dining room, Lex turned the corner and stopped as he got his first look at Lu.. The lighting in the bar was dim, but he could make out her features perfectly. Blue-black hair reached midway down her back falling in a straight line without an ounce of wave. Growing up, she had worn her hair either long or short. She would let it get long cut if off for "Locks of Love" and then grow it out again. But when he had left, it was short. She had always been tiny, but now, compared with his six-foot-two frame, her demure height of five foot two left her standing a foot shorter than him. She looked like a pixie, with her delicate features and her big, blue eyes.

All the angst of seeing her evaporated in the midst of a rainfall of memories. She was what was good about his childhood. She, like his father, had molded him into who he was. Without any hesitation, he moved quickly through the dining room and grabbed her. Wrapping her up in his embrace, he lifted her off the ground.

"Louisa May Knight, you have no idea how good it is to see you," he said. Reveling in the feel of her, he noted the changes in her body. She felt delicate but by no means did she feel fragile. Curvier than her sixteen-year-old self, she had filled out in all the right places and his body responded to hers almost immediately. Holding her in his arms, he met his brother's surprised look with the smile that made Lex Pellitteri Lex Pellitteri. But had he been able to process anything other than what it felt like to hold Lu, he would have noticed Pete's expression of concern.

Eight years fell away. Overwhelmed by the feeling of being in Lex's arms, Lu sighed deeply, breathing him in. His scent was different from the sweaty boy smell she associated with him. His tangy, fresh scent wafted around her and she knew she would forever attempt to remember it. The sinewy feel of him disappeared under the hard-worked muscles he had developed over the last few years. This wasn't Lex the boy she had known so well. This was Lex the magnificent man whose boyish angles had been traded in and up. Though she felt breathless in his embrace, there was a sense of relief when he set her down. Being in his arms felt too good.

Lex looked much like she had envisioned when she was a little girl. His dirty-blond hair still sported two very blond spots at his temples. Just as when he was a boy, those spots on his head stood like beacons of his time in the sun. Sprinkled across his nose and cheeks, freckles lent a boyish quality to an otherwise chiseled man. Set perfectly and fringed in amazingly straight black lashes, his green eyes still twinkled with constant mischief and irreverence.

"God, I am so glad that you are here," he practically gushed, boyish in his enthusiasm. "I have to go say hello to everyone, and bring my mother some wine, but I want to have some time to talk to you before you leave."

"I'm actually headed out soon, but we can catch up tomorrow," she said, too quickly.

He looked over his shoulder at her as he poured two glasses of wine. "Absolutely not. I'll deliver this to my mom and be right back. Don't leave or I'll show up at Willa's in the middle of the night," he said with a wink before he took off to find his mother.

⌒

Horrified, Lu turned to Pete and said, "I have to go. Can you grab Willa for me and tell her to meet me at the house?"

Pete, looking dazed, responded slowly, "Lu, you might as well just talk to him now. You know his ass will follow you to Will's just because he's Lex. Don't force his hand on this one."

"I can't, Pete. I just can't tonight. I'm exhausted and confused. I can't have a casual conversation with him. I need to fortify myself. Please just tell Will that I'll be waiting for her." With that, Lu made a break for the garage door through the kitchen—knowing it was the easiest and quickest way out. She hurried across the well-worn path between their two houses, yanked on their side door, and flew up the stairs to her room, where she grabbed her bag. She headed back downstairs and threw her bag next to the front door. Fighting against the pull of the past, she exited out the back door and followed their porch around to the opposite side of the house. From there, although hidden from view, she could see Willa's approach.

Sitting heavily in one of the white rocking chairs, Lu allowed herself a moment to catch her breath. Leaning her head back on the chair, she resisted the urge to rock. The big fat wooden planks groaned and creaked with the slightest movement. Paralyzed by her reluctance to give away her location, she sat stiffly, waiting impatiently, impotently for her sister to make a more graceful exit than she had. With a slight smile she remembered the look on Pete's face as her panic blew up on him. He had to wonder how she managed to mother his niece when she could barely manage to control her emotions.

Heaving a wavering sigh, Lu shut her eyes and concentrated on the night sounds all around her. She was searching for some quiet for her overactive mind. But the quiet allowed all of the memories in, and before she could stop herself from going there, Lu was remembering the moment she became friends with Lex. They had never attended the same school. Lex and Pete's parents had sent them to the Catholic school down the street. Lu had skipped second grade and found herself at the gifted school by the time she entered fifth grade. That move had earned her the nickname Harvard—another moniker from Lex. It was right about that time that Lu realized that Lex was a lot smarter than he let on to everyone.

"Hey, Harvard, how was school today? Did you skip any more grades this week?" he had teased. The teasing from Lex was merciless but mostly harmless. On this particular day, though, Lu wasn't in the mood.

"Shut up, Alexander James," she yelled because she knew the use of his full name annoyed him as much as the use of her nicknames annoyed her. "Why can't you just be normal?" she screamed. God, she mostly hated him, she thought as she took off toward the wooden play set at the back of her yard.

He juggled his soccer ball, flipping it up into his hand. With his other hand, he grabbed her arm, cocking his head to the side and said, "What exactly is normal?"

It wasn't that profound a statement. And being in the snit that she was in, she was surprised when her blue eyes met his green ones and she knew there was a lot more to him than she thought. Shrugging him off, she started to walk away.

"Come on, Harvard. Whatcha got?"

She kept walking toward the play set, Lex in tow. They sat up in the fort that day, just talking. Had anyone in the neighborhood seen the two of them, they wouldn't have believed it. The two became each other's confidant that day. And from then on, if Lex was in town and didn't have a game, Lu wasn't far away. She couldn't help it as a smile spread across her face, lost in the memory. Distracted.

⌒

It took him approximately twenty minutes to make his way back to the spot where he had left her. But when he got there, both she and Pete had left the bar. Looking around the kitchen, he located Pete but not Lu. Headed on a direct path to his brother, Lex was only waylaid once. He watched, fascinated as he saw Pete attempt to avoid him. He couldn't figure out what the hell was going on, but he let Pete do his dance because he had spotted Willa engaged in a conversation across the room with her mother. Figuring Lu had fled the scene, he changed directions and headed for the garage.

He knew exactly where she would be—which struck him as odd. When he rounded the corner of the deck, on the opposite side of the house Lex marveled that it didn't seem like anything had changed. What was it about coming home that made you feel like you were still the child you were when you left?

Spotting Lu in the rocking chair, he paused, taking her in. She looked tense, completely upright and stiff in the chair, not moving a muscle, with her eyes closed as if she wanted to shut out the world. But then a smile raced across her face. He wanted to know what brought that smile. So he crept, not really wanting to startle her, to the spot directly in front of her. As he sat down on the hard porch, he studied her. Luminous but guarded, her face caught the moonlight directly, almost an ethereal glow. And even though she smiled, she appeared stressed. He could have watched her forever, but his desire to talk with her overpowered him. So he moved, knowing that it would bring her around.

Which is how he sneaked up on her. And how she suddenly felt the planks creak and her chair move with the vibration. And how she opened her eyes to find Lex sitting directly in front of her, leaning back on his elbows, with his legs outstretched.

He cocked his head to the side, his laughing green eyes boring directly into her startled blue ones, smiling that smile. Left eyebrow raised, another Pellitteri trait, he said, "Louisa May Knight, I get the feeling that you are avoiding me."

6

Caught off guard by his appearance and that smile, Lu sat up too quickly, right as the chair rocked back. In an effort to counterbalance the movement, she shifted forward at the wrong moment and found herself thrust upward in the air. Overcompensating, she leaned back. The chair was moving forward and nailed her in the back of the head. She grabbed her head and leaned forward again. But this time there was too much momentum and she found herself landing with a thump, on her knees, between Lex's legs.

Head hurting, knees smarting, pride wounded, and nerves fraying, Lu glared at Lex as if he had gotten up and bodily thrown her out of the chair. He looked at her, and although she could see him struggling, trying not to, he burst out laughing. He couldn't help it. And maybe it was the release he'd needed, because he couldn't seem to stop. His elbows came out from under him and he fell onto his back, flat and hysterical.

"Ugh, Alexander James, why do I always manage to have embarrassing moments in front of you?" she couldn't help but ask, indignantly.

"Sweetheart, I've had a couple of women throw themselves at me, but not nearly as graceful as that," he managed before the laughter overtook him again.

Frustrated, and unwilling to give in to the desire to join him in his amusement, Lu smacked his leg. Attempting to disengage herself from him, she started to stand up and move away. But Lex's long arm shot out, grabbed her wrist, and pulled her down on top of him. For one blissful moment, Lu let herself lie there, one leg on the outside, one leg trapped between his. Her hair splayed over his chest, his right hand finding its way underneath to rest lightly on her back. The heat of his hand on her, him between her legs, his left hand still grasping her wrist—she let it all wash over her. She could have combusted. She felt the heat creep through her body. Then he released her wrist and wrapped his other arm around her. She followed. The deck impeded her arms from fully engulfing him, but she held tight, savoring his warmth and her memories.

"So, I'm intrigued now, Lu. What other embarrassing things have happened around me?" he inquired, wanting to keep the mood light. He needed light.

"Right, Lex. Like you don't know."

"I don't," he answered in his most innocent voice. "Tell me one, just one."

She giggled. God, she thought, I'm like putty. How does that happen to me? "No. I'm not going to relive my embarrassing moments just so you can have another laugh at my expense."

"Do you think that maybe it was the fart?"

Mortified, she struggled to get off of him. But his arms tightened like steel bands. She could feel his laughter rumbling in his chest.

"We are *not* having this conversation, Lex."

"Come on. I just lost my father. You are supposed to want to cheer me up."

"Really? Really? You are pulling the dead-dad card. You are horrible." Again she struggled to get away, but the struggling started to do things to her body that were completely inappropriate. Ugh, I can't do this, she thought.

"Yes, I'm shamelessly using the fact that my father died. What could have been worse than the farting incident?"

"You are such a bastard," she said but even she couldn't help smiling.

"Oh, I just remembered."

"Lex Pellitteri, I swear if you even say it, I promise you I will hurt you."

"That day, I remember thinking that it must really suck to be a girl," he teased. He loved being here with her. She was still so easy to goad.

"I swear, please, Lex. I am not sure I ever got over that."

"Big deal. What's a little blood—"

"I hate you," she said, cutting him off. "This is the problem with growing up next to boys. Please don't say another word."

"Are you blushing, Lu?" he continued. "Lemme see," he said as he grabbed her upper arms and lifted her up so he could see her face. Sure enough, the blush had crept up her neck and was staining her cheeks. He miscalculated, though. Seeing her like that, so beautiful and fresh, actually blushing from embarrassment about an incident that happened thirteen or fourteen years ago, bowled him over. And suddenly the mood wasn't light anymore. I want her, he marveled. Before he could think any more about it, he pulled her up so that his lips could meet hers.

It was merely a quick meeting of their lips. Not really even a kiss. But Lu pulled away from Lex so quickly that he had to wonder if she had a boyfriend, a significant other person in her life.

"Don't, Lex," she pleaded as she tried to disentangle herself. "Please let me up."

Reluctantly, Lex let go of her, allowing her to crawl off of him. He closed his eyes, lying prone on the porch, trying to figure out how he had misplayed that. He rolled over quickly and stood up. He walked over to grab another rocking chair from the front of the porch, angling it so that they could both sit and talk. Feeling the past thirty-six hours zing through his body, he sat wearily and patted the arm of the chair next to him.

"Take a seat. Willa will be here in a bit. She's helping clean up."

They both smiled, knowing Willa was hating that.

"Great. She'll be in a pleasant mood on the ride home," Lu observed as she sat, albeit unwillingly.

"You never answered my question."

Puzzled, Lu drew her brow together. "What question?"

Smirking, he said, "Are you avoiding me? Why were you hiding out over here?"

"Two."

"Huh?"

"That was two questions."

"Lu, I've been up for almost two straight days and my dad died yesterday. At least I think it was yesterday. I'm not in the mood to play word games."

Acknowledging his comment with a nod, she leaned back in her chair. "I'm not avoiding you." Shrugging, she continued. "Willa and I were trying to get out of here so we could get some sleep. It's been a long couple of days for everyone. And the next two are probably going to be even more trying."

Although skeptical, he accepted her logic. Before he'd seen her talking to Pete, he hadn't been itching to spend any time with her either. He hated to admit he was sorry that she didn't seem to feel the same compulsion he did. She hadn't been rocked by the sight of him. He silently acknowledged that he'd been spending too much time with groupies. She wasn't nearly as impressed with him.

"I know this will sound trite, but how are you?" he ventured, curious about her.

She smiled. "I'm good. Things are good."

"What are you doing with your life?" he asked, then laughed. "Shit, that doesn't quite sound like what I want to know."

Again, she smiled, knowing how awkward this felt. "It's OK. I know what you mean. And I'm finishing up my dissertation."

"Not shocking." Again, a pause, a smile. "What's it on?"

She hedged. "I'm getting my doctorate in psychology."

"Not English?"

"Ah, no."

"Fought that tooth and nail, huh?"

"Absolutely." She looked away. Of course he'd remember that she wanted to make her own way. Not be like her mother. "What about you? Is being who you are everything you thought it would be?"

"Just like you to start out with the hard questions." Shaking his head, he thought carefully about his answer. "Yes and no."

"Thought we weren't playing word games," she teased.

"My answer has evolved over time. At twenty, it was everything I thought it would be. Soccer all the time. Localized fame. Easy pickings." He stopped. "It's different now. I still love playing. God, I love it. It's like I was born just to do that. There's no greater high. But it's also a business. I used to just let my agent handle everything, but I wanted to be more involved with everything. Mostly because of my dad. He didn't like that I didn't always know what was going on. So I spend a lot of time trying to manage my affairs."

"So he got his businessman after all," she said knowingly.

Chuckling, Lex agreed. "Yes, he did. I hated it at first. And even though I know Caroline knows I'm not stupid, we had to jump through a lot of 'dumb jock' hoops. I had to prove myself to her. Which in the end felt good—but it pissed me off in the beginning. I almost fired her."

Lu laughed. "Oh, I'd have paid to see that. She made you work. Ha. Bet that felt different."

With a self-deprecating grin, he said, "It did." They were quiet for a while. Each lost in their own thoughts.

"I'm so sorry about Mr. P.," she said softly. "He was such a special person. I will really miss him." She reached out to Lex, grabbing his hand and squeezing it.

"Thanks, Lu." Reaching over with his other hand, he turned hers, lightly stroking her palm with his thumb. "I didn't know what it would be like to see you again. But it feels so natural sitting here with you. It doesn't seem right that we haven't had a conversation in eight years."

Danger, danger! her head screamed. She pulled her hand away. "I'm going to go rescue Will," she said hastily, as she stood up.

Standing also, he said, "Lu? Come on. She's fine."

Adamant, Lu started walking away. "I'll see you in the morning, Lex."

He started to walk the other way, but stopped and headed toward her. Covering the ground quickly, he grabbed her by the hips and moved her gently up against the HardiePlank of the house, his body penning her in. Her eyes held a weary message that he was unable to decipher. "Where's my good-night hug?" he asked, mischief dancing in his eyes.

"You are still the same—bully." God, could she not have exited gracefully? Annoyed but unable to resist playful Lex, she shook her head.

His arms snaked around her waist and he pulled her into his body. It was almost enough, he thought. Almost. But not! He pulled back enough for her to look him in the eye. Then his mouth captured hers.

7

It sucked.

Not the kiss.

The kiss she resisted. For the first time in hours, she thought about her daughter, Nina. She thought about Dr. J. She thought about the devastation that she was about to rain down on everyone. This was the wrong thing to do. To complicate the situation any more was wrong. Her mind was screaming at her to stop. Her lips were clamped shut. But it was Lex. And one thing she had never been good at was resisting him. But she tried, although there was nowhere to move. He surrounded her. His body caging her in, his arms, imprisoning her she was lightly trapped. But still waging the war.

Then her body took over and she felt her mouth open under his gentle probing. As his tongue entered her mouth, her body released a breath she didn't know she was holding. Lex coaxed her tongue with his. Her hands wound up his neck, stroking his nape, feeling the bristles of his short hair. Trying to get as close to him as she could, she pulled her body away from the wall and moved toward his, seeking his heat. She wanted this. She wanted him.

"What the fuck are you doing?" Willa snapped.

Lex pulled away from her gently, keeping her where she was but terminating the kiss. Lu ducked out from under his arms and looked at Willa sheepishly.

"Just saying good-bye," Lu said, walking toward the front of the house, the same path she had started to tread just five, maybe ten minutes earlier.

Looking back, she noted that Lex was still leaning against the wall, a playful smile on his face. Probably remembering, like they all were, the first time Willa ever saw them kiss.

"Déjà-fucking-vu! It's like a damn time warp being back here with you two," Willa said in her snappiest voice. "Get your shit. It's late. I'm pissed and tired."

Rolling her eyes, Lu stepped through the front door, grabbed her bag, and headed down the steps of porch, grateful for the escape.

Lex watched her walk away and turned wearily toward Willa, who was trying like hell to imitate the death stare. Waiting for the inevitable set-down Lex pushed off the wall and walked toward her. "Whatcha got, Will?"

"She's not made for this. For you. I'm asking you to leave her alone."

"You're right," he acknowledged, eyebrow raised. "Déjà-fucking-vu." Kissing her on the forehead, he went on, "She always has been so much stronger than you ever gave her credit for." He started to walk away when Willa grabbed his arm. Turning back to her, he waited.

"It's you I'm worried about. She won't resist you, but this time you'll both be shattered." With that, Willa walked away. And Lex stood, his hands on the railing, wondering what the hell was going on.

⌒

Willa and Lu were silent as they drove away from their house. Her condo on the beach was about twenty minutes away and Lu prayed that Willa would hold her tongue so that she could escape to the mindlessness of sleep. But ten minutes in, Willa unleashed her tongue.

"Are you fucking kidding me? What the fuck is wrong with you?"

"Language, Will."

"Nina's not here to hear me so I can say whatever the fuck I want. Seriously, Lu, what the hell are you thinking?"

"Trust me, Will. I know it was stupid. I tried to avoid him, but you took too long."

"Oh, so this is my fault."

"No. Not at all. It's mine. It's his." She looked out into the night as they crossed the north bridge, over the Intracoastal Waterway.

"You know this is going to make it all worse. Shit, Lu. This is not what you need to be doing."

"I know."

"Go home tomorrow."

"What?" she asked, finally facing her sister, staggered at the suggestion.

"You do not need to be around him. You are like magnets for each other. Go home. Get Nina. Tell him." Willa glanced briefly at Lu, who could no longer stop the tears from running down her face. She looked absolutely desolate. "Lu, it's the best thing. If you sleep with him and then shove his daughter in his face, he will never forgive you. He might not ever forgive you now." Consciously gentling her voice, Willa continued. "I know that somewhere deep in your soul you have always hoped that you guys would be a family. But it will never happen. You have lied to him for eight years. You kept his child from him. You gave her to everyone but him. How can he possibly forgive you for that?"

And that's what she was pondering when she fell asleep. How on earth would he ever forgive her?

⌒

As exhausted and emotionally drained as she was, Lu did not find her blissful silence in the night. She finally sank into dreamlessness around five in the morning, right about the time she was normally getting up. She felt the feather-light touch of a hand run up her arm and down her back. It swept up through her hair, then along her jawline. The warmth of it seeping into her bones eliciting a satisfied moan from her. Her eyes fluttered open and she found herself staring into the laughing eyes of Lex Pellitteri.

"Come, sleepyhead," he cajoled, "get up and come run along the beach with me."

Coming fully awake very quickly, Lu made a grab for the sheets as she turned and sat up. Fumbling for her glasses, she looked wearily at the clock. Six in the morning. With a groan of frustration, she threw herself back onto her pillow.

"Seriously, Lex. How did you get in here and why on earth are you up so early?"

With a shrug, he sat at the foot of the bed. "It's not six a.m. where I'm from. It's the middle of the day. I tried to stay in bed, but too much shit was moving around up in my head. I need to move."

"You always need to move. Guess that hasn't changed either," she observed.

"Nope. Remember when they tried to get Jo to put me on Aderall and she about threw a fit?"

"Yes, I remember."

"Ha. Sometimes having a force for a mother isn't such a bad thing."

"When was it ever bad for you?" Lu wanted to know.

"Jo? I don't know if bad is the right term. Just, you know how she is. She never backs down. It can be frustrating."

"Don't I know," Lu answered, then immediately regretted it.

Lex cocked his brow at her. "About Jo?" he asked, quizzically.

Backpedaling, she said, "No, mothers in general."

Looking past her, he said, "Dr. A. is different. Maybe it's that southern accent or genteel manner. I don't know. She just never seemed as intense as Jo."

"You still call her by her first name?" Lu laughed in spite of herself. "She must love that."

"She fucking hates it, but I just have to goad her." He smiled, that characteristic irreverence dancing in his eyes. "Come on. I need to run." Grabbing her foot, he pulled her leg out from under the sheet. "And don't try to tell me you don't still run. I can look at your leg and see all those muscles, long and lean. Get up."

Yanking her leg back, she groaned again. "I'm not going to be able to keep up with you. You're a world-class athlete. You keep in shape for a living."

"I'll go easy on you like I've always done anyway."

Lu's only response was to pick up the closest pillow and heave it at his head.

When it fell uselessly to the floor, he laughed, cocked the damn eyebrow, as a sinister-looking smile crept across his face. "Seriously?" Leaning down to pick up the discarded pillow, he quickly hit her with it in the legs, then jumped on the bed and gently straddled her. Conscious of their massive weight difference he pinned her arms with his legs, leaving his hands free.

"Lex, I swear if you do what I think you are going to do, I will *kill* you."

"Oh, you mean if the chicken comes to get you, as I'm pinning you, you'll kill me. And how are you going to manage that?" he laughed evilly and looked at his hands, then back at Lu. "You mean this chicken?" he asked as he showed her his two index fingers.

"Lex," she screamed as she wiggled to try to escape. Laughter spilling out of her mouth, she continued to try to buck him off of her. "Please don't!"

Images of their childhood played out in her mind. He and Pete had tortured her and Willa more times than she could count. Lex's hands started moving to her chest, dead center between her breasts. And he started drumming on her breastbone.

"Please . . . stop . . . please . . . Lex," she begged, trying to catch her breath and stop laughing. "Please . . . I'll run with . . . you . . . I . . . promise. . . . Just let me up."

Laughing, he rolled off of her and jumped off the bed. "Come on, then. You've got five minutes."

As she rolled over, trying to catch her breath, more laughter escaped from her. She couldn't believe he just chicken-pecked her. She laughed, thinking about the many times she'd teased Nina and done the same thing—much gentler. This is so not good, she thought, reveling in her feeling of happiness. Why could he make her feel like this after so long? Would anyone else ever make her feel this way or was she doomed to a solitary existence when he went home in seventy-two hours?

Glancing at the clock again, she tried to calculate how she could go running with him and still get back here for her seven o'clock call to Nina. Slithering out of bed, she quickly changed into some running gear, put her contacts in, and pulled her hair into a haphazard ponytail. Fortifying her soul before walking out of her bedroom door, Lu went off to the races with Lex.

8

When Jo made her way out to the deck with her coffee, she already knew that Lex had gone. He'd always been an early bird, never letting poor Pete sleep even though he preferred the night. She figured he'd gone to the beach to run. The moment he could drive, he'd get up before school, drive the eight miles to Siesta Key and run along the deserted beach. For the first time since he left home, she wondered if he missed the beach. She'd never asked and he'd never offered. He'd probably never offered because she'd never asked. Mike had probably asked. He probably knew if Lex missed it.

They had always been closer. Mike was easier to talk to, she imagined. She noticed most glaringly when Lex had gone to Mike for advice when he found out Lu was pregnant. They kept her in the dark for a while, Mike giving Lex the time he needed to think through his life-altering decisions. She'd been so pissed. Pissed that Mike had kept it from her, pissed at Lu for ruining Lex's opportunity, pissed at Amber for encouraging Lu. She'd been mad at the world. Lu's announcement had shattered her world.

Not like it was shattered now. But now, with Mike gone, the decision was still affecting her realm. The irony was not lost on her. Today they would start the process of burying her husband and here she was, dwelling on the past, waiting for the inevitable conclusion to the most horrible time in their married life. And soon, she would lose Lex too. She knew that. Knew it like she knew the sun was going to rise right before her in another twenty minutes. Creeping over the horizon, its light would filter through her large oaks, awakening all that was around her. And much like the rising of the sun, there was nothing she could do to stop the loss of her son.

"Good morning," Amber said as she shuffled across the deck.

Jo's eyes stayed focused on the rising of the sun. "Good morning."

Amber hesitated. She thought that anything that came out of her mouth would sound trite, or meaningless, so she opted for silence.

"He's with her. I imagine their feet are flying swiftly over the pounding surf right about now," Jo observed.

"Very poetic this morning," Amber said. Willa had texted her the moment Lex showed up at the house.

"Ha. Do you remember when we first found out that they liked each other?"

"Oh yeah. Our biggest fear realized. Of all of the kids around, all the pairs I imagined, Lex and Lu never entered my mind. She was always so serious and he—was not. Didn't seem like an obvious connection. And I think Willa and Pete were more surprised than anyone."

They both smiled at the memory. Willa and Lex were the wild ones, Pete thoughtful, and Lu mature. Lex's travels cultivated his fun-loving spirit. When he would return, he and Willa would go to parties, hang out with friends, run the same gamut. Although Lu had caught up to them in school, she just didn't have the social-butterfly gene. Content to stay home, she enjoyed a small, exclusive group of friends. Pete fluctuated between the two—sometimes partying with his brother and Willa, sometimes hanging low. They were an unlikely foursome, brought together by proximity. The boys were naturally protective of the girls, but no one ever noticed any proclivity between Lex and Lu.

Willa had been the first to notice. And no one was ever sure how far it had progressed. Not in the habit of having anything to tell her mother about Lu's social life, Willa came to Amber more out of a stunned bewilderment than out of a desire to rat out her sister.

"Mom," she began, "have you noticed anything . . . different about Lu?"

Amber, taken aback, tried to think about what, if anything, she would have noticed. There wasn't much to notice. Lu was to graduate with Willa and Lex, but because of her age, Amber was making her stay at home and take courses at the University of South Florida as it offered classes in Sarasota. Their house had been somewhat chaotic because of graduation and prom. As Amber thought about it, though, she had to admit that Lu had been scarce recently.

"Now that you've asked me, I guess she's been gone more recently. But so have you so . . . What's going on, Will?" Even Amber had taken to calling the girls by Lex's dubbing.

"A couple of weeks ago, Lu was pissy. I don't know why, but she snapped at everyone. Even her nerdy friends were annoyed."

"Willa Knight. That's rude."

"Sorry. Her sweet, unsocial, extremely smart friends. Is that better?" she asked sarcastically.

"That's enough, Willa."

Rolling her eyes, Willa continued. "This is going to sound ridiculous," Willa noted, shaking her head. "I really can't even believe that I am thinking this."

Amber was suddenly on high alert. "Willa, for goodness' sake, just tell me what's going on."

"Well, Lu was in a really bad mood. She was especially bitchy." Willa looked directly at her mother, "Sorry, sorry. She was in an exceptionally foul mood," she said in a very proper tone, while looking at her mother inquiringly.

"Just tell me!"

"She was really rude to Lex. It was weird. I've never really seen her be mean to him, but she was acting all high and mighty, Miss Smarty-pants, around him. Like she was pissed. But for the life of me, I couldn't understand why. I asked Pete, and he was just as baffled. Then, all of a sudden, everything's great and she and Lex are now together all of the time."

Amber got very still.

Willa, knowing she had a captive audience, put it out there. "I think something is going on with Lex and Lu. Something of a not-friend relationship."

Bewildered, Amber turned away from her, contemplating her news. Although Willa and Lu were different as night and day, they were close. That closeness added validity to Willa's claims. But she knew there was more, because Willa wouldn't have come to her unless she was sure. Turning back, she looked at Willa, "What else?"

Willa heaved a deep breath. "I saw them kissing."

Amber was horrified. She loved Lex, because he made it extremely difficult to not like him. But he was leaving. And as smart as Lu was, Amber imagined that when she let herself love, it was going to be the sticking kind.

Jarred back to the present when Jo stood up to get more coffee, Amber waited for her to return. "I was just thinking about the day that Willa told me about them," Amber told her.

"Yeah, I've spent a lot of time over the last couple of days thinking about that time in our lives. Even more than I've thought about Mike. Maybe it's avoidance."

"Or maybe it's the sense of resolution."

"You think this will be resolved?"

"I think you started that ball in motion with your conversation with Lu yesterday."

Jo could tell Amber was angry. "Are you going to go all Mama Bear on me?" she asked, sarcastic.

"No. The time for Mama Bear was eight years ago. I let you and actually participated in bullying my daughter. I won't do that again." Amber felt anger coursing through her, her shaking hands a reflection of its path.

"Hmph," Jo grunted. "Guess my thirty-six hours of sympathy have expired."

"Don't pull that on me," Amber hissed. "You deserve all the sympathy I have and you've got it. Being angry at you for attempting to browbeat Lu into doing what you want when you want is a separate issue. Why on earth did you order her to go get Nina?"

Jo cut her eyes at Amber. "Lu told you?" she asked, surprised.

"No, of course not. She would never talk to me about what to do about Nina, not after I didn't help her. Willa told me."

Jo got up from her chair, feeling the compulsion to move, something that she was sure Lex had inherited from her, not Mike. She wanted, needed, to explain to Amber.

"I was wrong," she said, still pacing. "I was wrong eight years ago, and I was wrong yesterday. I really don't expect to be forgiven for what happened before, but I hope you can forgive me for yesterday. I didn't intend to say that. I wanted to ask her to not say a word, to be there for me, Pete, even Lex if we needed her. But to wait for Lex to get over the loss of his father first before she told him. I know, knew that this was all going to come to a head, even before Mike died. The guilt he felt was enough for me to be thinking of a plan to bring Nina to Lex when Lu was ready." She paused and laughed, a brittle sound. "That's bullshit—when I was ready." She stopped again, making her way back to the lounge chair and sitting down heavily. "But when I opened my mouth, instead I demand that she go get Nina. Maybe I would have realized what I had done and perhaps even apologized, but she got up, regally, and left."

Amber, stuck between loyalty to her daughter and sympathy for her best friend, didn't know what to say. She longed for her husband to be by her side. She knew they could shoulder the grief for each other and that he could help her navigate this treacherous path. When he got back they would figure it out.

"Part of me," Jo continued, "part of me needs to have Nina here. Mike loved her so much. She was the light of his life. Sometimes I think that if I could get past the guilt, guilt that I didn't really know I was feeling, I could love her even more than I do. But when you look at her, she looks back at you with Lex's smiling green eyes and you just can't help but be happy. That's always been Lex's gift, aside from soccer: he just makes you happy. And Nina's the same. And, selfishly, always selfishly, I wanted her here for me." And then she broke.

All the angst, the sorrow, the desolation and devastation, the possibility of utter destruction overwhelmed her and she sobbed, burying her face in her hands.

Amber went to Jo and wrapped her arms around her, holding her while she melted down. Reduced to a shell of a woman who had lost her mate and was about to lose her son.

9

The day had flown by. Six hours of viewing had been filled with hundreds of people paying their respects to Michael Pellitteri. Overwhelmed by having so many people feel the need to say good-bye to his father, Lex spent the day in a euphoric fog, punctuated by the surprise appearance of a number of his teammates, past and present, and his agent, Caroline. Not once, throughout the day, had sadness descended—in fact, he existed in the glow of pride, humility, and happiness—the exact opposite of what he expected. Part of him knew it was because so many people obviously loved his father and they were surrounded with that love. The other part of him waited for the reality to set in, for the grimness of life without his father to take hold.

He didn't let Lu out of his sight the entire day. Her presence was like a buoy in the ocean, keeping him above the water of sadness. Having her near kept him smiling. His teammates were enchanted with her, and even Caroline, who tended to skewer any woman in a ten-mile radius of her athletes, gave Lu a wide berth. Lu radiated an inner joy and contentment that he desperately wanted. He hated that she had it already, without him. He wanted to be the one who lit her up from the inside out.

When his teammate Miguel made his way toward Lu and began

his mating ritual, Lex found himself feeling possessive. When he had Miguel's attention, Lex leaned in close and whispered, "Not her, she's mine." Miguel, a lover not a fighter, conceded with a roguish smile. "No harm, no foul," he said. Lu, who was close enough to hear Miguel's comment, looked at Lex quizzically. He merely cocked his eyebrow, smiled at her, and returned to the conversation he had walked away from.

Although the day had been far more manageable than he expected, he found himself watching his mother closely. Jo seemed excessively tense. And he was worried about her. The depth of her sorrow didn't surprise him. She looked sad. But there was something else too—a fragility that was unexpected and troublesome. Jumpy and easily startled, she seemed to be waiting for something bad to happen. But even Lex couldn't think of anything worse than the unexpected death of his father. He noticed that girls, Amber, Stacy, Cami, LeeAnn, and Natalie hovered around her like an honor guard of some sort, seemingly protecting her. Thinking about his and Lu's long friendship, Lex watched as his mother looked up and caught his eye. A deep, penetrating look passed between them and she mouthed "sorry" across the space. Confused, Lex could merely respond with a questioning look. He swore she mouthed, "I'm so sorry," again before she returned to the conversation swirling around her.

Lu appeared by his side right then, grasping his hand and squeezing, silently offering her support and comfort, almost as if she had observed the strange moment with this mother. Without really realizing what he was doing, he leaned down, as close as he could get to her ear and whispered, "I need to be inside you. Soon." Then he dropped a light kiss just below her ear. He could feel her body stiffen, and she pulled her hand from his before he thought to hold his tighter. Before he knew it, she was across the room and out the door, running from him again.

He wasn't sure what was going on with her. Unhappily, he gave in to the insecurities that had plagued him regarding Lu. He knew she— and, it seemed, everyone else—was keeping something from him. He didn't know how he knew, but the pervasive feeling of a great conspiracy jumped to the forefront. He felt like everyone was in on it. An undercurrent seemed to flow in every conversation he had with people. And when they saw him in close proximity to Lu, he felt their curiosity. Perhaps it was merely *that*—curiosity. Would the childhood sweethearts find their way back to each other? Everyone loved a feel-good story. But then he would catch sight of Pete or Willa watching him, and he couldn't help but wonder what they were holding back. He checked Lu's left hand, searching for a sign of an engagement ring, something that would explain her reticence. He found nothing.

Then, ruefully, he thought of what he had whispered to her and he smiled. What was he thinking? Lu wasn't some groupie. His comment had been bawdy and shockingly disrespectful to Lu. That was why she ran this time. But she wouldn't be able to run from him. Not tonight. He needed her. And he was going to have her. Consequences be damned.

Ducking into a small, unused viewing room, Lu quietly closed the door behind her. Flinging herself into one of the striped wingback chairs, she leaned back and closed her eyes. She was trembling with a heady combination of desire and fear. Her run with Lex earlier in the day had set the stage for the rest. Their easy camaraderie had reestablished itself as their feet pounded over the packed sand. When he left her at 6:55, he'd dropped a kiss on her forehead, much like he'd done to Willa the previous evening. And while part of her wanted more than that, great appeal could be found in maintaining Lex's friendship. The betrayal of a friend seemed so much simpler than that of a lover.

So when he'd leaned in close and whispered in her ear—what he'd whispered in her ear—shock and surprise overwhelmed her. And it had heated her. If she had stayed in the room, everyone would have seen the telltale blush run up her neck, she imagined, and creep over her cheeks. She'd felt everything in her body tighten and hum. So she fled. She expected Willa to find her at any moment as her panicked gaze had found her sister's on the way out of the room.

Lu had to hold out. As much as she wanted Lex, she couldn't allow herself to be with him in any way other than to support him. But damn he was irresistible, she conceded unhappily.

When she heard the door open, she looked over, thankful for her sister's concern. But Willa wasn't the person who walked through the door. It was Lex's stunningly beautiful agent, Caroline Thorvaldsdottir. Lu didn't know a lot about her, but she could tell Caroline was shrewd. Mike wouldn't have entrusted Lex's career to just anyone. The choosing of his agent had been a long, thorough process that Mike had agonized over for quite some time. In the beginning, he had managed Lex's career and money. But he was more interested in being a father than an agent, so when Lex turned twenty-one, Mike bowed out. And from what Lu heard, it had been a good move for everyone involved.

Lu watched warily as Caroline found a chair and pulled it up, in an effort to facilitate some kind of conversation. She had been introduced to Caroline earlier and she seemed nice enough, but now, Lu experienced a sense of foreboding that perhaps this wasn't a casual conversation.

Tilting her head, Lu acknowledged Caroline with a smile. "You must be exhausted from your travels," Lu began.

Caroline returned her smile, making her seem even more beautiful, softer somehow when she relaxed. "I am. It's been a long couple of weeks. Throw a transatlantic flight into any week and it's enough to make one tired."

Not having ever left the country, Lu nodded but didn't contribute anything.

"Are you OK?" Caroline inquired.

Taken aback, Lu nodded. "Yes. Thank you. Just a long, sad couple of days."

"It must be nice to have Lex back in town," Caroline ventured.

Lu smiled before she could stop herself. "Yes, it is. We spent our childhoods together, and it's nice to see him."

Caroline nodded, understanding reflected in her ice-blue eyes. Lu felt at ease. "I can tell he's looking to you for comfort. He hasn't been able to take his eyes off of you and he seems to like having you close by," she observed.

Caroline didn't seem to be looking for a response so Lu didn't offer one.

Caroline leaned forward, in a manner that made the two of them look like they were conspiring together. "When I took over the management of Lex, there were certain things already in place. And since Mike Pellitteri essentially hired me, I was bound by attorney-client confidentiality." She paused, smiled briefly, as if contemplating what to say. "Mike was one shrewd bastard."

"I think you might be the only person who knew Mr. P. who would think it OK to call him a bastard," Lu said, her annoyance clear in her voice.

Caroline merely smiled. "Don't misunderstand me," she said. "I don't mean it as a slight. Just that when it came to managing his son's career and money, he did everything right. When it came to Lex, he drove a hard bargain." Again, she paused. "He was a hard act to follow."

Lu knew this to be true. She never asked for details from anyone, but she knew that Lex was worth a lot of money. His soccer career had been storied. Lex's talent and his father's business acumen were a profitable combination.

"When I began going through Lex's accounts, which are vast, I noticed that a trust had been set up. Twenty percent of everything Lex made was funneled into the trust."

Lu got very still. When she thought back on this moment later, she would regret that she let her poker face slip.

"Mike never did tell me what that trust was for, but I can see from your expression that you know what it is?" she said, questioning Lu.

Lu, regaining her equilibrium, said, "No, I don't."

But she'd already shown her hand.

Caroline looked doubtful. For a moment, Lu thought she would let it go and relief surged through her. But it was fleeting.

"You don't have to tell me. I imagine I'll find out before too long."

Although her tone dripped with understanding and sympathy, Lu felt suddenly chilled.

"I can see the way Lex is looking at you. He wants you. Just be careful."

"You're worried about me?" Lu asked, skepticism clear in her words.

Caroline continued to stare at her. Lu could see that she would be good at her job, representing her clients with equal parts charm and confidence.

"That's an interesting question," she responded. "I'm very familiar with the way Lex operates. Right now, he wants you; that's plain as day. It's equally clear that you want him. But you don't really know him anymore. He's not the same boy that you knew. And his attention span is short. You are familiar and convenient. But he'll leave you behind. I'd hate for you to get hurt."

"I certainly appreciate your concern, Caroline. But I'm not after Lex," she reassured her, "not that it's any of your business, though." Lu just couldn't hold that comment back. She liked Caroline, but this really wasn't any of her business.

Caroline smiled, clearly not offended, and patted Lu's knee. Lu got the distinct impression that Caroline was patronizing her, but she didn't care as long as this conversation was reaching a conclusion.

"Just be careful," she murmured as she stood up to leave. She was almost out the door when she stopped and turned to Lu. "I almost forgot," she said, although Lu knew that she didn't 'almost forget' anything. "Mike left a letter with me for Lex in case anything ever happened to him. I imagine it holds the key to the mystery that is the trust. I'll give it to Lex before I leave tomorrow." With that, Caroline swept from the room.

Lu knew she'd be given notice. She had until tomorrow to tell Lex about Nina.

10

Willa found Lu sitting in the same striped wingback chair that she had escaped to thirty minutes before.

"Come on, *chica*. The hall is clearing out. We're headed to the Village." Taking up the seat that Caroline vacated, Willa threw herself into it. "You OK?"

"Aren't you sick of asking me that question?"

"Hell yes. Damn, just get over this mopey shit," she replied, reminding Lu of Sky and eliciting a smile. "Seriously though, why'd you bolt out of the room?"

"You don't want to know."

"Seriously? Of course I do. What happened?"

"I can't tell you."

"Why not?" Willa demanded. "What the hell, Lu? I saw Lex say something to you. What did he say?"

"Will, trust me," Lu said, not wanting to think about what he had said. But just talking about it brought the whispered words back to her and a blush crept up her neck.

Willa watched, fascinated. She laughed as she said, "Ooh, Lu. He said something dirty dirty to you, didn't he?"

"Stop it, Will!" Lu demanded.

"Tell me, please. It's been a while since I've gotten laid."

"Seriously, now you're encouraging this?"

"Absolutely not. Don't you dare sleep with him! It would be the stupidest thing you could do. But might as well enjoy the flirting. Now tell me what he said."

"Have you been drinking?"

"Not yet. But I will be. Come on, Lu. If you were me, watching you from across the room, you would so want to know what he said. Come on, Louisa May," Willa continued to cajole.

"I can't, Will. I'd be embarrassed to say it." She hated to admit that to her sister.

"Ugh. It must have been good."

Lu glanced at her watch. "Is Dad back yet?"

"Yup. Just got back from the liquor store. Are you done avoiding him?"

Lu smiled ruefully. "Not yet. I just can't have the conversation that he and mom want to have."

"Can you and I have it?"

"Yes."

"What's your plan?"

"Sky is bringing Nina tomorrow. She'll be here about one o'clock. Since the service is at ten, I figure that will give everyone enough time to get out of the house."

"So she's just going to knock on the door and say, 'Hi, I'm Nina Pellitteri Knight. You can probably tell from looking at me that I'm your daughter!'"

"Ha ha, Willa. No. I'm going to ask Lex if we can talk after the house clears out. I'll explain to him what happened and introduce him to Nina. And then I'll duck."

"Are you actually developing a sense of humor about this?" Willa asked, sounding impressed.

Lu smiled a weary smile. "No, not really. I'm just accepting the inevitable."

Willa reached over to give her hand a squeeze. "Are you telling Dr. J.?"

"I want to let her fucking suffer," Lu said with no malice, "but since I'll be destroying her son, I think I owe her a heads-up." Lu didn't tell her what else she had planned. No one needed to know that. It was between her and Lex, and it was the only way she could think of to save the man she loved some hurt.

Willa stood. "Let's go," she said. As they started to walk to the door, she added, "Is it OK if I strip Pete down and fuck his brains out?"

"Did you just admit that you want Pete Pellitteri?" Lu asked, not hiding her shock.

"Yes. I did. Are you surprised?"

"That you want him—absolutely not. That you are finally admitting it? Hell yes."

"So," Willa calculated, "will you tell me what Lex said?"

"Ugh, Will. You're relentless," Lu said, laughing, following her sister out of the funeral home. "Let's go find those pesky Pellitteri boys."

"Yes, lets!" Willa agreed. "Let's do that."

⌒

The Village had changed a lot since Lu's younger days. Since she left at seventeen, she'd never really hung out at the bars in the small commercial district on Siesta Key. She did recognize that it had been infused with some upscale boutiques, a couple of bars and restaurants. They chose the Daiquiri Deck because of its open-air venue. The beautiful night was clear, humidity free and cool enough to lure people to sit outside. They left the house to the adults and drove to the bar as quickly as they could exit. Willa and Lu were happy with the choice because it meant they could walk home. It wasn't like they could get too crazy, with the memorial service at ten o'clock in the morning.

Willa, Pete, Lex, Lu, Caroline, and Miguel were all that was left of the crowd. The talk of the table turned to soccer when Willa and

Pete went to get drinks. Lu excused herself and headed to the bar to join them. Walking up to Pete, she grabbed his hand, squeezed it, and leaned in to him. "You doing OK?" she asked.

"Yup, Harvard, I'm doing OK," he said with a sad smile.

"So many people were there today. Must have made your mother feel good."

"More humbling than anything," Pete responded. "But, yeah, I think it made a difference."

Willa looked at her watch. "I think we should call it a night. I'll get their drinks, then can we leave?" she asked Lu.

Lu didn't hesitate. "Absolutely."

"I'll come with you," Pete said. "Lex can swing by and get me when he's ready. I think they're talking business."

"I got lost about two minutes into the conversation," Lu said.

They each grabbed a drink from the bar and headed back to the table. Placing the drinks in front of their respective owners, Pete said, "We're gonna walk to Will's. Just swing by and get me when you're ready."

Lex looked at his brother, then at Lu. She was across from him, out of his reach. "You too?" he asked her.

"Yeah. I'm beat." Lex nodded his head, seemingly accepting of her decision. Surprised, but relieved, Lu walked over and wrapped her arms around his neck. "I'll see you in the morning," she said.

Lex merely turned his head, which was right next to her ear and whispered, "Before that." With the din of the music and the swirling conversation, no one heard him but Lu.

Quickly withdrawing, she looked uneasily toward Pete and Willa. "Ready?"

They said their good nights and walked the half mile to Willa's condo. Lu dropped back, lost in thought and trying to give Willa some space to operate. When they made it to the apartment, she quickly withdrew to her room, leaving Pete and Willa alone.

Willa was still debating, wondering if she should really try to seduce Pete. He interrupted her thoughts.

"I'm surprised Lex didn't put up a fight when Lu left."

"I'm not," Willa responded. "He'll end up here. He's just biding his time." Pete opened her sliding glass door and walked out on the balcony.

"Do you love hearing the water when you go to sleep and wake up?" he asked.

Standing a heartbeat away, Willa moved to his left and leaned on the railing, mimicking his stance. "You know I do." She wanted to talk to him about Lu's plan, but she wasn't sure how to broach the subject. Over the last eight years, Willa and Pete had, by mutual, silent agreement, avoided the subject of their siblings. It just seemed simpler not to talk about it. Willa had always been afraid that Pete secretly hated what Lu had done, what she agreed to, and she didn't want to have to defend her sister. But suddenly she needed to talk to him about it.

"What do you think Lex is going to do when he finds out about Nina?"

Dropping his head in his hands, he looked completely distraught. Rolling his head to the side, he caught her eye. "I feel like I am waiting for Armageddon to occur."

Willa didn't mean to, but she smiled. "Nice."

"Fuck, Willa. We're burying my father tomorrow. The people I'm closest to are going to come apart at the seams when this all gets revealed." He sighed and looked back to the water. "There's a good chance Lex will absolutely hate me, but I'm so relieved. I want him to know Nina."

Willa knew there was more, so she stayed quiet—which was damn hard.

"Can we fast-forward past tomorrow and just get to the aftermath?" Pete asked.

Willa couldn't resist any longer. She pulled his hand out of its clasp and locked her hand with his. She pulled him close, into a hug. She felt him stiffen, then relax into her. "Damn, Willa. What the hell are we going to do?"

"We'll figure it out," she murmured.

They didn't talk for a while, just held each other. Pete's hand started to move up and down her back and she willed herself to let him dictate this.

"Will," he whispered, close to her ear, making her shiver with desire, "would it feel at all incestuous to you if I tried to kiss you?" He drew back and smiled at her.

And she burst into rippling laughter. "Ah, Petey, you really know how to get a girl hot."

He laughed too. Then, he grabbed her gently by the back of her neck, pulled her forward and kissed her. And it was good. Very good. Not at all incestuous and not at all the little Petey that she had grown up with. When he ended the kiss, she grabbed his hand and led him to her room.

"Stay here tonight, Pete."

"OK. But Willa"—he stopped her, grabbed both of her hands, and kissed her briefly—"this can't go any further tonight." He kissed her again to take the sting out of his words. "Tomorrow we are going to be operating in a whole new world. We need to take this slow."

Willa was about to protest. Pete stopped her by laying his index finger across her lips. "Listen to me. I already love you. We have an amazing niece together. But my brother and your sister are about to destroy each other. I just can't do this now when—" He stopped. "Armageddon. I know this isn't you, but can we do this my way?"

Willa was burning up with desire. Always the impulsive one, she wanted to have him now. But Pete was the reasonable one—the one who tempered Lex. And just as he was the voice of reason so much when they were growing up, what he said made sense. Her blue eyes burned hot.

With his finger still on her lips, he begged, "Please don't make this harder for me than it already is."

His big chocolate eyes were impossible to resist. She reached up and gently took hold of the hand that had rested lightly on her mouth. "OK.

But you better be really fucking good," she said with characteristic bluntness.

Laughing, he leaned forward and branded her with a scalding kiss. "You don't need to worry about that!"

Willa led him to her room. She got ready for bed, he texted Lex. Then he wrapped himself around her and fell into a contented sleep.

11

Lex couldn't remember ever being so exhausted. The last couple of days had finally caught up with him. But as he crossed the threshold of Willa's condo, a startling energy coursed through him—his proximity to Lu instantly registering. He needed her. Surprised to find the living room empty of his brother, he sat lithely on the couch.

He'd been warned off by everyone, his mother, Caroline, Dr. A., and Willa. The vehemence of their positions gave him some pause. Their concerns were valid. They beat at him now as his body continued to strum with unreleased desire. He would return to England, she would stay here. While baby genius Lu was super intelligent, she wasn't worldly. He would hurt her. His world wasn't made for a tenure-track professor. How could he leave her behind again?

He'd heard it all and he'd listened. He'd even thought briefly about leaving without making love to Lu. But how could he? Maybe Pete was right about this being just familiarity and grief. Did he just want her because he was home and it felt like he should be with her because his memories of Sarasota were all wrapped up with her? He didn't think that was it, but he couldn't be sure of anything at this point. His objectivity on the subject didn't exist.

He thought back on the day. She had been there for him every moment he needed her. As if she could sense his lapses of composure, she would send him an encouraging smile or lightly touch him (which about drove him insane). Even having Pete around didn't bring him the kind of peace that Lu's presence provided. What did that mean? Why did his fingers itch to touch her and his heart long to know her? A little unnerved by the direction of his thoughts, governed by an innate sense of self-preservation, Lex thought about the one thing that gave him balance. She still needed to explain what happened when he left. He needed to know why she gave up on him and their plan. Remembering that betrayal helped him rein in his overwhelming feelings for her.

Suddenly noticing that Pete wasn't sleeping on the sofa that he was sitting on, he wondered if he had misread the text Pete sent him. Pulling his phone from his pocket, he looked at it again. Confirming what he thought he knew, he wondered where Pete was sleeping. Then it dawned on him. Pete was sleeping in Willa's bed. Lex let out a soft chuckle. Finally. In the midst of all this confusion, things seemed right in the world.

Running his hands over his face and leaning deeper into the couch, he contemplated leaving Lu alone. He was convinced that she was deeply involved with someone. It was the only explanation for her reticence. Because, let's face it, he knew she wanted him too. Smiling at his arrogance, the trait his father liked best and least about him, he stood up and made his way to Lu's room.

The sight that greeted him didn't disappoint. She was so innocently sexy that she sent his heart sputtering in his chest as he imagined himself sliding into her. He closed the door to her bedroom and leaned back on it. Lying on her stomach, her black hair fanned out behind her over the pillow with strands covering her neck. Her right leg, long and straight, while her left leg was bent and a pillow spanned her stomach—a habit he remembered from when she was six. He knew his hand would be traversing those long legs momentarily and he was instantly hard. As he imagined all the ways he would have her, her eyes opened and she looked directly at him. She was wide awake.

"Playing possum, Lu?" he asked. Although he wanted to go to her, he remained where he was, leaning on the door.

She smiled warily as she moved to sit up.

"Don't!" Lex said, a little too sharply.

Lu froze, watching him with wide eyes. She wasn't lying down anymore, but she wasn't sitting up.

Lex pushed himself off the door and made his way to her. "I was just imagining running my hands up your leg, from toe to thigh." Still moving toward her with panther-like grace, his voice soothing, he gently pushed her back down onto the bed. Then he knelt on the side and starting at her toes, he ran his right hand all the way up the length of her leg and back down again. He repeated the motion, but this time continued up her body, groaning when he encountered her thong, but seeking her back and lightly stroking her. "We need to lose this shirt and these," he whispered, running his hands under her thong, then leaning over and pulling her ear lobe into his mouth.

Lu, who had continued to watch him warily, closed her eyes as desire overwhelmed her. She didn't know where the thought came from, but her brain continued to fight, while her body was screaming, "Resistance is futile!" She smiled, which Lex immediately noted. Kissing her neck, between her lobe and her jaw, he continued with his perusal.

"Turn over for me, baby," he said, moving his hand down her back. When she did, he lifted her tank top up, prodding her to lift her head up. He threw the shirt to the side, then moved down and discarded her underwear. Then he took in his first glance of her body. "God, Lu, you are beautiful," he murmured. He couldn't stop his hands from gliding over her, exploring her breasts. With a devilish smile, he looked directly at her and noted, "I liked your sixteen-year-old breasts, but these"—he looked down, then back up at her while his hands found her nipples— "these are a definite upgrade."

Mortified but not surprised that Lex was cracking jokes, she briefly considered sitting up. But Lex anticipated her reaction and bent down to take a nipple in his mouth. As he gently drew on her, he watched her with his laughing eyes. Lu was powerless to do anything. He watched her melt into it, her eyes heavy with desire, and his laughter died, just like that. He had an overwhelming need to kiss her. Pulling his mouth from her breast, he stood up. Lu, confused, opened her eyes and looked up at him. She still hadn't said a word.

He pulled off his shirt and pants, stripping in a fluid motion, like he did everything else. Then he was beside her. And then on top of her between her legs, his face even with hers. He kissed her gently. "Lu, I want to take this slow and worship every inch of your body."

She heaved a stuttering breath, her body so wet and ready for him that she didn't think she could take much more.

"But I can't wait that long. I meant it today. I need to be inside of you," Lex said.

Again, Lu didn't say anything. She merely watched him with her too-old eyes. Her fingers were stroking his head, playing with the bristles of his hair.

He kissed her again. He knew she was ready for him. Her heat surrounded him. He could smell her desire.

"Talk to me, baby," he prompted, but then he kissed her again, stealing her breath. His hips moved between her legs, bringing him in contact with her heat. "Lu?" he said, the question evident in his voice. He realized then that he needed her to want this. He wanted her to want him as much as he wanted her. And ego aside, he needed to hear it or see it or feel it.

Lu continued to stare at him. His arms were starting to shake as he held himself back. Then the most bizarre thing happened. Her eyes filled with tears and he groaned in frustration and fell on top of her, rolling out from between her legs.

Neither one of them said anything, and the room filled with an uncomfortable silence. Then Lex rolled out of bed, pulled on his pants, and walked out onto the balcony.

Lu stayed in bed, fighting the urge to go to him. If she went to him, they would have sex. All he needed was for her to say yes. He'd been breaking her down, slowly, surely. But he had needed her to capitulate totally—that was just Lex. It was always, had always been, all or nothing with him. She wanted to, but how much worse would it be when she told him about Nina? And how many times could she have this argument with herself?

Not able to stand the distance between them, she got out of bed and picked up his shirt off the floor. Slipping her arms in, she quickly fastened a couple of buttons and walked out to the balcony. She leaned against the door jamb and took in the view.

Perfection. His elbows resting on the railing. He gazed out at the gulf as it rolled gently against the sand, beating a gentle rhythm. Sliding in and rolling back out—erotic images filled Lu's brain, and she thought she might combust right there. His athlete's body rippled with muscle. Ink scrolled all over his back. She hadn't known he had any tattoos. Fascinated, she moved closer. Without meaning to she began tracing the lines of the intricate pictures detailed on his body.

She felt him stiffen, but he didn't say anything, so she didn't either. Her fingers continued to peruse his back. A weird band spanned his upper back, from his left shoulder blade to his right. Probably Celtic, but she couldn't be sure. His number, seven, was on the lower left side of his back. He had Italian and Cuban flags, intertwined, a tribute to his heritage. It should have appeared crowded and incongruent, but somehow it all fit together.

"You followed Dr. J.'s tattoo rule?" she murmured, fascinated with her exploration of his body.

He didn't answer her at first and she didn't blame him. He'd tried to get her to talk and she'd left him hanging.

"Yes," he said simply.

She stopped moving her hands, allowing them to rest lightly on both of his hips. Then, as if in a trance, she moved forward and kissed his back, on his spine. Then slid her tongue down his body until she reached the waistband of his pants.

His body grew taut. She could feel him struggle. She knew his frustration with her; she was frustrated too. But she knew she needed to be with him. Before she did anything else, she wrapped her arms around him and leaned into his back. "I need you to promise me something," she said.

He drew a ragged sigh. "I don't think I can make you any promises, Lu. I wish I could."

"Let me say this, Lex," she begged, her forehead resting on his back, her arms still around him, but a small gulf existed between their bodies.

Taking another fortifying breath, he said, "I'm all ears, Lu."

At any other time, she knew, he would be saying that with a smile. "I need you to promise me that after the memorial service tomorrow, when everyone clears out, that you can give me some time."

She could feel his hesitation.

"Lu, I've let it go. We don't need to go back over the past." He didn't want this to be about the past. He needed to hold on to that to keep some perspective.

"Lex, please," she begged.

He turned in her arms so he could see her. Her eyes and face must have told him what her words did not. "OK, Lu. I promise." His hands were gripping her shoulders. "Promise," he said again, giving her the reassurance he knew she needed, always anticipating what she needed.

She looked at him, then at his mouth. It was probably his one imperfection. His lips were mismatched. He had a full bottom lip but a very thin upper one. It didn't matter, of course. Drawing up her every reserve, fortifying her heart, she looked directly at him and murmured, "I want you inside of me, Lex."

She hadn't finished her sentence when he pushed her back against the wall of the balcony. His mouth ravished her, the forcefulness of the kiss making their teeth hit. Grabbing her upper thighs from between her legs, he lifted her up against the wall, securing her with his weight. By mutual consent, Lu wrapped her legs around his waist. He slipped his hand in his back pocket and pulled out a condom. He held it to her mouth and she gripped the corner in her teeth. She was naked except for Lex's shirt, so no barriers marred his access. He was inside of her in seconds, filling her in a way she didn't think possible. He pounded into her with more finesse than seemed right, with a wall at her back. He reached between them. It took one touch of his finger to send her over the edge. He held her as she clenched around him.

Then, still sheathed in her warmth, he moved her to the bed. He slipped out of her when he set her down. Kneeling at the edge of the bed, he turned her over on her stomach and pulled her down so her knees were at the edge and her ass was up in the air. Stifling a groan as he looked at her, his eye caught her tattoo. He wanted to ask her about it, but his thoughts were scattered. Unable to wait any longer, he entered her from behind, grabbing her hips and pulling her back into him. They cried out together at the contact. He couldn't hold out any longer. With pent-up desire exploding, Lex filled her again and they found their release together.

12

They feasted on each other all night. A pattern developed. They would have sex, wrap themselves around each other, doze off, talk, and start all over again. Lu found herself liking him more and more. He asked her about everything, joked with her, and made her want him with a passion she hadn't known existed. Exhausted and sated, they learned the ins and outs of each other again. He didn't hold anything back in his questioning of her, even when the questions made her blush or think before she answered. Like his body, his mind was insatiable.

"Lu," he said as he rolled her onto her stomach and moved his hands up and down her body. "Tell me about this tattoo? Why do you have a tramp stamp of a ship?"

Slightly mortified, Lu didn't know how she forgot about her tattoo and that he would see it. His fingers outlined it over and over, running up and down the four masts, tracing the lines of it.

Breathless from his perusal, she answered carefully, "First of all, when I got it there, the term 'tramp stamp' didn't exist."

He moved his body down so that he lay between her legs, his mouth even with her tat. "Baby, that term has been around for a long time." His tongue mimicked the lines that his fingers had run.

When he called her baby, she felt her whole body heat up.

"So, why the tribute to Columbus?"

She hated that he was intelligent sometimes. Why did he have to be graced with all things good? "It's not a tribute to Columbus."

"OK. What is it?"

She didn't know how to throw him off. Her body and mind were completely pliable.

"It's the *Niña*," she said. Not really believing that she told him, she buried her head under the pillow, hating that he could make her stupid.

"And?"

"And what?"

"Why are you so stubborn?" he asked, smiling. "I know that I can get you to talk." He murmured. He moved one of his fingers inside of her. "And why?" he prompted again. When she remained silent, he slid another finger inside her warmth. "You are so tight and wet, Lu," he murmured.

"I can't think when you do that," she spat out, moaning despite herself, her hips starting to move against his hand.

He laughed. "Me either, actually," he agreed before completely distracting both of them.

As he made love to her again, she forgot about her tattoo, his desire to know what it meant, and her reasons for trying to hold anything back from him.

~

Lex looked at the clock, startled to find that it was four in the morning. Neither one of them had slept much. He knew that he should, but he didn't want this night to end. He wasn't ready to face the reality of his father's death and Lu provided an amazing distraction. He wondered briefly if it was Lu specifically or if any woman would have worked. But then he felt her move closer to him, like a heat-seeking missile, and he knew it wasn't that he lost himself in a woman. It had everything to do with that woman being Louisa May.

And suddenly he needed to know.

"Lu, are you involved with someone?"

She stiffened in his embrace. "Why would you think that?" she asked, sounding pissed.

"I'm not sure," he answered truthfully. "I feel like you're holding something back. That you're keeping something from me."

She pulled away from him, putting space between them. Leaning on the headboard with the sheet wrapped around her body, she responded, "Do you really think I would sleep with you if I was involved with someone else? Are you that jaded and conceited that you think I'd sacrifice a relationship solely to sleep with Lex Pellitteri?"

He couldn't help himself—he laughed. "Yes. I am jaded and conceited. Two traits that you have known about since you were six. So it doesn't really count."

She closed her eyes, frustrated and trying to block out his radiance. She didn't want to argue this point too much. Because she did have a secret.

He tried to pull her closer to him. But she resisted. "Come on, baby. Talk to me," he said, his eyes busy with mischief. He moved down the bed, grabbed her ankles and pulled her so that she was lying down again. His attempt to dislodge the sheet at the same time failed, so he gave it a good tug, leaving her exposed to his view. Settling himself between her thighs again, some place he found that he enjoyed an awful lot, and looming over her, he tried again.

"I thought maybe you were involved with someone because I'm not sure if you noticed but there seems to be this conspiracy to keep us away from each other—a conspiracy, I might add, I think you are involved in." Leaning down, he kissed her spot, the one right below her ear lobe, right by her jaw, and like always, it turned her eyes to liquid desire. "So, at first," he continued, "right up until the moment I was inside of you, I thought you were seeing someone." Again, he got distracted by her eyes and her mouth. He moved in, kissing her hard and quick. "But when I got inside you, you were too tight and sweet to be sharing this," and here, he moved down her body and licked her, running his tongue between the folds of her sex, "with anyone on a regular basis."

He dropped his head again between her legs and licked her. Then he moved his hand, plunging two fingers into her, making her cry out with desire. Caught up in her cries, he spread her with his other hand and sucked on her clit, making her come hard and quick, shaking with the force of it. He looked up at her wide-eyed stare and smiled that Lex smile, eyes dancing, mouth coated, watching her. He moved back up her body then, bringing his mouth down hard on hers again, sharing her taste. "So, baby, come on. Tell me what it is?"

For a moment, just a brief moment, she imagined telling him, right then, while he was between her legs and he could still taste her. Maybe she'd have a chance to make him understand. Perhaps he could forgive her and they could be a real family. But just as the thought of the three of them appeared in her mind, the bubble of her dream burst around her. He hadn't thrown words of love at her. Lex had become a typical athlete as far as she could tell. Her observations—and there hadn't been a lot—were of him with beautiful women, none of them lasting for long. And hadn't Caroline told her that his attention span was short? She couldn't get caught up in him. She had known that when she walked out onto the balcony. So she did the only thing she could think of to do. She turned the tables on him.

"So when do you head back to England?"

If her question caught him off guard, he handled it extremely well. "What's today? Friday? I think I go back on Monday. I have a game on Tuesday. I want to be back for it."

"Are you going to stay away for another eight years?" she pushed, trying to shift his attention, take the focus off of her.

He looked questioningly at her but didn't seem to be uncomfortable yet. "I don't know. I haven't had time to think about any of this."

He dropped his head, kissing his way across her collarbone.

She went for broke then.

"So this, tonight, it's merely a distraction for you?"

Lex's head snapped up and his body tensed. Lu breathed a sigh of relief. Pushing away she could do.

He didn't say anything for a moment, merely stared at her. She knew he was trying desperately to frame an agreeable response, even though his face never gave anything away.

"No, Lu. Not a distraction. A homecoming," he answered, his green eyes deadly serious, boring into hers.

He took her breath away. She couldn't speak, couldn't respond. She merely returned his stare, unable to look away.

"I don't know what that means, Lu. I just know that being here with you, inside of you, feels damn good. And don't we have a conversation scheduled for tomorrow?"

At her nod, he said, "Let's leave all this for that time, OK? Can you do that for me?" he asked earnestly. Oh God, she thought, I know this look and those words. Before she could close off her thoughts, a vivid memory of Lex leaving her flashed through her mind. They were standing at the airport, the final boarding call echoing through the small terminal. Lex had pulled her into a hug, shifting so he could lay one hand on her stomach and keep her close with the other. "Take care of yourself and our baby," he said. "Can you do that for me?" Did he remember too? She felt panic racing through her body. It made her squirm against him and that quickly got him aroused again. He took from her movement what he wanted to take from it and entered her quickly, sheathing himself in her heat.

"God, Lu," he murmured as he moved inside of her, faster and harder, looking for his release.

She closed her eyes, protecting herself from his gaze, not wanting to get lost in his green depths. For the first time in her life, she wanted, needed, to get away from Lex. She wanted this to be over, she wanted him out of her. She needed their connection to be broken. But this was Lex and he wouldn't settle for that. All or nothing.

He stopped moving, and before Lu knew what was happening, he took hold of her chin. "Open for me Lu," he said, "open up and look at me."

She shook her head slowly, imperceptibly. Refusing.

"Lu, please. The only way I can get closer to you right now is to be able to look into your eyes. I need you to look at me." His cajoling tone, the one he'd teased her with all night, was gone. His last words were a desperate plea. "What can I do, Lu?"

She thought about him pulsing inside of her and how unfair she was being, but she just couldn't go there again with him. She couldn't orgasm while staring dreamily into his eyes knowing that tomorrow he wouldn't even want to look at her. It was all about the depths of his eyes for her. Sometimes, she felt like she could touch his soul. But she couldn't leave him hanging either.

She pulled back from him, forcing him out of her. Without looking at him, she turned over and invited him to enter her the way he had earlier in the night. He accepted her invitation with a groan and filled her immediately. This way, he didn't see her tears hit the sheets. And Lu didn't have to see the look of confusion in his eyes.

13

When Lu felt Lex slip into a deep sleep, she got up. She walked over to the alarm clock on the nightstand in the room, picked it up, and set it for seven o'clock. Then she soundlessly entered the bathroom, grabbing her running clothes out of the stockpile of gear that she left there as she unpacked. Picking up her running shoes, she grabbed her funeral clothes and her makeup bag, and hurried out of the room, down the steps, to her car. She drove down to the next beach access, parked, and began her run. The moon still shimmered on the water and the stars continued to light the night.

She ran to the jetty and back, busting out three miles in a little over twenty minutes. Sweaty, salty, and sandy, she jumped back into her car and headed to her parents'. She'd shower and get ready at their house. Willa, Pete, and Lex could catch up with her. The less direct, solitary contact she had with Lex, the better. She hated that she felt like a coward running away from him, but she'd worked it out in her mind. And this was the best way. It didn't stop her from longing for more—some way for a perfect ending to their story. But it wasn't to be.

She pulled into her parents' driveway at five forty-five. Following the porch around to the back of the house, she entered through the kitchen. She hopped in the shower in the vacant guest room, towel dried her hair, and donned some sweats. Glancing at her phone, she typed a quick text to Sky.

Are you on schedule?

She'd hoped for an immediate answer. When she didn't get it, she slipped the phone into the pocket of her sweatpants and slid her feet into her flip-flops. Taking a deep breath, she made her way back out of the kitchen, across the path to Dr. J.'s.

Cresting the last step, she stopped in her tracks. Apparently, the avoidance game was over. Sitting in the chairs were her mother, her father, and Dr. J. Just what she needed—a fucking audience.

"Figured you'd be up and at it. How was the run?" her father said, amusement apparent in the lines of his face.

Rolling her eyes, Lu began her trek across the deck. "Got any coffee?"

"There's a mug on the counter waiting for you," her mother replied.

"That's just fucking great," she mumbled, softly enough that no one could make out what she said. As she made her way into the house, she felt her phone vibrate.

Sky: Yup. But I can't text and drive so I couldn't answer you right away.
Lu: Haha. How's my girl?
Sky: Excited to see you and family.
Lu: ETA?
Sky: 3:00
Lu: Be safe.
Sky: No shit Sherlock.
Sky: Are you ok?
Lu: Are you driving and texting?
Sky: No Mam. I pulled over. Are you OK?
Lu: Just fucking peachy.
Sky: Need to see your girl?
Lu: You have no idea!!!
Sky: Do anything stupid?
Lu: Yes. Eight years ago.
Sky: Can't change that now. See you soon.

Lu tucked the phone back into her pocket and grabbed her coffee. She took a few sips. Biding her time. Then, knowing it was now or never, she took a long, deep breath and headed out to the firing squad.

When Lu came back out, Dr. J. and her parents halted their whispered conversation. Not that she cared what they were saying.

"Can I presume that my children were with you ladies last night?" Dr. J. asked.

"Yes," Lu replied absently, not offering any other explanation but she caught sight of her mother's questioning look. And she ignored it. She took another sip of her coffee, letting the silence become their fifth companion. She didn't think she was trying to let them stew, but she may have been. It struck her when she saw them all together, waiting for her, that she was pissed. For the first time in eight years, she realized that she hated each of them just a little bit. It wasn't overt. It wasn't even enough to make note of—until right then.

"Dr. J., I want you to know how sorry I am for you. I have always admired your relationship with Mr. P. There always seemed to be this understanding between you two. And it was so obvious that he loved you and you him. When I used to dream of having a relationship, yours was one that I held up as the pinnacle. And since I've had Nina, he has been my greatest supporter. Greater than the three of you combined."

She stopped and turned away from them. Gathering herself. Thinking of and talking about Mr. P. was hard. She hadn't meant to sound like a bitch or take anything away from any of them, but she wanted them to know how much his loss was going to affect her. She wiped away the tears from her face and slowly turned back to them. She looked over them—not *at* them, because she didn't want to see the emotions playing across their faces.

"To see him with Nina made my heart sing. I don't know how else to describe it. I know he found joy in all of the mannerisms that she inherited from Lex. I know he loved her because he could see his son in her. But it was so much more than that. He loved her because she was Nina. I think he died regretting the decisions that were made eight years ago."

"Louisa May," her mother said, shooting up out of her seat. "That's enough. You are being incredibly insensitive."

Lu stood there, trying not to glare at her mother. Please be on my side, she thought. Without meaning to, she looked directly into Josephine Pellitteri's eyes. They weren't green like Lex's, but the soulfulness of his eyes he got from his mother. Jo reached out and patted Amber's arm.

"It's OK, Amber. She's not saying anything I don't know. And I bet she's been sitting on this for a long time." Jo never took her eyes off of Lu. Inclining her head, she granted Lu permission to continue.

Bitch, thought Lu. I'm reprimanding them and she's giving me permission.

"I'm doing this my way. That's what I came over here to tell you. Although I was going to tell you all separately, before you ambushed me."

"Lu, we knew you'd come when you'd figured out what you wanted to do. This wasn't an ambush."

"It's neither here nor there," she said waving away her mother's comment with her hand. "Sky is on her way here with Nina. Nina won't be at the funeral. I haven't even told her about Grampa Mike because I didn't know how." She paused, hating that she hadn't been able to sit down with Nina before she'd had to rush here. "I'm not going to share much more than this with you. What I do today is what I think is best for Nina and Lex. I haven't asked for your opinions about it because I'm not sure that I care."

Angry and surprised by her anger, Lu took another moment. She turned away from them. How is it that I didn't realize that I held them responsible? she thought. Trying to get a grip on her anger, she walked to the edge of the patio and looked out into the dawn. The possibilities of the dawn. Her mother could probably quote great works of literature that paid tribute to the new beginnings promised at the start of each day. But as Lu looked out over the horizon, she only saw endings for her. Lex could get a beginning. She was going to do everything in her power to ensure that he got the endless possibilities today. And Nina would get a beginning. Lu smiled at the thought of Nina and Lex discovering each other. They would fascinate each other. But she only saw dusk for herself. She would once again feel the loss of Lex. How was it possible that she had to experience that earth-shattering loss twice in her lifetime? And she was forced to admit that she would lose some of Nina today. It wouldn't be the two of them against the world anymore. She would have to share her daughter. Another loss. And she would be saying good-bye to Mike Pellitteri. Mr. P., who had sensed the depth of her loss because he had lost too on that day so long ago. Her heart ached. And her anger bubbled. It was then that she knew she was losing her parents too. Because quite suddenly, she wasn't sure that she would be able to forgive them.

Turning back to the three friends, knowing there should also be a fourth, Lu moved toward them again. "I'm doing this my way. I'm making it up to the seventeen-year-old girl whose destiny was chosen for her. You are not to interfere." She met the eyes of each of them. She saw their reluctant acceptance. She drew herself up, and as a parting shot she looked back on them. "You better hope that Lex and Nina find a way to connect. Because if my daughter gets hurt in any way, I am holding the three of you personally responsible."

As Lu made her way off the deck, silence descended again. Before Jo could stop it, laughter rippled through her. She looked at Amber and Chris, her dearest friends.

Amber was clearly horrified. She sat stunned, ripped open by the vehemence of Lu's anger. Although it was justified, Lu had never given them any reason to believe she was that angry with them. She looked over at Chris, wondering if the bewilderment she was feeling was the same for him. Chris looked just as stunned as she felt.

"I never thought she was so angry with us," Amber said as she got up and walked to where Chris was sitting. She knew this was a conversation they needed to have privately, but she couldn't contain her thoughts.

Chris shook his head. "I don't know. We probably should have known. She's always been good at letting you think you know what's going on in her head. She's too damn smart."

"Think about her holding that in for this long."

"I don't think that's what's going on, Amber. I think she just realized how mad she is. Everything coming down on her with no warning. She's striking out and we're convenient."

"Think there is any way that today can end well?" she asked, rhetorically.

Chris chose not to answer.

Jo remained silent, lost in her own thoughts. Listening but not really listening. Letting them deal with their family as she knew she would have to deal with hers today. If Lu was this angry, she couldn't imagine Lex's wrath. It took a lot to get Lex mad. In fact, she couldn't really remember a time when he let anger rule him. He had always found a way to laugh things off. Even on the field, no one ever got the best of him. The most popular descriptions of Lex were words like *mischievous, fun-loving, irreverent. Intense* usually played into it too, but no one could claim to have ever seen Lex angry. Jo worried she would see it today though. Today, she would see a side of Lex Pellitteri that no one had ever seen.

Her thoughts drifted to Lu. And she felt proud. She had been magnificent—an avenging angel. Taking back what she lost those years ago. As she thought of Lu taking control, it dawned on her.

"Lex," she said out loud.

Amber and Chris turned to her, waiting for her to continue.

"Lex brings it out in her. That confidence we just witnessed. That 'swag'! He's the one person who could ever tap into that. I have a feeling that today isn't going to be anything like we think it is. She's got something planned. Something no one else would have even considered. She's going to do something to save my son."

As the three of them contemplated the coming day, they lapsed into that now-familiar silence, each lost in their own thoughts. When Lex, Willa, and Pete walked up the deck steps, they shattered the pensive

LEX and LU

mood. Willa made her way to her parents, offering hugs and kisses as Pete and Lex bent to greet their mother. The three of them shared a look of concern. They weren't sure what they'd missed, but their parents looked shell-shocked and the day hadn't yet begun. Willa and Pete looked to Lex, begging him to do something about the mood.

"What's going on out here?" Lex inquired, taking center stage. "You all look like you're going to a funeral."

And just like that, the bubble of tension burst and everyone laughed.

14

Everyone except Lu had made it for breakfast. Lex waited, watching as the door continued to open to admit people, but Lu never appeared. Miguel, Caroline, and Pete stayed close to him. Miguel and Caroline to offer support, Pete to siphon it. They'd always taken turns, but today, Pete was leaning hard. When it wasn't on Lex, Willa was close by, and for that Lex was grateful. But it also made him angry because Lu seemed to have disappeared. Lex desperately longed for a run to drag the anger from his system. He couldn't remember the last time he had been as pissed as he was right now. Two hours before saying good-bye to his father, and he couldn't think of much other than waking up alone. He longed for Lu to be with him. He'd tried to play it off, but Pete and Willa knew. They knew he had spent his night with Lu, and it was obvious she'd slipped out before Lex had gotten up when he strolled out of Lu's room alone. Although he'd slipped easily into his role of lightheartedness, he resented having to be the one to help everyone feel better while he slid further toward darkness. He needed Lu now, and he couldn't figure out where she'd gone and why she'd left without him.

Right before they left for the service, he pulled Willa to the side.

"Where is she?" he asked, as he attempted to maintain his façade of utter coolness.

Willa didn't try to pretend, which he appreciated. "She went to the church to help take care of things so your mom could stay here with you and Pete." She reached out and rubbed his arm. "I'm not saying she didn't take an opportunity to avoid you," she paused, "but she was trying to help your mom."

Somewhat mollified, he gave her a brief smile. "Thanks," he said, pulling her into a side hug and kissing her forehead. "I've missed you, ya know."

She slung her arm around his waist. "It's good to see you too, Lexifer," she said, laughing at her very old pet name for him.

He threw back his head and laughed. "I totally forgot about that." Leaning in, he said softly, "Go easy on my boy, OK?"

"I'll try. But as you know, I'm not easy."

"Ha! Oh, I know."

"You OK?" she asked, knowing the question wasn't a fair one.

"It's all relative, right?" At her nod, he said, "I think I am in shock still. I don't really believe that he's gone. I mean, I believe it, but it hasn't hit me."

Since she had nothing to compare it to, she simply nodded.

"You ready?" he asked.

"Yeah. I'll go grab Pete. I can drive."

"Thanks."

⁓

The service was beautiful. Isn't that what you are supposed to say about a memorial service for your father? he thought. Lex felt the sympathy around him. A tangible euphoria, as if everyone in the church was having the same memory of his father, enveloped him in all of his happy memories of the most amazing person he had known. Besieged by different images still alive in his heart, he focused in the defining moment of his childhood. He'd always been closer to his dad than to Jo. So when Lu told him that she was pregnant, Mike was the person he sought.

"Pops, I need to talk to you about something," he'd said when he found his father alone in his office Lex was fairly certain that his father assumed he wanted to talk to him about his upcoming trip. He'd made the U-20 National team and would be leaving soon.

"OK. What's going on?"

Lex tried to come up with something witty and Lex-like, but his Lexicisms failed him. "Ah, I'm not quite sure what to say."

"Just spit it out. I can read it."

"Lu's pregnant," Lex said quickly.

Mike's eyes got wide, he rubbed his hands over his face, and then turned away. "Can you say something else?" his dad quipped.

"I could, but this is what I need to talk to you about."

"How is she?" Mike asked. Lu might as well have been one of his children. And Mike could imagine her intellectual anxiety, which would be far more potent than with most sixteen-year-olds finding out they were pregnant. "And don't think I'm questioning you, but how did you handle it?"

The smile that was so much a part of Lex's charm split his face. "I told her I'd be back as soon as I could and we'd play it from there. I'm not leaving Lu behind. You know that, right?"

Mike smiled, but it was tight, worried.

"So, how do you think Dr. A. and Mr. Chris will take it?"

Mike didn't even know how to respond. He wasn't sure how *he* was taking it. "Have you guys discussed options?"

"Like what? Abortion?" Lex laughed. "You know Lu. In all her intellectual glory she knows exactly what abortion is. And ya know, she knows what she'd be giving up, but she doesn't want to have an abortion. She said, and this might be word-for-word, 'Lex, I know I'm supposed to go on to greatness because I've been "blessed" with this crazy-smart brain, but I can't have an abortion. I know my mom will freak because she's done everything in her power to raise smart, independent thinkers. Her picturing her sixteen-year-old daughter pregnant will offend all of her feminist sensibilities. But I think I can have our child and still make something of myself.'

"Seriously, Dad, how can I argue with that? It was like listening to Dr. A. When Lu talks like that, I feel like I am totally out of my league."

"We're all a little out of our league around Lu. But if it wasn't for you, Lu wouldn't be who she is. You bring out the best in her."

"Well, I think it's more like I bring out the stupid in her," Lex said with a very Lex-like self-deprecating smile.

"How did this happen, Lex? Your mother's been handing you condoms since you were fourteen."

"Well, it's like I said. I bring out the stupid. The only time we had sex without a condom was when I found out I made the team. Can we leave it at that?"

"And when did you two start having sex?"

"Is this something we really need to talk about?" Lex asked as sheepishly as he could.

"Yes. Because, really, Lex, she's only sixteen." When Lex started to protest, he said, "I know her birthday is soon, but, really, Lex, you are both children."

"Dad, I stopped being a child the day you let me leave the country on my own," Lex said indignantly.

"Regardless, you think you're not going to have to answer these questions? What happens when Chris hears about his sixteen-year-old daughter having sex with you? And not that I think this will be an issue, but you are over eighteen, Lex. Technically, they could press charges."

"Dad!" Lex looked mortified for the first time in the conversation. "Do you think they would do that?"

"No, I don't think so, but they could. I'm just trying to point out to you that this is serious, Lex."

"You think we don't know that? You think I'm not scared shitless. Jesus, Dad. I'm about to go off to follow my dream. It was hard enough leaving Lu behind, but now I feel like a piece of shit even thinking about leaving."

"Not leaving is *not* an option. I know I should be noble and be ready to trade your dreams in, but you've worked too hard. And if there are any two kids—because you are kids—that could make this happen, it's you and Lu. But you have to promise me that you'll follow this path that you've been on. If you don't, I think you'll be damning you and Lu to failure. Do you understand me?"

"Yes, sir. Lu said the same thing."

Mike smiled a sad, weary smile. "I love that kid," Mike said.

"Me too," Lex responded. "So, how do you think Mom's going to take this?"

Mike blanched. "Not good, buddy. Not good at all."

Lex snapped back to the present when he felt someone grab his hand. He looked down to see Lu sliding in beside him in the pew. Smiling over the irony of his memory, he squeezed her hand, happy she'd come to him at last. He tried then to pay attention to what was going on around him. Now that she was there, he could focus on the present, getting through the day, instead of thinking about the past.

Soon enough, the service was over and people were surrounding them to offer condolences. His mom and her girls had decided to hold the reception at the parish hall so that the house couldn't be overrun with people. So they made their way next door. Although Lex knew it was hard for people, they kept their comments to expressing their sympathy for his loss even though he knew they wanted to talk to him about his life. He appreciated it. After coming to him during the service, Lu had been scarce. He saw her helping in the kitchen, putting stuff out, generally helping the girls make everything as easy as possible for his mom.

His mom looked to be holding up fairly well. He'd kept his eye on her and Pete, gauging their actions, ready to dole out some comic relief if needed. But neither one of them seemed to be looking for him to step into his role. Pete fed off of Willa, which made Lex happy. They were good for each other. He hoped Pete could keep up with her. And his mom was surrounded by her posse. One of them was always at her side, boosting her up if she needed it. They'd always been like that. The Supper Club girls. They'd been a part of his life since he was eight. They knew each other so well, and it helped him to know that when he left in two days, she'd have the support she needed.

As much as Lex appreciated that they both seemed to be OK, it dawned on him that they didn't need him. Shocked by the realization, he thought back over the years he had been gone. They had still been a close family unit. Pete and their parents made frequent trips to see him, sometimes together, sometimes individually. Once Pete started med school, his visits became less frequent. But he'd always relied on their unit for his support, love, comfort. Lex felt a little shaken. Perhaps because of how he was feeling, the moment would forever feel like a turning point in his life.

Caroline approached him. "I have to get going soon. Do you have a couple of minutes to talk before I leave?"

Lex smiled. "Of course." He had a healthy respect for Caroline. When he and his father finally settled on an agent, after an exhaustive search, he'd been very happy with their choice. She'd continued to make him a lot of money without whoring him out to every sponsor that asked. She kept her advice to a minimum. Once she told him what she deemed important, she allowed him to make the decisions, without ever trying to sway him. She also kept him out of trouble. She'd cockblocked him a couple of times for good reason and had saved him from making a number of stupid mistakes.

He knew there were some rooms in the parish hall so he grabbed her arm and escorted her to one. He didn't notice Lu watching them as they walked inside.

Lex pulled her into a hug. "I really appreciate you coming. And I know you rallied some of the guys to come with you. Thanks."

"I respected your father a lot. I wouldn't have missed it. And I couldn't have kept Miguel away. The others too. I didn't rally them. Just made it easier for them to get away."

"Thanks," he said again, wanting her to know what it meant to him. "What's up?"

"You have your itinerary?" At his nod, she continued. "I can get you out of Tuesday's game if you need me to."

He shook his head. "No. I need to play. I don't need any more idle time."

"Are you sure?"

"Absolutely," he responded. He definitely didn't need any more time. He wanted to play.

"OK," she said. They had ended up in one of the Sunday-school classrooms. There were little pictures all over the room of Jesus rising from the dead, obviously left over from Easter. The chairs were small and the tables low. But Caroline walked over to one of them, sat down awkwardly, and patted the seat next to her.

Lex looked at her quizzically but made his way over to the table. Pulling the chair back, he sat down, with his knees spread, trying to get comfortable. "What's going on?" he asked, sensing that this wasn't one of their normal conversations.

She opened her clutch and pulled out an envelope. Handing it to him, she began, "Your father left this with me when he and I first worked out the terms of your contract. As you had set him up with your power of attorney, there were some parameters set that were protected by rules of confidentiality. Your father was no fool. He knew that by hiring me, there were some things that could be protected."

Lex felt the beginning of panic set in. "Caroline, I appreciate the history lesson, but I'd rather you get to the point."

"Your father had set up a trust. Twenty percent of everything you have earned from playing soccer, not your endorsements, is funneled into the trust."

"Who's the trust for? Is it for my mother?" He was thoroughly confused. Why did he need to set up a trust? Lex was not stingy with his money, although no one ever asked for it. He'd paid Pete's tuition because he wanted to, but even then, they had given him a hard time. "Are you trying to tell me my father planned to steal from me?" He'd heard stories about parent managers who had ended up skimming off of their children's accounts, but he couldn't imagine his father would have done that.

"No. No. The trust is set up for your child, to be used for tuition and then for whatever she wants on her twenty-fifth birthday. It's ironclad. We can't change it."

Lex stood up. "Why would he set something up for my future children? Did he not trust me to make good decisions about my money? You're not making sense here, Caroline."

"Lex, it's not for your future children. Lu didn't have an abortion eight years ago. You have a daughter."

15

For a time—and Lex would never know how long—he sat, dazed, in the Sunday-school classroom. His mind empty. Although he wanted to focus on what'd he'd just learned, he sank deeper into a murky existence. Thoughts flew around, but he couldn't quite grab on to anything. Images and memories assailed him. His conversation with his father a couple of days ago, Lu refusing to look at him the last time they'd had sex, his mother's eyes glistening with unshed tears, Pete and Willa standing together all day, Dr. A. watching him with a weary gaze as he left the room with Caroline, his mother telling him that Lu had an abortion, his first goal scored in Premier League soccer. A constant barrage of scenes over the last eight years, all which he experienced by himself, continued to pelt him like hail falling from the sky. How different would his life have been had he known that he had a child? How was it even possible that he had an eight-year-old daughter and he didn't know it until today? How could Lu have slept with him and lied to him over and over again? How could he have been so wrong about her? Even after not seeing her for the last eight years, he felt he knew her. He'd fallen right back into his childhood. Teasing her, cajoling her, bringing her out, seducing her. And all along, she'd held back. He felt robbed. He felt like a fool. He wanted to hurt her, make her feel what he was feeling. Afraid to move, thinking he might somehow shatter, he remained there.

Pete found him. But Lex didn't hear the door.

"Lex!"

Lex looked up and saw his brother. "What's up?" he managed.

"I've been looking for you for twenty minutes. And I had to say your name ten times!"

Lex shook his head, as if to clear it. "Sorry."

Pete studied him. "What happened? Are you OK?"

"Yeah," Lex said, pulling himself together. "I just needed a minute." He stood up from the tiny chair he'd been perched on for however long he'd been there. "You OK?" he asked his brother, hoping to divert his attention.

Pete eyed him wearily. "I'm OK," he said, nodding his head as if to reassure himself and Lex that he really was. "Are you ready to go? They've started heading back to the house."

Lex thought about going back to his house; his connections to the past blew up in his mind. He didn't want to taint his house with the conversation he knew he needed to have with Lu. He needed to preserve that piece of his childhood. "Is Lu still here?"

"Uh, I think she is back." Pete paused. "She ran some food to the house, but she came back a couple of minutes ago."

Lex drew a shaky breath. Here, he thought, looking around, I want this confrontation to be here, not at my home, not where my memories of my father are enshrined. "Can you get her for me?" he asked, staring his brother down, hoping to intimidate him into doing his will. As much as Pete loved him, Lex knew that he instinctively wanted to protect Willa and Lu. Lex was the same way.

Pete cocked his head to the side, studying Lex. Then Lex smiled at him, that Lex Pellitteri smile, and Pete knew that he was OK. "Sure. Do you want me to wait for you?"

Shaking his head, Lex said, "Nah, Lu can get us back."

"Are you sure?"

"Yeah, man. We're good."

Pete started toward the door, then turned back, "What were you and Caroline discussing for so long?"

"Contract stuff," Lex said nonchalantly. "You know Caroline. She's all business."

"All right. You sure you're OK?"

"Bro, I'm good. I just needed a moment." Nodding toward the door, he said, "Go get Lu for me, please."

⌐

Lu had just finished packing up the rest of the food when Pete found her. He draped his arm around her shoulder and leaned in for a quick hug.

"Your presence is being requested."

Lu looked at him curiously, questioning him with a look.

"Lex asked me to come find you. He needs to talk to you."

"Oh," Lu said.

"You've avoided him all day, Lu. What did you expect?" As much as he loved her, he was unimpressed with her behavior today, and it showed in his tone.

"You're pissed at me?" she asked, without any fight in her voice.

"I'm disappointed. How could you abandon him today of all days? He needed you. I could see it in his face."

She stepped away from Pete, needing some distance. "I couldn't, Pete. I couldn't lie to him up close anymore."

She sounded so defeated that Pete took pity on her. "So then don't, Lu. Tell him. Free yourself, for God's sake," he responded rather vehemently. "This shit's gone on long enough."

Eyes floating with tears, Lu ran her hands through her hair, tucking it behind her ears. She couldn't stop fidgeting. Pete took note and moved closer to her, grabbing her hands and stilling them.

"I've tried to stay out of this. But everything changed when my father died. He wanted Lex to know. I know he never said anything to you—he'd never pressure you, but it's what he wanted. He'd always wanted that. I know he got outvoted all those years ago." Pausing he continued holding her hands. He moved closer and captured her eyes with his. "You have to tell him."

Lu yanked her hands out of his. "Do you think I don't know that? Do you think I don't look at Nina every day and long for her to know him? What kind of person do you think I am? I thought you knew me."

"Don't do this, Lu. I know you, and I love you with all my heart. And I know what you want, deep down in here," he said, placing his hand over his heart. "But, sweetheart, there's no chance." Before she could protest, he continued: "And I know you know that. But you slept with him, and you've been with him for two days, trying to hold on to that dream. You have to let it go. You have to tell him, and you have to give some of Nina to him. I know it's scary. But it's time."

He drew her to his chest and wrapped his arms around her.

It felt just like he imagined it would feel. Blanketed in a constant feeling of impending doom, Pete held on to her. He knew he was on the verge of losing his brother. He'd been a part of the great conspiracy. As much as it would hurt for Lex to know of his betrayal, it would be worth it the moment he saw Lex with Nina. He'd sacrifice his relationship with Lex so that Lex could know his daughter. It was that simple. But he knew that today he'd be burying his uncomplicated, deep relationship with his brother just as he was burying his father and it left him feeling dizzy and immensely sad.

"Lu," he said, "I want you to listen to what I'm about to say. I know you won't want to hear this right now. So I'm asking that you put it away, lock it up somewhere where you can easily retrieve it when you're ready to face it. Can you do that for me?"

He felt her take a big, deep, shuddering breath. "OK," she answered weakly.

"For eight years, I've watched you be this amazing woman and mother. You've raised Nina to be a thoughtful, caring child. And you've still managed to achieve what you've needed to achieve with that crazy, big, powerful brain of yours. But you've held on to this childhood fantasy of you and Lex. It's paralyzed you. You haven't moved on." He stopped, letting her digest what he said as he continued to hold and soothe her. "You are carrying a tremendous weight on your shoulders. When you let this go, when you tell Lex, you will be free. I know it's going to take time, but you'll heal and you'll move on. And you'll meet someone else who can make you happy." He felt her stiffen in his arms. "The Lex you knew has been grown up for a long time. He looks familiar to you and he feels familiar and he's safe because in your mind he's that eighteen-year-old boy that you loved your whole life." Pete pulled back from her but took her face in his hands. "The Lex I know is worldly and sophisticated. He's rich and smart. He's used to everyone around him catering to him. He would stomp on your tender heart. He wouldn't mean to, but he would tear you apart." He saw her flinch like he'd slapped her. "Let him go."

He kissed her on the forehead and hugged her again.

He pulled away. "Lex is in the Sunday-school room. It's the last room at the end of the hallway."

She nodded. Still looking shell-shocked, she gave him a tremulous smile.

"I feel like I'm sending you into the lion's den," he said with a sad smile.

"You are," she agreed, "but I'm the one who gave the lion his teeth." With that, she turned and began her death march.

Pete watched her walk away, his heart heavy. When he felt Willa's arms come around him, he leaned back into her, seeking comfort and warmth.

"How much did you hear?" he asked.

"Enough," she said, hugging him harder. "I heard enough to know that you are amazing. And I want to fuck your brains out because the way that you love knocks the breath out of me."

He laughed and turned in her arms. Grasping her face in his hands, much like he'd done with Lu only moments earlier, he kissed her quick and hard. "Let's make sure we get to that tonight. I'm going to need that."

16

As Lu walked away from Pete, her heart took a tumultuous tumble. She'd listened. She'd heard. She'd told herself the same things over and over again in her mind all day. After her confrontation with her parents and Jo she'd needed some time on her own. Setting up for the day had given her a task. She'd been helpful to everyone here except Lex. The one moment when she could fight his pull no longer she'd joined him in the pew and held his hand. They didn't speak. They didn't look at each other. But the exchange of communication in that touch had been meaningful—both helpful and destructive. It had been their one inter-action, and when she'd walked away from him, she had been breathless and broken.

She had practiced in her head all day. She hadn't gotten it right yet, but she'd told him about his daughter in a thousand different ways. Not one of them made any sense. Not one of them exonerated her in its retelling. She wasn't sure if she should try to describe Nina or just intro-duce them and let him discover her for himself. She wanted to give him the high points. Tell him what she was good at, what her insecurities were, tell him that she'd tried to raise her like she thought they would have raised her together. She definitely hadn't gotten it all right. What the hell had she known at eighteen about being a mother? But she was proud of Nina every day, so she felt she had gotten most of it right.

As she walked with a purpose, yet aimlessly, toward the Sunday-school room, she thought of Pete and what an incredible friend he was to her. She knew that he had taken it the hardest when the edict came down that Lex shouldn't be told. He and Lex were tight. She also knew that he did everything he could to be there for Nina. He hadn't missed an event, not even once he started medical school. But what he just did for her, telling her the cold, hard truth when she least wanted to hear it, ranked right up there with showing up for Nina's Christmas play the year before, in the middle of exams, when she'd been one of forty sheep. His heart was so good. And he would be so good for Willa if she'd let him. Knowing that the two of them might be able to make a start from the ashes of her life made her feel like something good was coming from it.

She reached the Sunday-school room and paused as she reached for the door handle. She knew what she needed to do to help preserve Lex's family. Fortifying her heart with her hopes for her daughter and Lex, she turned the knob and walked inside.

Lex turned away from the window when he heard the door open. He watched Lu approach, apprehension clearly written upon her face. Like a blinding light, anger scorched through him. Lex worked hard to keep the emotion, unlike anything he'd ever experienced, off of his face. It cost him a tremendous amount of effort. Anger was an alien emotion for him. So this blinding rage left him shaking, unsure of how to control it. It dawned on him that he was scared for Lu because he couldn't find any balance.

He waited.

He watched as concern clouded her eyes, her eyebrows drawing together. She walked toward him. When she was directly in front of him, she reached out and touched his cheek. "Are you OK?" she asked.

Shaking, Lex grabbed her hand, drew it away from him and as gently as he could, he got her out of his direct line of vision. Moving past her, he went back to the window and looked out. Able to reign in some of his emotions when she wasn't in his face, he tried to answer her calmly.

"Why wouldn't I be OK?" he responded.

"You don't look OK."

Still facing the window, he said, "What did you want to talk to me about?"

"You want to talk here?" she said, apprehension in her voice.

"We're in a church. As good a place as any," he said, a harsh laugh escaping. "This is where people come to confess their sins."

"OK," she said, drawing out the syllables. "Do you want to sit down?"

"I'm not sure that would be best right now, Lu. Tell me what you need to tell me."

"Lex, I need you to come sit down and talk to me. Please."

"Like I needed for you to look at me when we were fucking last night?" he asked scathingly as he turned toward her and blasted her with a look of pure hatred.

Lu jerked back.

He started walking toward her. He didn't feel in control of anything that was happening. His anger was dictating this show. He wanted to hurt her. He wanted her wounded, like he was wounded. He watched fear begin to crowd her face and it made him happy. Stalking across the room to where she sat on the chairs he and Caroline had abandoned, Lex stopped directly in front of her.

"Stand up!" he demanded.

Lu's blue eyes bulged with disbelief.

"You already know, don't you?" she asked, finding her voice.

"Know what?" Lex asked, deceptively calm although he felt anything but. "What do I already know?" He reached down with both hands, slipping them around her arms like manacles. He pulled her to her feet. He managed to restrain his anger. He didn't want to hurt her, but suddenly he wanted her. He knew it was dangerous, with his rage bubbling up within him, but seeing her, being in the same room with her, continued to make him want to take her.

Lu continued to eye him warily as he moved her backwards toward the wall. When they reached it, he leaned forward and nipped her by her ear. "What do I know, Lu?" he said raggedly in her ear, sending shivers of apprehension and desire through them both.

"Lex, please stop. We need to talk."

"I'm waiting for you to talk, baby," he said as he continued to hold her by the arms and explore her neck with his mouth.

"Lex, I can't have this conversation with you doing that." She tried to move away from him, but he wouldn't let her. "Lex! Stop it. You're scaring me!"

He jerked his head up and his eyes blazed into hers. He released her. But he could see that she was flushed with desire, that she wanted him. Even though she'd betrayed him all these years, she wanted him and he wanted her. And still he felt that relentless drive to hurt her. Not touching her, he leaned down and said low, close to her ear, "You want me. Like I want you. I can see it. Your underwear are probably soaking wet. Aren't they?"

She shook her head vigorously, but they both knew she was lying.

"Should I check?" he asked, dropping to his knees in front of her. "Since the cat seems to have your tongue." He smiled.

He ran his hands up her leg but she clamped her thighs shut.

He laughed. "Come on, Lu. You so want this." Relentlessly, he moved his hand up, forcing her legs to part until he found what he was looking for. He groaned. "Fuck, Lu." He moved her panties aside and plunged two fingers inside of her and she cried out. He knew he had her when she spread her legs, allowing him greater access. He didn't look at her. He stared at the wall behind her, trying to keep everything in check. He was seething, but all of his energy was with her, in what he was doing to her. He pushed her to the limit and right as she was about to clench around him, he pulled out of her.

"That's right," he said, not in his sweet lover-like voice from the night before but in a driven, hard voice that Lu had never heard before. "You don't like to look at me when you come, do you?" He turned her around toward the wall.

Lu knew she should protest, but somehow she thought that this was what he needed, and she was prepared to sacrifice a lot to be there for him. He could feel that in her. He knew she was allowing this because she wanted to put off telling him. So he drove her on, punishing her for her weakness. Before she realized what was happening, he was inside of her. He thrusted into her, not thinking of anything other than exacting some type of revenge for the hurt she was about to inflict on him. He finished quickly, his rage carrying him onward, driving him into her in a relentless rhythm. He reached around her, touched her intimately just once, and she shattered. As he held her while she climaxed, his eye was drawn once more to the picture of Jesus rising from the dead. It was at that moment, with a clarity that astounded him, that he saw the irony. He had just died inside.

Lu pushed away from the wall and, keeping her back to him, fixed her dress. She longed for a bathroom so she could expel him from her body, but she knew that she could prolong this no longer. Before they could decimate each other, Lu found one of the small chairs and took a seat. Composing her face, she looked up, searching for his gaze. She noticed then that he'd been watching her, maybe waiting for her to rail at him. Unsure, she reached over and patted the chair beside her.

"I think it will make this easier for you if you sit down. But I also know your penchant for movement, so perhaps you should do whatever it is that feels right." She paused. Her nerves were reflected in her voice as her speech began the climb to formal. Lu always reached for the big words when she was nervous.

He continued to lean on the wall, one foot bent and braced so that his leg was at an angle. Looking at him, she was reminded that he took her breath away. Determined to move forward she started. "On July 4—yes,

Independence Day, which I always find ironic because I seemed to have lost my independence on that day—your daughter, Nina Pellitteri Knight, was born at 8:00 p.m. after about an hour of labor. Apparently, I was made to make babies. Which again I find ironic because my mama wanted so much more for Willa and me than teenage pregnancy. But ya know, of course, shit happens." She knew she was rambling, but all of the speeches she'd rehearsed were somehow getting strung together, so her flippant side was intermingling with her superintelligent side. It made her head hurt to try to control the jumble, so she let it flow from her mouth. When Lex didn't protest or tell her to fuck off, she knew that he'd already been told about Nina. She knew Caroline had told him and she was pretty sure it wasn't presented in a delicate manner, so she knew she should continue her story.

But nothing came out of her mouth; she didn't know how to continue. Neither spoke. They simply stared at each other, Lu not knowing what to say and Lex refusing to make it any easier.

Finally, Lu found her footing again and remembered that she was trying to save Lex's family for him. She continued, or maybe she started over. She was not really sure. "We knew that if you knew I was having the baby, you would come home from Europe. Nobody wanted to stifle your chance. So it was decided that we'd tell you I had an abortion. If we'd said I lost the baby, you would have come home. But an abortion, that ensured that you wouldn't need to come home."

At this point, Lu couldn't sit anymore and she couldn't look at Lex anymore. She was at a crossroads, one she knew she would eventually reach. Here, she could condemn herself or she could condemn their parents. Knowing that placing the blame where it truly belonged would essentially orphan Lex, she looked up to the heavens, hoping Mr. P. was smiling down on her.

"When you didn't try to reach me or check on me, I was hurt and angry. So I issued an ultimatum to everyone. The only way I would allow them in Nina's life was if they promised not to tell you. I was young and stupid and I felt a little powerless at the time. And later, I was afraid to retract it because I wasn't sure how to tell you."

She tried to meet Lex's eyes then, but he was staring off into some distant spot. His body remained against the wall, completely rigid. Finally, after what seemed an eternity but in reality was probably not very long, Lex pushed away from the wall. He walked directly to her.

"When can I see my daughter?" he asked.

Lu swallowed audibly. "She's at your mom's house now."

Nodding his head, Lex reached out and traced a finger down her cheek. His touch was achingly gentle and Lu couldn't help but lean in to it. Lex leaned too and they were almost embracing except that the only part of their bodies that were touching were his finger and her cheek. He moved slightly so that his mouth was close to her ear. "I'm sorry about earlier," he whispered, then drew back so he could see her. He looked directly into her eyes. "But I figure, one good fuck deserves another, ya know?" he remarked, eyebrow raised, Lex Pellitteri in full force. But it wasn't a Lex that Lu recognized.

She stepped back, feeling very cold, scared of this man in front of her.

"So we're clear on where we stand: This is the last conversation you and I will ever have. From here—until the end of time—anything you have to say to me goes through my attorney." He raked her from head to toe with a murderous look. "I will never forgive you for what you've done," he said in a voice that was scarily calm. He turned away from her and left the room.

Shaking from head to toe, Lu lowered herself into a chair. She was damp and sticky, and her nostrils were filled with the smell of him. She knew she needed to move, to get to Nina, but she couldn't stand on her shaky legs. Looking around the room in a daze, she saw all the leftover Easter pictures of Jesus rising from the dead. And just like that her body shuddered with sobs. Surrounded by pictures of resurrection, Lu knew that her life wouldn't get a second chance.

17

It was Willa who finally came to get her. Like Lex earlier, she was not sure how long she sat in the Sunday-school room, back in the little chair. But when Willa walked in, Lu looked at her through a haze of unhappiness.

Instantly alarmed by the look of her, Willa practically ran to her and dropped down in front of her. Grabbing her hands, Willa rubbed them vigorously, attempting to infuse some warmth into her ice-cold fingers. Willa was shocked by Lu's appearance. Her face was tear-stained, her eyes and nose red from what looked like a serious bout of crying, her hair mussed as if she had repeatedly run her hands through it. "What happened, Lu?"

Lu flinched, almost as if she didn't realize that it was Willa sitting in front of her.

"Where's Lex?" Lu asked.

"He's back at the house. When you didn't come back with him, Sky and I came to find you."

"Has he seen Nina?" she asked impatiently, suddenly alert.

"No, Lu. When Pete saw Lex walk up to the house, he knew something was off. He took Nina to our house. He didn't want their meeting to take place without you." Willa stopped when she heard the door creak open again. Turning, she met Sky's look with a worried one of her own.

"Sky's here," she said soothingly to Lu.

Lu looked at Sky and Willa and tried to offer up a smile, but it was one that didn't work, and they both became more alarmed.

"Lu," Willa said, "What happened? Maybe if you tell me, you'll feel better."

Lu laughed a maniacal laugh and said, "I don't think I'll ever feel better."

"Yes, you will. It will take time, but you will."

Shaking her head and looking sadly at the ground, she started to ramble about what happened. "He was so angry, Will. But he knew before I told him, so when I walked in here, he already knew. Who would tell him? I mean I know who told him but I wanted to be the one to tell him. I'm not saying he wouldn't have been angry, but I don't think he would have been so ruthless."

Suddenly on edge, Willa asked a question she wasn't sure she wanted the answer to. "Lu, what did he do to you. Did he hurt you?"

Again, the maniacal laugh before she answered. "We fucked." Laughter. "I wish I could say it was something more meaningful than that, but he wanted to hurt me, and I let him."

Willa stood up, pissed. "I will rip his fucking dick off!"

Lu reached up and grabbed her hand. "I wanted him. One last time. I needed him. It was as much my doing as his."

"Stop it!" Willa shouted. "You don't deserve that."

"Willa, I kept his child from him for eight years. Then when he comes back, I don't tell him. And to top it off, I sleep with him while holding all of it away from him. And he asked me. He knew I was lying to him and I still didn't tell him. Somehow, I thought that I could lessen the blow. I'm wrong here, Will, not him."

"He's going to pay for that."

"Willa, think back for me. I've been sitting here trying to think about this. Do you ever remember seeing Lex mad about anything? Have you ever seen him angry? I haven't until today. I brought out this completely foreign emotion in him. To look at him and not see his laughter in his eyes, it was like a stake to the heart. And I did that."

Willa allowed herself to appear calm and collected. "We have to get you cleaned up and back to the house. You look like hell."

"I don't want Nina to see me like this, OK?"

Willa and Sky exchanged a look. "Yes. Come on. We've got to get back."

Willa and Sky helped her out of the little chair. They left the Sunday-school room behind.

When they returned to the house, Willa sent Lu with Sky to get cleaned up. Willa made her way over to the Pellitteris'. Not finding Lex or Pete in the kitchen mingling with the guests, she headed to the office. The office had been Mike's sanctuary. The dark-paneled walls and plantation shutters blocked most of the light, giving the room a serious mood. The places that were painted were a dark wine color. It was one of the few rooms in the house with carpet, but it was plush and made you feel like you were bouncing when you walked. The built-in cabinetry flanked the back wall. Directly in front sat Mr. P.'s massive desk. When they were little, this room seemed to be forbidden. Part of that came from the fact that they rarely entered as children unless they were in trouble. Pulling open the pocket doors, Willa barged in to find Lex, Pete, and Jo huddled, talking quietly. Lex was leaning against the desk, his arms crossed in front of him. Jo and Pete were sitting in the chairs.

Sliding the doors closed so that they banged and reverberated around the room, Lex looked up, while Jo and Pete turned to see who felt compelled to intrude. Watching their expressions, Willa took note of Lex's weary gaze, Pete's shy smile, and Jo's quick flare of annoyance. Stalking through the room, Willa walked between the chairs to stand directly in front of Lex.

She could see his curious look as he raised his eyebrow as if to say, "What do you want, Will?"

Before anyone knew her intention, she drew her hand back and smacked him across the face. "What the fuck is the matter with you?" she seethed.

At first there was stunned silence. Only the sound of Willa's agitated breathing could be heard. Then, all at once, everyone moved. Jo jumped to her feet, Lex stood up from the desk, and Pete wrapped his arms around her so that she couldn't move hers. Backing her away, he whispered to her, "What are you doing?"

But she didn't hear him. "What the fuck is the matter with you? How could you hurt her like that?" she screamed, fighting against Pete. Willa was so mad at Lex that she couldn't calm down, even though she could hear Pete murmuring soothingly to her.

"This isn't our fight, Will," he whispered, moving her slowly toward the front of the room, out of Lex's reach.

But Lex kept moving toward them, and Pete could feel panic rising in his chest. All he could hope for was not to be put in the middle. Don't make me choose, he thought to himself, pleading in his eyes as he held on to the struggling Willa and watched Lex move toward them.

Suddenly, Lex stopped, as if Pete's silent pleas had reached his ears. He took a tentative step toward them. "Will," he said in a voice surprisingly soft, "how am I the bad guy here?"

Willa froze in Pete's arms. Glaring at him with residual adrenaline rushing through her, she said, "When you pulled your little sexual power play."

He nodded. "Point taken."

Pete glared at him. "What the hell did you do?"

"That's enough!" The three of them stopped as Jo walked into the middle, between Lex and Pete, who was still holding on to Willa, even though she had stopped struggling. "Just stop it. This isn't the time nor the place for this discussion." Looking at Willa she said, "It's not your place to get in the middle of this mess with Lex and Lu. They've got to figure this out without any interference from the rest of us."

Willa, still livid, couldn't hold her tongue. "Like you've been so good staying out of it?"

Jo, caught off guard by Willa's blast of anger, glared back at her. "That's quite enough, Willa." At the same time, Pete tightened his hold on Willa, begging her to stop, and whispered "please" in her ear.

Willa pulled out of Pete's arms, needing distance from him. She knew somewhere in the back of her mind that she couldn't put him in this impossible situation, today of all days, but she couldn't help sticking up for Lu. He felt her pull away but knew he couldn't do anything about it. Lex, already regretting his encounter with Lu, was flooded with guilt, and Jo, who was trying desperately to do the right thing for Lex, wanted to smack Willa. Pete, the only one in the room with diplomatic skills, knew he needed to do something to save the situation, but his mind was blank. When a tentative knock sounded at the door, they all grabbed on to it as if they were drowning and the knock were a life preserver.

"Come in," came the chorus, as all of them answered.

The pocket door slid open and standing just outside were Lu and Nina.

Pete, Willa, and Jo all shouted at once, "Little Bit!" "Nee!" "Nina!"

A big smile broke over her face. She was the perfect blend of Lu and Lex, but didn't really look like either one of them. She had gotten Lu's black hair, Lex's green eyes, Lu's full lips, Lex's height but Lu's slender stature. The whole room was enchanted.

Nina bounded forward, as was normal for her. She greeted her grandmother, her aunt, and her uncle. Lu, who could tell that the atmosphere in the room was heated, entered the room gingerly, and closed the doors behind her. Although she would have preferred to be anywhere else, this was the inevitable conclusion to the turmoil of the day. Without trying to, she found herself watching Lex. He was struck still.

After Nina finished hugging Pete, she stopped in front of Lex. Lu was about to make an introduction, but Nina stared up and him and said, "Hello."

Lex, still dumbfounded by her presence, managed a "Hello."

"I'm Nina," she stated matter-of-factly.

"I guessed that," he said as that smile of his lit his face.

"Are you Lex Pellitteri?" she asked.

He nodded. "I am."

Willa, Pete, Jo, and Lu all watched, fascinated with the exchange, each holding hope in their hearts that somehow this could reach a happy resolution.

"Grampa Mike told me all about you," she continued.

Everyone was surprised, but no one more than Lex, and it showed in his expression. Feeling awkward towering over her, he went down on one knee, resting his elbow on the other leg, and leaned forward.

"What did he tell you?" Lex asked, completely curious.

"That you are really special. You play soccer." She held her hand out and with each point, she counted them on her fingers as if trying to remember everything. "He said you're smart and funny. But he said the most important thing about you is that when I finally get to meet you that you are going to be a really good dad."

They all reacted to this. Jo choked on a suppressed sob, Pete smiled, suddenly feeling lighthearted, Willa looked to Lu, concern lining her face. Lu just watched Lex. She saw how that one sentence seemed to lift him up. It restored his swag. And then she couldn't watch anymore. She found Willa's gaze, silently asking for help, then slipped from the room.

Lex, who had thought he couldn't love his father any more, felt his heart fill. Leaning in to his daughter, he said, "You know how he knows that?"

She shook her head.

"Because he taught me, and he was the best father in the world," he confided to her, his eyes damp.

She smiled, obviously agreeing.

"Granny was getting me some ice cream. Do you want to have some ice cream?" she asked.

"I'd love some." Lex stood up then got back down. "Can I ask you a favor first?"

"Sure," she answered.

"Any chance I can get a hug?"

She didn't answer. She just threw herself into his arms.

18

Jo found her some time later, sitting on the refurbished swing set that had been updated to accommodate Nina when she came to visit. Lu sat with one foot gently pushing, slowly, the moment it encountered the ground. Lost in her thoughts, Lu didn't see Jo approach and jumped in surprise when she spoke.

"Well, that certainly went better than I expected," she observed as she sat in the swing next to Lu.

Lu nodded without taking her eyes off the toe of her shoe. "Yeah," she said shortly.

"Are you OK?" Jo asked, concern obvious in her voice.

Lu glanced up ruefully at her. "Shouldn't I be asking you that?"

"Probably," Jo concurred. "But I'm thinking the changes in your life are going to be more numerous and just as difficult to deal with as mine."

"Yeah," Lu said again. "But you can't change what happened."

"Neither can you."

"Are we going to argue about whose situation is worse too? Because, not to make you feel bad, but yours is much worse."

Jo laughed, a genuine laugh. "Yes, I suppose it is."

Lu smiled at the picture Jo made, sitting on the swing with her sad eyes smiling. "Did you know that he told Nina?"

Jo shook her head. "No, sweetie, I didn't. We didn't really talk much about the situation. It's crazy to think about now, with him gone. Which, let's face it, I'm never going to get used to that." Shaking her head, as if to clear it, she continued. "It was the one thing in our marriage that we never resolved."

"That seems weird to me," Lu commented.

"Me too. But nevertheless, it is what it is. And now there's nothing I can do to fix it. But you can."

"I've done my part. They're together now. How we're going to sustain that, I'm not sure."

"She took right to him. They're in there eating ice cream, chatting like they've always known each other." Neither one of them spoke for a couple of minutes. They sat, gently swinging, each lost in her own thoughts. "What do you think the plan's going to be?"

Lu kicked the dirt with her foot in frustration. "Who the hell knows? He lives in England for God's sake. And to top it off, he hates me."

"Lex could never hate you, my dear. He's angry, which is not something he's had to deal with, ever. When he's had some time to think through everything, when he gets some distance, he'll forgive you. It's not his nature to hold a grudge. He devotes too much energy to other things to try to sustain a grudge."

"It doesn't matter as long as he and Nina can figure their way around each other."

"That will take time too," Jo said sagely.

"Do you think it's odd that Nina never told me that she knew who her father was? I mean, she never even asked me."

"I thought about that briefly. I wish I could shed some light. I wish Mike had told me that he'd spoken to her about it. From what she said, it seemed like they had spoken about it often. She was just so comfortable and confident about him being her father that I feel like it's something she and her grandfather spent a lot of time discussing."

"I agree. I was completely thrown when she said that to him. It felt like I was watching a Hallmark Channel Christmas special."

Jo laughed. "Well, let's hope we get our happy ending."

"Problem with that, Dr. J., is that I'm not sure what a happy ending would be."

"Don't you?" Jo asked.

"No, not anymore. What my happy ending was forty-eight hours ago and what it would be now are totally different," Lu said, staring out at nothing.

"Louisa May?" Jo said, calling in the motherly tone.

Lu looked up directly at Jo, a slight smile on her face. "Yes?"

"What exactly did you do? Why is Lex not mad at me?"

Had Jo asked her that question at another time, a time when she felt stronger or more hopeful or more generous, she would have answered differently. But she didn't have any strength, hope, or generosity left in her reserves to call upon. So she looked directly at Josephine Pellitteri and said, "I sold a bit of my soul to save all of yours." With that, she pushed herself off the swing and moved away, seeking solitude so she could sulk without an audience.

⁓

Lex sat at the counter with Nina, totally enthralled. He had a difficult time thinking that he had a part in her creation and he wondered how often his parents had thought that throughout his and Pete's childhood. In the brief time he'd spent with her, she seemed to be equal parts him and equal parts Lu. The combination of their features in her physical appearance made him wonder how those genes got all mixed up and spit out. It seemed to work on her and he vaguely wondered what his life would be like as the father of a sixteen-year-old who looked like her.

He saw his mischief reflected in her green eyes, but he could already tell that she had Lu's thoughtfulness and innately cautious nature. That in itself would be a most interesting combination. She would have Lex's craziness but would temper it with actually thinking through her actions. He smiled, thinking again of the teenage years.

Lex hadn't spent much time with children, so he felt a little out of his league. Ice cream he could do, but he'd sputtered a few times trying to think of appropriate things to say to her and to ask her. She always picked up the slack, asking questions that had sometimes caught him off guard. He was able to handle the "Why do you play soccer?" and "How much do you practice?" He managed "What's England like?" and "Do you have a best friend?" He'd completely blanked on "Will you always play soccer?" and "What will you do when you don't play soccer anymore?" Did all eight-year-olds talk like this or did she have Lu's super brain?

He'd already fallen in love with her, but when she asked if he thought Grandma Jo was going to be OK, he felt his heart grow, like the Grinch's.

"I think Grandma Jo is going to be OK. But it might take some time," he answered.

"I'm gonna miss Grandpa Mike," she said sadly.

For the first time since he'd met his child, her face was marred by a frown. Again, feeling out of his league, not sure what to say, he hoped he could manage this conversation without having to resort to calling his brother over. "Me too. I will miss him every day."

She looked at him quizzically, her eyebrow cocked. Oh shit, Lex thought, she inherited the eyebrow.

"But you didn't see him very much because you've been gone for so long."

Lex felt wounded, but wasn't sure if that had been her intention . . . Running his hand over his short hair, Lex fumbled through an explanation. "Well, I'll still miss him. Even though we didn't see each other every day, I talked to him almost every day, and he was one of the closest people to me."

"Oh," Nina said. "So is that what we'll do now? Will we talk every day?"

Lex wanted to reach out and pull her in to a hug, but he didn't know how that would be received. He wanted to assure her that they could have a good relationship even with an ocean between them. He wanted to know the right thing to say and do, but without the last eight years of experience he felt helpless. And that's when he got pissed all over again. That's when the seed of his plan began to take root.

Lex called up his reserves: his patented smile and charm, which had seen him through every difficult situation in his life. Smiling the same smile that she would use, he said, "We're going to figure all of that out. We're coming up with a plan. OK?"

He thought the look she gave him was calling bullshit. But, again, without knowing her the way he should have, he couldn't be sure. He wanted to reassure her, but he didn't want to have it be a lie later. So he kept it vague. "Your mother and I are working on it. Promise."

"OK," she said with a shrug.

Reluctant to step away from her, Lex looked around, hoping for an out so that he could get some control of his anger. Pete wasn't far away. Throwing him a "please help me" look, which he knew his brother would catch, he waited for Pete to walk toward them.

"Hey, Little Bit. Does Uncle Pete get some time today?" he asked, with a natural ease that came with familiarity.

Unreservedly, Nina got up off the bar stool and went into his arms. "Can we go on the swings?"

"You bet." Looking at Lex, Pete said, "OK if I steal my favorite niece away?"

Nina giggled. And Lex knew this was an inside joke with them.

"Uncle Pete, I'm your *only* niece," she responded in a well-rehearsed way.

"Oh, that's right," he said, looking sheepish, as was part of the joke. "You're just too smart for me, Nina."

Another giggle.

Lex watched it all, fascinated. His brother was obviously a permanent fixture in Nina's life. A streak of jealousy shot through him. This was fucking torture and too much to take.

"We're going to head outside," Pete said, asking his brother for permission with his look.

At Lex's nod, Pete turned to leave. Lex stopped him. "Know where I can find Will?" he asked.

Pete looked at him questioningly, remembering their last encounter.

Lex rolled his eyes, indicating it was OK. So Pete acquiesced. "She ran next door. You may want to wait until she gets back."

Lex knew that code. "OK. Can you let her know I need to chat with her?"

"Yup. I'll send her over."

Pete left and Lex made his way back to his father's office to wait for Willa. Closing the doors behind him he moved to Mike's desk. Sitting there, he took stock of everything. He was angry. He was jealous of everyone's relationship with his daughter. He was infinitely sad over the loss of his father. He'd never felt so out of control in his life. Emotions completely foreign for him beat at him from every angle. He longed for a return to normalcy—practice, a game, a focus. But even as that thought flew through his mind it dawned on him that his normal had been infinitely redefined. Struggling with a new vision of what his life would look like, the soft knock at the door indicating Willa's arrival caught him completely off kilter.

Willa never waited for permission from anyone, so when she sat down in the chair across from him he smiled at her out of a great appreciation for the woman that she'd grown to be. They'd been close. His intimacy with Lu had changed that, but not in a bad way. Now, facing her across his father's desk, Lex knew that any road back to that closeness would be littered with causalities of this war that he was about to wage. As he gazed at her, he felt a millisecond of regret, but then that unfamiliar anger that had become his companion today took over. Fuck it, he thought.

"I guess I should apologize for slapping you earlier, but I just can't bring myself to do it," she started.

Again, his appreciation for her bluntness overtook him. He smiled the Lex smile, showing her that he got it. "Well, that seems appropriate as I'm not going to apologize for what happened. And for that matter, I'm not going to apologize for what is about to happen."

Willa looked at him, truly looked at him for the first time. She didn't look at him as the harbinger of the last few days. She looked at him as one would in taking stock of an adversary. And that made her sad. He was everything that their youth had promised. Successful, confident, intelligent. He hadn't given in to his own appeal. He continued to work at who he was and what he wanted to achieve. She respected him. And it made her proud. But she focused as she would in a courtroom because she knew this was not a friendly conversation. She felt the energy radiating from him. It wasn't a positive force. Suddenly a little fearful for her sister, Willa sat back in her chair, attempting to radiate confidence.

"Much of this conversation is something I should be having with your sister, but I'm afraid I can't trust myself to be in the same room with her right now."

Willa simply nodded, knowing he wasn't expecting a response.

"Although I haven't had much time to think about this or attempt to come up with a better solution, I have come to a conclusion. I'm going to tell you so that you can talk to Lu. Then, on Monday, you will receive the documents from my lawyers. We can do this the easy way or the hard way, but be assured that I'm going to win."

Willa didn't say anything. But she admitted to herself at that moment that she feared this Lex. She'd forgotten how determined he was. And Lu didn't have that kind of fight in her. Mostly, because of her guilt, Lu would make this as easy on Lex as possible. It might destroy her, but the way she loved him, she'd do it for him. Although looking across the span of the desk at him, she wasn't sure that this was a Lex that Lu knew enough about to love.

"I don't want to be away from my daughter," he continued. "That's a given. When I look around and see the familiarity she has with everyone but me . . . I don't think I can describe the anger that I feel." He paused, obviously not very happy that he had let her know anything he was feeling. "So the question becomes, how do I get an opportunity to know her with an ocean between us? The answer is, of course, I don't.

There's no way I get any shot at a relationship with her when she lives here and I live there."

Willa's whole body tensed. He was going for custody, she thought. Fuck! Lu won't allow that. Willa saw their two families embroiled in a fight to the finish. She saw any shot with Pete dissipate before her eyes. She saw Lu as a broken shell of a woman. But she kept her panic masked.

"I'm also not ready to retire from soccer. The day will come, but it's not here yet. And when I do, I'll go into coaching or front-office work. I'll be doing something and America's not there yet. I have to do it from across the pond. So the only solution is for Nina to come to me."

Willa couldn't help it, as she spat, "You motherfucker!"

He smiled the Lexifer smile. "Temper, temper, Will!" he said, shaking his finger at her. "As much as I hate Lu right at this moment, I'm not going to drag her into a custody battle. Although, just so we're clear—I have the resources and power to do it." He let that statement hang in the air as he watched Willa ingest it. "The only solution is for Lu and Nina to move to England."

When she made to protest, he held up his hand. "I'm not done," he said in a voice that resounded with the power and resourcefulness that he had just referred to. "I realize that a move like that will take time. So I'm giving her six months. She's smart," he said with a smirk, "and resourceful. That should give her time to come up with a plan that will be beneficial to her career. My attorney will help with the visa process, and I'll make sure they have a place to live. In the meantime, I want joint custody. I deserve time to get to know my daughter. I want school vacations for now. I'll pay for transportation for Nina and a family member. I don't want her to travel alone, and I don't know that I'll be able to get away to make the flight back and forth. So I'm going to need for you all to be there for my daughter again. We'll work out a more formal agreement that discusses holidays and weeknights later. It will be settled before she moves so that we aren't dealing with any ambiguities."

Most of this had come to him as he was talking, but he knew it was a good plan. It was the only way. He wasn't particularly happy that

Lu would be within reach, but he wasn't prepared to separate her from Nina. He wasn't that much of a bastard, no matter how pissed he was.

"Do you have any questions?" he asked after giving her some time to think about what he had said.

"Do you know how much of a dick move this is?" Willa asked, anger pulsing from her.

"About as much of a dick move as keeping the knowledge of my daughter from me for eight years?" he asked with feigned innocence.

At that moment, Willa hated him. She wished for a do-over so that she could punch him instead of bitch-slapping him. She hated this idea, she hated that she had to present it to her sister. But if she looked beneath the anger, she saw that it was only fair. Unfortunately, she wasn't there yet.

With as much bluster as she could manage, she stood. "I hope to hell you know what you're doing!" she said before she exited.

She didn't hear him say "Me too."

19

Willa couldn't face Lu on her own. She knew her limits. The seething anger she felt towards Lex wouldn't do anything to assuage Lu's fears, so Willa went to find Pete. Willa understood she would be putting Pete in a difficult spot asking him to explain to Lu what Lex wanted. Willa didn't understand why Lex thought she would be a better messenger than Pete, unless Lex assumed Willa would represent Lu in their custody discussions. They all knew that Pete was a better diplomat. Knowing Lu was still licking her wounds from earlier, she headed to find some reinforcements—a bottle of wine, Pete, and Sky.

Willa found her mother first. "Mom, I need for you to keep Nina occupied for a bit."

Amber, noticing the bottle of wine in Willa's hand, looked at her questioningly. "What's going on?"

Willa knew that Amber would find out soon enough, but she wasn't willing to be the messenger twice. "Just think Lu needs a pick-me-up," she answered vaguely.

No fool, Amber knew there was more going on, but she wasn't willing to try to pry it out of Willa in this setting, so she merely agreed.

Before Willa walked away she asked Amber if she'd seen Sky and Pete. "They're on the patio with Nina," she answered.

Willa walked toward the patio with the wine in hand. The sight that greeted her stopped her in her tracks. Pete, Sky, and Nina were sitting at one of the tables, playing cards. They looked very comfortable together, and Willa experienced a jolt of jealousy she didn't expect. Shit, she thought, this is not good. Making her way outside, she approached quietly, attempting to make out the conversation and gauge any attraction between Pete and Sky. But as soon as Pete saw her, his eyes lit up. She could see it, and the jealousy evaporated. Thankfully. He looked at her with questions in his eyes, but she smiled to put him at ease.

"Hey, Nee, Granny wants you," Willa announced.

As they had just finished their game, her timing was perfect.

"OK," Nina said, jumping up from the table and running inside.

"Does she walk anywhere?" Sky murmured, watching her.

"No," Pete and Willa answered at the same time.

They all laughed.

"What's up?" asked Pete.

Willa sighed. "I need you both. I just talked to Lex, and he's come to some decisions that he wants me to present to Lu." At Pete's quizzical look, she sat down heavily in the chair. "I can only imagine he was speaking to me as her lawyer, but I can't be sure. If he wanted a diplomat, he would have asked for you," she said, reaching across and taking his hand.

Pete nodded his head. "Maybe he didn't want to have to face me with his ideas," Pete said, knowing his brother well. "Will I be disappointed in him when I hear this?"

Willa looked away, not sure how to answer. Shrugging her shoulders, she barreled forward. "The fucker's giving her six months to get everything together to move to England. He says he can't see any other solution. Selfish ass!"

Sky reacted first. "You can't be serious. She's just supposed to pick up everything and move over there. What about her life here?"

Pete remained quiet. Willa watched him, waiting for his reaction. She wanted, expected him to react to the audacity of Lex's plan. But the longer he stayed quiet, the more she began to fear that his reaction wasn't going to be what she wanted.

"Pete?"

"I don't know, Willa."

"What don't you know?" she said, knowing that his contemplation meant he agreed with Lex's position.

"It's not such a bad idea," he answered.

She pulled her hand away from his.

Reaching for her, he said, "Don't . . . Don't . . ." while he attempted to reestablish their connection.

Willa stubbornly refused to acknowledge his plea.

Knowing he wasn't winning this right now, he chose not to argue with her. "What do you want from us?" he asked, looking towards Sky.

"I want you to be with me when I talk to Lu."

Pete felt the pull—the loyalty to his brother, the desire for Willa. Struggling against the tide of his conflicting feelings, he braced himself for the force of Willa's anger. He winced. "I don't think I should be there, Willa."

She'd known he was going to say that, but it hurt nonetheless. She didn't even look at him. Turning to Sky, she silently waited for her answer.

"Of course," Sky said, "I only have one horse in this race."

Willa looked at her gratefully while Pete flinched. Not even acknowledging his presence, Willa rose from the table, waited for Sky to join her, and went off to talk to her sister. Pete leaned his head back on the chair, frustrated. As much as he wanted Willa, he didn't think they would be able to do this with the gulf widening between their families. Equal parts thankful and regret-filled, he thought of his decision not to sleep with her last night and wondered if it was the best or worst decision he'd ever made.

Willa and Sky found Lu at the computer in Amber and Chris's office going through email.

"Anything interesting?" Willa asked as she put three glasses on the coffee table, pulled out the corkscrew, and opened the wine.

"Just some feedback from my professor on my dissertation."

"Did you and Lex ever get around to discussing your work?"

Lu turned away from the computer and walked toward them. Sitting on the floor, she thought over their conversations. "No, it never really came up."

"He wasn't curious about what you were doing with your life?" This struck Willa as odd and annoyed her.

"Oh, he asked. I just avoided it. I didn't want him to think it had anything to do with him, I guess."

Willa digested that but didn't say anything. "You think he would have thought that?" she asked.

Lu smiled. "This is Lex we are talking about."

"True," Willa said, returning her smile. Willa studied Lu for a moment. "You look better than you did earlier today," she observed.

Lu didn't say anything for a moment. Drinking some of her wine, she thought about her conversation with Jo, the time she'd spent with Nina. She no longer felt devastated, as she had after returning from the church. "Maybe what Pete said was true."

When Willa and Sky looked at her questioningly, she said, "I feel less . . . weighed down. I'm not sure if that's the right term, but I feel better that he knows. I've always wanted him to know. It was so unfair to both of them."

"You forgive him for what happened at the church?" Willa pushed.

"Willa, there was nothing to forgive."

"Why do you let him do that to you?"

"Will, I don't see it like you. I'm not mad at him. I know you want me to be, but I'm not. It's over. He knows about Nina, and what comes next is going to be dictated by him. However he wants to get to know her, I'm not going to fight him. He deserves that from me."

Willa and Sky looked at each other. Sky nudged Willa to tell Lu with her look.

"He talked to me about what he wants. And maybe it won't be as much of a shock to you as it was to me. At least that's what it seems like right now." Willa took a sip of her wine. She was pissed. Why was she more angry than Lu? Did she expect more from Lex than her sister did? Or was her anger all wrapped up with her feelings for Pete?

"Oh. Why didn't he talk to me?" Lu asked, hurt despite the fact that she knew she shouldn't be.

"He said he didn't think he could be in the same room with you."

"Ah. Wonder if that will ever change," she said softly.

"I don't think so. Not for a while at least," Willa answered bluntly.

Lu knew she couldn't blame him. Not after what she'd told him. This was the price and she'd be willing to pay it. If it seemed odd that he was willing to blame her and not even consider being upset with anyone else, she congratulated herself. This was the outcome she'd been working for so that he didn't feel betrayed by everyone.

"So, what did he say," Lu asked, bracing herself. She couldn't even come up with a thought on how he would want to handle this.

"He wants you and Nina to move to England."

Lu drew a deep breath. "You can't be serious!"

"Oh, I'm completely serious. He said he would give you six months to work it out. His lawyers will help with the visa issue. He'd find a place for the two of you to live. In the meantime, he wanted joint custody. He seemed to know that joint custody would mean school holidays only. But once you moved there, you would be splitting weekends, weeknights, holidays." Willa stopped, allowing all of this to sink in. "He wants the custody agreement worked out before you move there so that there is no ambiguity." She put air quotes around *ambiguity*. "He had it all worked out in his head."

Lu looked stricken again. "Shit," she muttered. Grabbing her wine-glass, she got up and walked to the window. Taking a sip of her wine, she thought about his request. Of course, after everything that had happened, it was more of a demand. Could they really move to England? Why would he want her close to him? Before she could even think about that, she realized that he didn't want her close to him. He wanted Nina close to him and he would tolerate her to accomplish his goal. Moving didn't really worry her. She needed time to complete her dissertation. But when she was done, she worried about finding a team to be able to continue her work.

"Lu," Willa said, dragging her back to the conversation, "are you OK?"

Lu walked back and sat down on the floor.

"What are you thinking?" Sky asked.

"I'm thinking it could be worse."

"Seriously?" Willa and Sky asked at the same time.

Lu looked at both of them. "Seriously."

Incredulity reflected back at her from both sets of eyes. "Look, how else is he going to have access to Nina? It's not ideal, but for the next year, I'll be writing my dissertation anyway. I can do that from anywhere. My research is mostly complete. Besides, there are worse places to go. Dr. Ziegler was a Rhodes Scholar and I know he still has contacts there. If I need to come back to do some work, I can work that out." She paused, looking at both of them. "Nina will adapt. She's far more adaptable than we are."

Willa wanted to be delicate in the way she said this, but she just didn't have it in her. "He's never going to want you."

If her bluntness hurt Lu, she didn't show it. She grabbed Willa's hand. "I know that. I'm letting it go. Can't you see that?"

"You're moving on?" Willa asked, doubtful.

"Yes, I'm moving on. I'll even date. I'll make you both proud."

Sky and Willa exchanged doubtful glances.

Lu acknowledged the looks. "Seriously," she said, trying to convince them. She turned away, not wanting to face their skepticism. "I know we all came home to bury Mr. P. But my childhood fantasies died right along with him."

Neither Sky nor Willa had any response to that.

20

As the last of the guests left the Pellitteris', Amber, with Stacy and Natalie's help, wiped down the counters and cleaned the rest of the kitchen. Jo and Chris holed up in the library, discussing the terms of Mike's will. Lu, through Pete, had encouraged Lex to come over and read to Nina before she went to bed. Amber couldn't be sure about Willa. She'd left a while before in a huff but had refused to tell Amber anything. When everything was clean, they grabbed a bottle of wine and set out for the porch.

Pouring a glass for the three of them, Amber sat back, exhausted. Closing her eyes, she let her head fall back on the chair. "I still can't believe he's gone," she said to no one in particular.

And no one responded. What was there to say? Their twenty-year friendship had seen it all—all except death. How did they recover from it? What would it be like without Mike? Would Jo still come around? Once, long ago, they'd talked about death. But it was a subject that one avoided in the throes of life. Amber distinctly remembered Jo saying that she wouldn't want to be around all the people who were constant reminders of her life with her husband if he were gone.

"Do you remember—" Natalie began.

Both Amber and Stacy responded "Yes!" quickly, effectively halting the conversation. They all knew that the cornerstone of their relationship had begun to crumble.

Lu walked up to the morose group right then. In hindsight, Amber would think that if she had caught her at a different point, she might have reacted differently, things might not have gone the way they did. But she didn't.

"Ladies," Lu said as she made her way around the table kissing them all. "I know this glass is waiting for Dr. J., but since she and Dad seem to be in deep discussion, can I hijack it?"

Natalie lifted the bottle, filled the glass, and pushed it toward Lu.

"How ya doing?" Stacy asked. They all knew the story, had in fact been intimately acquainted with most of the details of the "tragic teenage pregnancy," so their inquiries seemed natural.

"OK," Lu said. Leaning back and capturing her mother's eyes, she continued, "In fact, I received a rather interesting proposition."

Amber looked at her, waiting to hear about all the undercurrents that had been bouncing through the house that day.

Lex and Lu had always strategically told their parents information. The pregnancy, for instance—they told them about that following Supper Club one night. By the time they were teenagers, they'd figured out that Supper Club meant their parents were probably pleasantly buzzed and generally in a good mood. So they'd waited at Lu's house for their parents to get home. As their parents pulled the golf cart into the driveway, Lex had run across and asked them to come over. The only one of the four of them who knew at that point was Mike. Mike's buzz dissipated right then and there. It had softened the reaction, but not the blow. The problem, they all said later, was that Lu was too smart and Lex was too worldly.

Perhaps they'd been wrong in their assessment. Either that or Lu had learned from the master.

"Lex wants Nina and me to move to England," she said matter-of-factly.

Amber stilled. "What? Why?"

Stacy and Natalie exchanged glances and started to get up from the table.

"You can stay," Lu said. "It will save her from having to recount the story later."

Amber looked at them and nodded her assent. "How do you feel about that?"

"It's the only thing that makes sense. He has a career that isn't mobile right now. I don't. He wants an opportunity to get to know his daughter. He can't do that from over there. And quite frankly, it wouldn't be fair to Nina to have to constantly fly back and forth across the ocean."

Frustration lanced through Amber like a sword in the back. "So once again you put your life on hold to accommodate the dreams of Lex Pellitteri? How did I raise you to be at the mercy of a man?"

Lu flinched. Suddenly embarrassed to have an audience for this conversation, she glanced to Natalie and Stacy, who had already begun to remove themselves from the area.

"I am not at his mercy," she hissed furiously. "How can you say that?"

Amber's anger made her rigid, almost robotic in her movements and speech. "For the last nine years I have watched everyone bend over backwards to make Lex's life easier. At first, I thought we were too much of a force for you. Imposing our will on you. Now, I see that you're weak. And we made you that way."

Lu stood up out of her chair so forcefully that it flipped over behind her. *"Weak?"* she yelled. "I'm weak. The fact that you can even say that to me just illustrates how little you know of me. If you had been stronger, strong enough to stand up to Dr. J., I wouldn't be in this situation. But you weren't. You fed me and your unborn grandchild to the fucking wolves. So don't sit there and call me weak. I've managed to accomplish a lot while raising a pretty amazing daughter. Your precious prodigy has surpassed expectations, even after having a child at seventeen." She paused to take a deep breath and to calm down. "What I'm choosing to do now is what's best for my child. A concept you know nothing about."

With that, Lu turned and walked back through the house. Amber sat, anger mounting, as she thought back over those fateful couple of weeks when they'd made the decisions that continued to shape the lives of her daughter and Lex. So focused was she that she didn't hear the scrape of the chair. When his hand reached out to grab a glass of wine, she noticed Lex watching her.

Amber blinked. She found herself looking into a pair of green eyes, flashing with anger.

"That was pretty magnificent," Lex said, in an eerily calm voice.

"What did you hear?" Amber asked, not really caring.

"Just that last part. About doing what was right for her child." He slowly swirled the wine in his glass. "Let me be very clear on this, Dr. A. No one is to interfere with my family anymore."

"Family?" she spat. "What do you know about family? You haven't been here in almost ten years. You don't know anything about the mother of your child, nor your child. Don't you dare talk about your 'family' when you've known about the birth of your child for less than twenty-four hours!"

"And whose fault is that?" He stood up, looking down on her through a haze of contempt. Then, leaning down, so that his face was directly in front of her he said, "I'm going to say this again, so that you don't misunderstand my meaning. You. Are. *Not*. To. Interfere."

As Lex walked away, Amber watched, angry at the world. She knew that she had had a hand in everything that had happened. She knew she hadn't protected her daughter as she should have. She knew that she'd given in because she had been so angry with Lu for throwing away her future. She knew all of that and even accepted that part of this was her fault. But she couldn't help it. She blamed Jo. They'd all bent to her indomitable will. She'd just been more stubborn and determined than the rest of them. Much like her son. That apple hadn't fallen far from the tree. Seething with anger, she stood up and headed to the library.

Chris and Jo looked up at the same time as she entered. Chris smiled, but quickly registered concern as he noted the look on her face.

Without preamble she said, "He's making her move to England."

If Jo and Chris were surprised, it didn't show. They both digested the information. Nodding slowly, Chris said, "That actually makes a lot of sense." Had he been able to properly gauge her anger, he would have kept that comment to himself.

Jo noticed and kept her mouth shut.

"Makes sense? Are you fucking kidding me?" Amber said, anger rolling off of her. "Once again, her life has to change to accommodate the great Lex Pellitteri. What is the matter with everyone?"

Chris, suddenly realizing his mistake and finally noting the magnitude of her anger, walked toward her, hoping to stop her from saying anything that would irreparably harm their decades-old friendship. "Amber, this isn't the time," he said as he stepped in front of her and grabbed her hands. "Not now," he whispered, hoping Jo didn't hear him.

But Jo, bracing herself for what came next, waited. As much as she liked to kid herself that Amber had forgiven her, she knew that underneath the foundation of their friendship existed a sinkhole of bitterness that threatened to pull it all under.

Amber stepped around Chris. "This is your fault. All of it. The outcome would have been different if we hadn't all agreed to sacrifice my daughter for the benefit of your son. Once again, he's dictating her life. He got that from you. That sense that the whole world is at his command." Amber took a breath, not even trying to control the anger that threatened to destroy everything between them. "You need to do something. You need to fix this." Pointing her finger in Jo's direction, she wisely didn't move any closer to her. "If he hurts her again, like he did today. If I ever see that look on her face again, I'll find a way to hurt you just as bad."

Chris grabbed her around her upper arms and whispered to her, "That's enough!" as he pulled her from the room. He glanced up at Jo and mouthed, "Sorry," even though he knew that wasn't enough to fix what had just happened.

When they had cleared the room, the door sliding shut behind them, Jo sank into Mike's chair. Resting her head in her hands, she let go. Finally, seventy-two hours after the death of her husband, she gave in and cried. She cried for her loss and her children, she cried for the death of her friendship, and she cried for the collision course that she had set for Lex and Lu all those years ago. She wanted to fix it. She wanted to make it right for them. She owed it to them and to Mike. But she didn't have a clue as to how to do it. For the first time in her life, she felt powerless.

PART 2

21

Six months later

Lu bent over to pull the turkey out of the oven. She may have moved to England without putting up a fight, but she was determined that Nina would take part in the American traditions. Taking a sip of her wine, she tried to fight the nerves flaring up in her stomach. Walking a tightrope, she worked to find the balance between matchmaking and interfering. She owed Willa and Pete, though, and this represented her chance to help them find their way back to each other.

Lex's demand that Lu move to England had dealt the deathblow to Willa and Pete's fledgling relationship. Willa wanted Pete to get involved. His refusal pushed her away. Like Lex, Willa went hard. All or nothing. Pete taking Lex's side—or not trying to talk some sense into him—had felt like Pete wanted nothing. It didn't matter that she essentially asked him to choose. She couldn't see beyond his support of Lex. Lu knew it wasn't right for Willa to hold Pete to that standard, but that was Will. And for her relentless support of Lu over the years, Lu wanted to give her what she needed. The problem being that Pete wasn't what Will wanted right now. Which meant Lu's impromptu Thanksgiving meal could be over very quickly.

It had been easy to get them over there. Both Willa and Pete had time. Pete had a short break from school and Willa got the weekend off from the practice. Nina and she had been in England for a little over three months because Lu hadn't wanted Nina to start a new school year at home. Lu had taken the summer to get everything together, and they were in London for the start of school. Nina's aunt and uncle hadn't seen her since they left. A visit was due.

Pete continued to call weekly to check on them. He'd told Lu he was coming over for his break. Knowing that, Lu had put the pressure on Willa to visit. She'd resisted at first, which is why Lu played her ace in the hole and put Nina on the phone. It took one simple request from Nina and Willa capitulated. So they were both in London and in about thirty minutes, they would both be in her flat, a term she was still trying to get used to.

Hurrying to make sure everything was ready, Lu slid the turkey back into the oven to keep it warm. She'd sent Nina and Willa on an errand so that she could have some peace before she set off the fireworks tonight. After grabbing her glass of wine, she made her way across the room to the table she'd set for four—another reason she'd sent Willa away. She didn't need her asking questions. Sitting down, she got lost thinking of the events over the last several months. True to his word, Lex still hadn't spoken to her nor seen her. Everything had been handled by his attorney. Lu allowed them to handle the visa issues but had put her foot down on Lex having some minion pick the place where they would live. Lu did much of it via the Internet and finally settled on a two-bedroom flat across the city from Lex. There had been some bumps, mostly having to do with transferring Nina between the two residences. Lex hired a woman to help him with transporting. He'd even allowed Lu to be a part of the selection process. But again, all communication came via Heathgard, Masters and Hughley, Esq. Sometimes, when Lu wasn't looking, she got hit with the pain of his abandonment. While it took her breath away, she always managed to find her footing.

Lu had adapted quite easily to living in London. The history of the city interested her, while the vivacity captivated her. Who knew she was a city girl at heart? But being in this country meant a lot more exposure to Lex, who enjoyed some notoriety over here. He graced the gossip magazines frequently enough for Lu to know he dated amazingly attractive women. And she marveled a bit at how much of a celebrity footballers were in this country. While it hurt, she was beginning to grow thick skin. She and Lex had settled on joint custody, which meant Lu had a lot more time on her hands than she was used to. And true to her word, she had started to date. It wasn't anything to write home about, but it was fun to get out there.

Lex's schedule was rather amazing. His season spanned August to May but over the summer, he'd played on the U. S. national team, which meant a lot of travel. He was gone often, which meant an amazing amount of coordination on the part of his attorney and her. They were becoming fast friends as they spoke to each other almost daily. The hardest part of the whole move was learning to share Nina. Nina embraced Lex's presence in her life with her whole being. Never a reticent child, again more like Lex than Lu, Nina skipped over all the awkwardness and just enjoyed having another person to share her life with. Nina talked to Lex daily, even when he was traveling. Lu found herself listening to these conversations reluctantly. And over time, she realized that Nina shared different things with Lex than she shared with Lu. Lu often wondered where Nina had been storing these parts of her life over the last nine years. She couldn't help but question her skills as a parent as she watched Nina blossom as she never had before. The newfound presence of her father helped soften the loss of her grandfather, whom she had been exceptionally close to. Nina took it all in stride, reminding Lu that she had a healthy dose of Lex's easygoing genes. She handled it all. If she found it odd that her parents were never in the same room, she never mentioned it to Lu.

Lex's schedule had made it easy to steal time with Pete. He had been in town when Pete arrived yesterday, but he had to leave today. It was the opening Lu had needed and why she had insisted that they all celebrate Thanksgiving as if they were back home. Hearing a commotion outside, she downed the rest of her wine, banking on some liquid courage. Pulling open the door before anyone could knock, she lit up at the sight of Pete.

Throwing herself into his arms, she hugged him close.

"It's so good to see you," she said, refusing to let go of him.

"You too, Lu," he said, hugging her back. Letting go of each other, Lu led him into her apartment.

"How's school? How's your mom? We talk to her every week, but it's so hard to know how she's really doing." She said it all in a rush.

"Slow down. All of a sudden, it's like trying to keep up with Nina," Pete teased.

"Sorry," Lu said, embarrassed. "I don't think I realized how much I missed you until you were right in front of me."

"I miss you too. But, Lu, you look amazing," he said, giving her a once-over. "London seems to be agreeing with you."

Without meaning to bring up any heavy topics, she launched into an explanation she thought he deserved. "Pete, remember the day . . . Well I don't have to explain that part, but the conversation we had before I went to confront Lex?" At his nod, she continued. "You were right. I feel so much freer now. It's like for the last eight years the guilt of keeping everything from Lex had become this weight on my shoulders. Even though we don't talk at all and he dictated this new life, I am so happy that he knows and that he can be a father to Nina. I feel like a different person."

She smiled, and Pete almost had to catch his breath. She was beautiful. It wasn't that she wasn't beautiful before, but the inner glow that had always made Lu stand apart was back. He smiled. "Well, a guilt-free existence works for you." He looked around. "Where's Little Bit?" he asked.

"She should be back any moment." Walking toward the kitchen, she called, "Can I get you a drink?"

"Absolutely," he answered, following her.

"How's your visit so far? What do you want? Scotch?"

"Good and yes."

"How's Lex?" she asked, then stopped herself. "Sorry, taboo subject. How's school?" She reached up to grab a glass and got the bottle of Glenmorangie that she always had on hand for Pete.

"School's good. Finish in May. Trying to find a place to be an intern."

"I have the date on my calendar already," she said.

"That means you and Lex will have to be in the same place," he said in mock horror.

Lu chuckled. "I'm to that point, ya know. I can handle joking about it."

He took a sip of his Scotch. Sobering, he said, "How's Will?"

Lu smiled inwardly, but turned to him without a hint of a smile on her face. "She's Will," she said simply.

"Yeah. That I already know," he responded with a grimace. "But how is she?"

Knowing suddenly how he felt, stuck between his brother and her sister, she said, "She's Will and she's OK. Probably wondering what if, but definitely not sharing that with me or anyone else."

"She's tough, Lu," he said glumly.

Looking for a change of topic, Lu went back to his internship. "So what hospitals are you looking at?"

"Not so fast. Tell me about your dissertation. Done?"

"I am," she said, smiling widely. "Submitted and accepted. Degree conferred in December."

"And work?"

"Slow. It's hard without having a pro team nearby. After I graduate, I'll probably have to do some traveling back. The team has been calling for consultations. Technology is an amazing thing. We've been Skyping, so I've managed to keep working."

"Lu, have you considered trying to work with one of the soccer teams over here?" Pete asked, a question he'd been hanging on to so that he could ask in person.

She looked stricken. "Absolutely not. Not a line I'm crossing. The last thing I need to do is try to get into Lex's world."

"Sweetie, you are amazing at what you do. You had teams clamoring to get you to work with their athletes. Don't you think the English would snap you up if they knew you were here and available?"

"Discussion over, Pete," she snapped at him.

"Fine." Taking another sip of his drink, he stopped when he heard the door open.

Nina walked in first. Turning toward the kitchen she let out a scream of excitement. "Uncle Pete!" Running across the room, she threw herself into his arms.

Preoccupied with twirling Nina around, he didn't notice Willa follow her in.

But Willa saw Pete. "What the fuck are you up to, Lu?" she said accusingly.

"Language, Willa!" Lu yelled, as Pete turned around to face her.

Dumbstruck at Lu's conniving, "Hey, Will," was all he could manage.

22

Seething at her sister but ever conscious of her niece watching the exchange, Willa tamped it down and headed to get herself a drink. Nina filled the awkward silence with a running commentary on the shopping she had done with her aunt. When she paused to take a breath, Pete managed to slip in a question and send her off in another direction.

"How's school, Bit?"

"Good. It's different."

"Do you miss your friends?"

A small frown formed on her face.

"Way to go for the jugular," Willa muttered from her place across the kitchen.

Pete glared at her. Lu jumped into the uncomfortable silence. "Dinner's almost ready. Nina, why don't you tell them what you can do with my phone."

At this, Nina smiled big. "I FaceTime with my friends at home. It's really cool. We can see each other and everything."

"Ah," Pete managed. "How come we don't get to FaceTime?"

"Mommy says you're too busy with school and you have an antique phone."

"Antiquated," Lu corrected.

"Antiquated," Nina mimicked.

"Only nine-year-old in the world to use that word," Willa muttered again.

"True," he acknowledged, while shooting Willa a death look. "What about your grandparents? Are you getting them to FaceTime with you?"

"No," she said. "We Skype with them."

"Wow, you know more about all this stuff than I do."

"Well, you're cutting up dead people so you can be a doctor, Uncle Pete."

They all laughed. Pete looked at Lu with a baleful glare.

"Sorry," she said, unapologetically. "When we don't talk to you for a couple of weeks, that explanation always seems to make her feel better."

"Great. You're teaching her to be morbid."

"Whatever works!" Lu replied saucily.

Pete rolled his eyes. Lu smiled sweetly at him and shoved the turkey into his hands. "Put this on the table, please." Doling out dishes for everyone to take to the table kept the tension to a minimum. Lu grabbed another bottle of wine for the table and refilled Pete's glass with Scotch, hoping the alcohol would keep things from getting too tense, although she knew the chances of that were slim to none. Willa couldn't pretend if her life depended on it. And Lu thought she may have misjudged how truly hurt Willa had been as she took note of the rage emanating off of her.

Rather than put Pete and Willa next to each other, Lu put them across from each other, hoping that Nina and she could provide some buffering. Pete couldn't do mad, but he did hurt pretty well. Lu could tell that Willa's anger was killing him. Lu tried hard to keep the conversation moving, but the tension continued to mount. Somehow they made it through dinner. Lu sent Nina off to shower and forced Willa to do the dishes so she could have a few more minutes with Pete. Pulling him over to the couch, they sat down to chat.

"Do I get story time tonight?" he asked.

"Of course." Taking a deep breath, Lu plunged forward. "I'm sorry. I misjudged Willa's anger."

Pete smiled. "To be honest, I think I did too." He sighed. "Do you know why I held off for so long?" At Lu's shake of her head, he continued. "Because of all of this. This craziness between our families. I knew, before I even got this ball rolling, that we wouldn't be able to separate ourselves from it."

Lu smiled sadly. "I'm sorry."

"It's just too complicated," he sighed. "Have you and Lex really not spoken?"

"We have not spoken," she said, a little sad. "It's OK. I've become quite friendly with his attorney." She smiled, letting him know she was really OK.

"I wish I could tell you that he'll break at some point."

"He won't. There will come a time when we'll have to discuss something pertaining to Nina. Until then, he's going to be stubborn." She paused then, thinking about how she wanted to say what she felt she had to say. "I know you have a lot going on with school and your future. But I hope you don't give up on Willa."

He laughed. "Come on, Lu. She's a female Lex. She'll never forgive me for not stepping in."

"She's wrong."

"So's Lex."

"No, he's not."

"Stop defending him. Damn it, Lu!"

Taken aback by his anger, Lu decided to wait him out.

"He's wrong to be taking all of his anger out on you. How is he not mad at everyone else? I don't get it. I've tried to talk to him about it, but he shuts down whenever I bring it up. I've never seen him like this. It just doesn't make any sense."

But Lu knew that it did and she wasn't going to let him wrangle it out of her. She sent up a silent thanks that Lex hadn't told Pete about their conversation.

SANTIAGO

"Do you ever wonder how different things would have been if you and me had fallen in love with each other instead?" Pete asked.

They both studied each other. Then simultaneously burst out laughing.

⌒

When Pete had gone and Nina was in bed, Lu went to talk to Willa. Willa had changed into her pajamas and sat, curled up with her Nook, in the corner of the couch. Lu watched her for a moment before approaching. They resembled each other. When they were children, people often mistook them for twins. But puberty had wrought different changes in them. Willa grew. She'd inherited their father's height and towered over Lu's tiny frame. Will's eyes had changed too, to a dark blue. She kept her dark hair cut short, in a pixie that not everyone could pull off. Her demeanor made her features look harsher than Lu's. If they had been paintings, Lu would have been a watercolor with soft, smudged edges, while Willa would have been an oil with strong, well-defined lines.

Sitting on the couch, Lu reached out and touched Willa's leg. Looking up, Willa impaled her with a glare.

"I'm sorry," Lu said candidly.

"You should be," Willa said. "How could you set me up like that?"

Lu smiled guiltily. "I thought you would be overcome with joy and would leap into his arms."

"I don't believe in fairy tales like you do, Lu," she said pointedly.

"Ouch," Lu said, drawing her hand away.

"Sorry," Willa muttered. "Look, Pete and I were never anything. You don't need to feel guilty about it."

"But you could be something. You've both held back because of Lex and me. And it's not fair. You would both be so good for each other."

"Right. Like we've been so far," she said sarcastically.

"Look, Willa. I've never tried to give you advice on anything because my shit was so fucked up that I didn't think anything I had to say would mean anything."

"That's pretty sad, Lu."

"I know, but it's true. Pete's the best there is. He loves you. You being mad at him is killing him."

"He'll survive. He hasn't even tried to talk to me. I think he's doing just fine."

"Willa, who really tries to talk to you when you're mad?" Lu pointed out. "And I think you're wrong to be mad at him."

"How am I wrong?" she asked, genuinely perplexed.

"You're mad at him for not wanting to get in the middle of Lex and me. You essentially asked him to choose. Not even Lex did that to him."

Willa thought about that crazy time six months ago. "I didn't ask him to choose!" she said, defending her position wholeheartedly.

"Tell me what made you mad enough at him that you haven't spoken to him in six months."

"I wanted him to be with me when I told you what Lex wanted. I thought it would be better coming from him."

"Not even Lex put him in that position."

"But . . ."

"No buts, Will. Lex knew that if he asked Pete to go to me with his plan he'd be shifting the responsibility of representing Lex to me. He didn't want to do that because he knew how Pete felt about you. He knew you'd be pissed as hell at Pete for going along with Lex's plan. He was trying to give you guys a chance."

"Oh, I get it now," Willa said, laughing harshly. "This is about you trying to make Lex into the good guy."

"Ugh!" Lu groaned in frustration. "Do I look like I'm trying to hold on to Lex? Shit, Willa, you are *wrong*! I know it's hard for you to see that, but you are. You put Pete in an impossible situation of choosing between you and Lex right after he lost his father. What did you expect him to do?"

Willa suddenly looked as if she'd been hit. It finally sank in. "I didn't do that."

"You most certainly did."

Willa sat in stunned silence, trying to figure out if she'd truly put him in that position. She tried to explain. "I just thought it would be better coming from Pete. His delivery is so much more appropriate."

"No. That's not what happened. You wanted him on your side. You wanted him to agree with you that Lex was making an outrageous demand. Had you come in there with Pete behind you, you assumed I would assume that he agreed with you. You were testing him."

Willa shook her head, trying to make that statement not true.

"Willa, I love you dearly. But you love hard. It's all or nothing with you. You think that if you're with Pete you'll be giving up part of you. I think my history has tainted your view of things. You wanted to make sure that he would love you as much. It was your way of pushing him away before you let him in. I get it. And I think Pete gets it. But you were wrong. And you need to forgive him, because he's the only person in the world that gets you like you need to be understood."

Willa looked at her little sister for the first time in a long time and thought, Holy shit, my girl is all grown up. "You think you're so damn smart!" she said without any rancor.

"So my IQ says," Lu responded with flair as she got up and started toward her room.

"Lu," Willa called out to her. When Lu turned around she said, "I love you."

Lu shrugged with a smile. "I know," she said.

23

Pete unlocked Lex's door and jumped in surprise when he found Lex standing on the other side of it.

"Shit! What are you doing here?"

"Last I checked, I lived here," Lex said drolly.

"I know, but you weren't supposed to be back until tomorrow."

"Yeah, I came straight home."

Pete followed him into the kitchen. Feeling uncomfortable about where he had been, he blurted out, "I just came from Lu's."

If Lex was surprised or angry, he didn't show it. "Nina will be here tomorrow. You didn't have to go see her," he said, explaining his lack of a response.

"Well, I wanted to see Lu too."

"Yeah," Lex replied, waving him off. "So how was the night?"

Pete felt trapped. He'd completely avoided any discussion of Lu whenever he talked with Lex. He'd tried for months to get Lex to talk to him and had finally thrown in the towel when he noticed Lex calling less frequently, trying to avoid any unpleasant discussions. "It was interesting. Nina's amazing."

Lex smiled that trademark smile. "Yes, she is."

"How's it going with you two?"

He ran his hands through his longer hair. "Slow." He walked over to a bar stool and sat down. "We have fun together, but I don't necessarily feel like her father. I mean, I don't know what to say all the time, and I feel like she sees me as a fun uncle rather than her dad. Which should be lots of fun when we get to the teenage years."

Pete studied his brother. "Gotta be the first time in your life that you've been unsure of how to act around a female."

Lex chuckled. "Yeah. Most important one. Go figure."

Pete let that thought linger between them. It dawned on him that he was worried about Lex. He just didn't seem to be himself. Even when he watched his brother play soccer, he seemed to be lacking that luster that had made him so much fun to follow. "You OK?" Pete asked.

Lex didn't say anything at first. He scrubbed his hands over his face again. He sat for such a long time without responding that Pete thought he wouldn't.

Finally, he said, "I'm not really sure." No longer able to sit, he got up. This was familiar to Pete, more like the Lex he knew, with the frenetic energy and the need to move constantly.

"Everything feels off. There have been so many changes that I don't know what to blame it on. Is it Dad dying? Is it suddenly having a child? I can't pinpoint it. But it's starting to affect my play. For the first time in my life, soccer is not helping me find my balance."

Pete wanted to respond, but he didn't know what to say.

"I thought having Nina close by would be a good thing, but I can't seem to find my footing with her. She hasn't done anything to warrant it yet, but what happens when she does something and I need to discipline her? I don't feel like I have the right. It's totally frustrating. Or what if something happens at school? I have no idea if Lu would include me in the discussion. Sometimes I wonder if it's just too late."

"You really think that? That it's too late to be a father to her?"

"Yeah, most of the time I do." He looked at Pete then and said, "And you know what happens when I think about that? I get mad at Lu all over again." Frustrated, he walked to the window, leaning his hands on the ledge. "So how's that for some shit?"

"That's some shit," Pete agreed, having no idea how to help his brother work through all this. But he had a small opening and so he tried to push the advantage. "Maybe if you and Lu could talk. Maybe then you could work through this together."

Lex turned slowly to face his brother, incredulity written all over his face. "Are you fucking serious?"

"Look, I have no idea how to even think about what you must be going through, but I think Lu could help. I know you are angry at her, but if you were able to forgive her, maybe it would be easier to see yourself as Nina's father." Pete knew he was treading on sacred ground, but he also knew that Lex needed help. It was the only way he could think of to help him get his equilibrium back. But as he watched Lex take it in, he knew he'd made a mistake. Lex moved like lightning and got right in Pete's face.

"I can't fucking believe you can stand in my house and take her side. What the fuck is wrong with you? Why are you defending her after what she did?"

Pete, suddenly fearful of the damage he might be doing to his relationship with Lex, wanted to change direction, but it was too late. So he plunged forward.

"I'm not defending her. I just think that if you are ever going to be a father to Nina, you are going to have to learn to parent with Lu."

"You don't know shit about being a parent, so you should stop while you're ahead."

"You don't know either," Pete said before he could stop himself. Before he could react, Lex slammed him up against the wall.

"Don't fucking mention her name to me. Don't try to fix this with your thoughtful logic. I'm well past logic on this." Rage was making Lex shake, and Pete could feel the anger vibrating through him. He'd never been afraid of his brother, but now, he was afraid of the person in front of him. "If you want to have a relationship with me, you are going to have to make a choice. Do you understand me?"

"There's no choice to be made, Lex. You're my brother."

Lex released him, turned away, and left Pete standing there.

Pissed at his brother and himself, Lex needed to get out of his apartment. He slid his feet into his running shoes and slammed his way out the door. The leftover adrenaline from the fight with Pete had his hands shaking. He'd never raised his hand to his brother. Even as kids, he couldn't ever remember fighting with him. Their differences had made them the best of friends.

He started running at a grueling pace, hoping to chase away all of demons that had been haunting him over the last couple of months, that had disguised themselves in questions of what ifs and hopes of if only. This anger that beat at him constantly was such an odd emotion for him that it constantly threw him off kilter. His mother had once asked him why he didn't get mad at another player on the field who had targeted him. He'd said to his mother, "It's a wasted emotion. Why be angry when I can just beat him down the field next time? Being mad throws me off my game."

So this torrential anger that dug its claws into him, that pulled him around like the dizzy bat game and left him unfocused and unsure, felt wrong. But no matter what he did to try to combat it, something would kick up the dirt again. In the end it all came down to Lu. It was the conclusion he drew every morning when he woke up and every night before he went to bed. If he could let it go, or figure out a way to not be mad at her, he felt he could somehow get his control back.

Smiling in irony over the discussion he'd just had with his brother, he allowed himself the leeway to forget that he'd just physically harmed his brother for saying the same thing. The problem, though, came down to how he could try to talk to her. Just the thought of seeing her made his blood boil. He broke into a sweat when he thought of being in the same room with her. And since he was being so honest with himself, he had to admit that it was more than just keeping Nina away from him. Although that was enough to convict her in and of itself, it wasn't enough to keep the flame of his anger from extinguishing itself. Because when he thought about those decisions made so long ago, he knew she didn't have the wherewithal to fight their combined sets of parents without him. And he'd left, even though he knew she was pregnant. For that, he could probably find it in his heart to exonerate her.

Her claim to have held them all hostage if they told him about Nina—he knew that was bullshit. She'd been convincing and, at the time, he wanted to believe that. But he knew she wouldn't do that. They had all made a decision to protect the secret because they didn't know how to tell him. They all withheld the knowledge of his daughter to protect themselves. He thought it sucked, but he got it. When is there a good time to tell someone he has a child who's been concealed from him?

So why was he really mad at her?

It was the sex. How did she open herself up to him when she kept the most important thing in her life from him? How did she let him inside her body while blocking off her heart? Was it just his ego that was hurt? Could he be that much of a dickhead? The Lu he thought he knew was genuine and sweet. So who had he been with six months ago?

24

The excitement and uncertainty of Willa's visit had begun to fade and life began to retreat into a normal pattern. School seemed to agree with Nina although, much like her father, her constant need to move had resulted in a few phone calls to Lu. Here she balked. How did she include Lex? She found no answers in her super brain and also found that she had no one to talk to about the situation. Everyone in her life was too involved and too jaded. It seemed as if suddenly the issue of Nina had divided their two families. She still spoke to everyone, reluctant to let Nina's relationships with them waver. But when looking for direction on how to include a parent who had been deliberately excluded for nine years, she found herself whipping in the wind. This was the only negative in her new life.

The approach of Christmas found Lu preparing for her transatlantic trip home to receive her degree. She had to finish packing Nina so that she could begin on her stuff. The mindless task allowed her thoughts to wander. With all that had been happening, it seemed inconsequential to go back for her graduation, but she knew that she'd worked hard and should enjoy the sense of accomplishment. Her PhD at twenty-seven seemed to say that she had lived up to the promises of her youth. Even her teenage pregnancy hadn't held her back from potentially achieving greatness. There was part of her—and if she was honest, she would admit it was a large part of her—that wanted to take her diploma and rub it in her mother's face. But the parent side of her recognized the immaturity of that sentiment.

After a long, arduous discussion with Lex's lawyers, an agreement was worked out for Christmas. Lex wanted to take Nina on one of his trips so she could see some of England and watch him play. Lex's nanny would chaperone her during practice and games. It made Lu nervous, but she didn't think she could hold him back from taking her. He'd patiently waited for her to have a break from school. It had come time for him to have her for an extended period. With their very separate lives, Lu still felt as though she were parenting alone. She envisioned a time in the near future when she would have to discuss it with Lex— not his lawyers—but she continued to give him the space he desired. On her return from the States, Nina would begin a two-week stint with him.

There were times when Lu questioned her own cooperative attitude. She found herself wanting to demand more, but she would work herself up for it and all the bluster would fade away. So much for that doctorate in psychology, she thought. She knew she felt guilty for keeping Nina from Lex and for not avoiding intimacy with him. But at some point, being a parent had to outweigh being a woman, right? That's what she was banking on—for this primal maternal feeling to kick in so that she could kick some English attorney ass. It almost made her laugh that she could continue to be pissed at her mom but couldn't work up the energy to fight Lex. Perhaps because she wasn't sure what she'd be fighting for.

Finished with Nina's bag, Lu moved into her room to get her things together. As she dragged her suitcase off the top shelf in her closet, her phone rang. She raced for it because in the middle of the day, the possibility of a call from Nina's school loomed large. Skidding to a halt in front of her desk, she picked it up but didn't recognize the number.

J. SANTIAGO

"Hello," she answered.

"May I speak with Dr. Knight?" said the voice on the other end of the phone.

"Either you're looking for my mother or you are a week early."

"Ah, a week early?" he paused. "I was hoping to speak with Louisa Knight."

She laughed, "This is Louisa Knight."

"Good. Louisa, I am calling from the EPL."

Lu paused. "EPL?" she questioned.

"The English Premier League."

"Oh," Lu answered. She should have known those initials. "How can I help you?"

"I should probably introduce myself. My name is Malcolm Helms. I happen to know Michael Ziegler," he said, matter-of-factly.

"Ah," Lu responded. "He told me that he'd passed my name along to a couple of people. He just didn't tell me who."

"He pointed me in your direction and after reading some of your papers, I'm interested in your work. I was hoping that we could meet so that I can discuss it with you."

"Mr. Helms, I'm flattered, but if you are familiar with my work then you know that it is specific to football," Lu explained patiently, "American football."

"Yes, yes, I understand. But I had assumed that you would want to continue your work. And there is no American football here in England," he pointed out.

Lu paused, suddenly struck by that statement. Was this how Dorothy felt? She wasn't in Kansas anymore. How long was she going to be here? She hadn't even thought about that. Did Lex think that they would stay here forever? It was at that precise moment that she finally felt all of the indignation that Willa had expected of her six months ago. She had uprooted her entire life without so much as a peep. It was fucking amazing what good sex could do to your brain.

"Miss Knight?" Mr. Helms said, bringing her out of her stupor.

"Yes. Um, I am headed to the States on Friday for my graduation. Why don't we plan on lunch sometime next week?"

"You'll be back so quickly?"

"Yes, sir. We'll be back on Monday evening."

"Let's say Tuesday, then, shall we?"

"Perfect. Where would you like for me to meet you?" Her phone beeped, indicating she had another call. Pulling it away from her face, she saw the number for Nina's school. "Hold on one moment, please. I have a call coming in." But as she went to make her pick between her three iPhone options, she hit the wrong one and ended up hanging up on the school.

"Mr. Helms, I apologize, but I have to go. Can you email me the arrangements and I will make sure that I am there."

"Yes, that works well. What is your email?"

"It's lmknight@langate.ggsu.edu."

"I will get that to you promptly."

"Thank you," Lu said before disconnecting. She wasn't sure if it was the accent, but it all seemed so proper to her. Who used the word *promptly* in everyday conversation?

Quickly dialing the school, Lu waited to be able to talk to someone, her stomach in knots. Immediately, she was put on hold. Finally, after waiting for five minutes, her call was answered.

"This is Louisa Knight," she said. She'd long ago learned that in any nonsocial situation, her full name got her places that her nickname just couldn't reach.

"Oh, Miss Knight, please hold. Our headmaster has been trying to contact you."

Again she waited, but this time, her nerves made her rusty mother's intuition sharpen. In her mind, her daughter had been seriously injured. She'd never had the headmaster call her.

"Miss Knight, this is Mr. Seddon. Nina is fine."

Breathing a sigh of relief, she responded, "Hello, Mr. Seddon."

"I'm afraid I am going to need you to come in and collect her from school today."

"I thought you said she was fine," Lu said, confused.

"She is physically fine. Are you able to come now?" he asked, his tone rather short.

"Yes, sir. I can be there in twenty minutes."

"Wonderful. Mr. Pellitteri said the same."

"Ah, Mr. Pellitteri?" she asked apprehensively.

"Yes. When I was unable to reach you, I called her emergency contact. So I'll see you shortly?"

"Yes, sir. Thanks so much." Lu disconnected the phone and fell heavily into her desk chair. Without realizing it, she took inventory of what she was wearing and tried to remember if she'd put on any makeup or done her hair. Realizing the foolishness of the sentiment, she stood up, gathered her coat and purse, and headed out the door. The rolling that had started in her stomach the moment the school called churned up so that she could almost feel the acid sneak its way into her throat. Her newfound hostility chose that moment to lodge itself, right alongside her worry over Nina. Aside from her daughter having to be picked up in the middle of the day, she was about to see Lex for the first time in seven months.

⌒

Lex had just finished showering after practice when his phone rang. He'd never received a phone call from Nina's school, but he had long ago programmed the number into his phone. Glancing at the name lighting up the screen, he answered without hesitation.

"Hello."

"Mr. Knight?"

Smiling, he said, "No, Pellitteri."

"Ah," said the voice, as if suddenly everything made sense. "Mr. Pellitteri, this is Mr. Seddon, the headmaster at Nina's school."

"Yes?"

"Well, I'm afraid I have to have someone come pick her up, and I was unable to reach Ms. Knight."

Suddenly alarmed, Lex said, "Is everything OK?"

"Yes, everything is fine. Are you able to come collect her?"

"Of course. I can be there soon."

"Great. If you could just ask for me in the main office, I'll be waiting."

"OK," Lex said. He grabbed his bag and headed for his car.

On the way there, thoughts flew at him like the oncoming traffic. He suddenly found himself thrust into being a father for the first time. Although the reason for the phone call remained a mystery, he was the second phone call. When Lu couldn't be reached, they'd called him. It astounded him, this feeling of responsibility. Such an inconsequential action, one that no one at Nina's school had given a second thought to, had for the first time made him feel like he was actually her father. Why this of all things?

She'd called him Dad from the start. He thought he probably owed that to his father, not to any action that he had taken that made her feel like he was really her dad. He could tell that she had been conditioned to accept him. His dad had taken care of him from the grave, it seemed. Somehow his father knew that his ego needed for her to just accept him. He didn't mind working for every bit that came after that, but to have to win her over from the start, when she had a nine-year headstart on him, would have crushed him.

So as he made his way into the school, he felt a myriad of things. Pride because someone other than himself recognized him as Nina's dad—even if that recognition had only been granted because of a form that said he was the emergency contact. Apprehension over why he was there—he wasn't used to walking into situations he hadn't been apprised of or orchestrated himself. And, he had to admit, anticipation because, after seven months of self-imposed absence, he might see Lu.

25

Lex had never been sent to the principal's office, which tended to surprise people who knew him. School had been a pleasant, albeit short, experience for him. By the time he was fourteen, he had missed great chunks of time from school for training camps and tournaments. When he was at school, he spent a lot of time charming his teachers, who in turn spent time catching him up. His mother didn't believe in home schooling, which meant he'd had to do a lot to meet the requirements for the hours he spent at his desk. Walking into Nina's school now felt foreign to him.

He was immediately shown into the outer office, adjacent to the headmaster's. Sitting in a chair, with a look of defiance plastered across her face, was Nina. When she saw him, she merely glared, offering no smile. Lex didn't have long to contemplate his reception, because Lu entered the room immediately after he did. Watching the scene unfold, he noted that Lu returned Nina's glare. He realized in that moment that he had never seen them interact. He'd be so hurt at the funeral that he'd avoided all interaction with Lu. And since then, everything had been accomplished by his lawyers. As Lu and Nina faced off in front of him, he felt awestruck.

Lu looked like she was fifteen years old again. In jeans, fluffy UGG boots, and a big purple cable-knit sweater, she had a gray scarf tied around her neck. Her black hair was pulled back in a haphazard pony-tail and a smudge of lip gloss coated her full lips. This is the girl I fell in love with, he thought. But she was all woman and indignant mother right now, scowling at Nina, which she had a right to. I don't have that right, he acknowledged to himself. Once Lu made sure that Nina knew she was angry, she walked over to her and dropped a kiss on her head. Lu was just about to sit down when the door to the headmaster's office opened and Mr. Seddon invited Lex and Lu inside.

"Nina, please wait while I talk to your parents."

Zing, right through his heart. He was her parent. He looked back at Nina, winked at her, and followed the adults into the room.

"Mr. Pellitteri, Miss Knight, please take a seat."

The office looked like Lex would have thought it was supposed to look. A big oak desk was situated in front of a window and two chairs sat directly in front of the desk. Lex had to remember for a split second that he wasn't the one in trouble here.

Lex waited for Lu to pick a chair and then sat. He felt he needed to portray the image of a concerned parent, so he made sure to sit on the front of the chair, alert and rigid. Fake it till I make it, he thought.

"I have to say that my phone call to Mr. Pellitteri explained some of the questions that I was going to ask you, Miss Knight," Mr. Seddon began.

Lu glanced in Lex's direction but not at him directly. He didn't blame her. He wasn't ready to fall into those cornflower depths just yet.

"I'm afraid I don't understand, Mr. Seddon," Lu replied. "Perhaps you could explain what is going on, without being cryptic,"

Lex almost smiled.

"Certainly. It appears that Nina has been, what's the proper Ameri-can word, 'fleecing' some students of their money."

Both Lex and Lu reacted. Lex felt the eyebrow go up, and Lu flinched slightly.

"At first, I didn't really understand and I thought the offense was more serious. But after learning of Mr. Pellitteri's involvement in her life, it has diminished in gravity."

Sperm donor, thought Lex. That's about the extent of my involvement. But he needed for Mr. Seddon to spell it out for him.

"Mr. Seddon, maybe you should just tell us what happened," Lex said, reiterating Lu's earlier request.

"Nina has been peddling some of your possessions for cash."

"I beg your pardon?" Lu said at the same time that Lex said, "What?"

"From what I have gathered from some of the students and a couple of the parents who have called me, Nina has taken some of your things—T-shirts, wristbands, socks—and sold them to your adoring fans. Like I said earlier, I thought it much more serious before I realized that she was your daughter."

No one said anything for a moment. Lu recovered first.

"Nina has profited from her father's name?" she said, trying to clarify it for herself.

"Yes. This is what I have pieced together. Some of our students are huge football fans, as I am sure you know. As the season started up, they began talking about it. At one point, Nina told them that you," he looked at Lex, "were her father. But they didn't believe her. So she retrieved an old jersey from your house and brought it in to prove her claim. There was a validation, which I only found out later. My computer-science teacher told me that the students looked up pictures of you on the Internet to indeed verify that the jersey belonged to you. Once they believed her, they wanted stuff. So, the jersey, the first article to sell, went for cheap. But then the prices started to go up. One wristband was signed and went for, I think, twelve pounds."

Lex leaned back in his chair, remembering when Nina had asked him to sign the wristband. She said she wanted to take it home with her so she'd have something of his. And he'd bought it. Hook. Line. Sinker.

Lu looked at him and he nodded his head. Shaking her head, she looked back at Mr. Seddon.

"Of course Nina will return all of the money."

"Yes, well apparently the students are reluctant to give back the merchandise."

"They can keep it," Lex offered. "She'll still return the money."

"Very well," Mr. Seddon said. "Mr. Pellitteri, Miss Knight, I know that there have been a lot of changes in Nina's life recently. And she is so pleasant that I'm sure everyone was secure in the knowledge that she was just adapting. But it seems that she is not as comfortable as she appears." He paused. "I am not here to tell you how to parent. I am a parent myself and I often long for a manual to raise my own children. But perhaps you may want to talk to Nina and help her through this tumultuous time."

"She has had a rough seven months," Lu remarked. "We are on our way home for a couple of days. I will make sure that we spend some time talking about this."

Lex said nothing. He had nothing to contribute, once again. He felt like an ass. He made them move here. And not at any point had he considered how it might affect his daughter. He'd been so caught up in his hurt and the betrayal he felt that he'd come up with a plan that worked for him. Maybe she'd have been better off not knowing about him.

Lu was furious. Once Mr. Seddon released them to collect Nina, Lex followed her from the office. She couldn't believe that her nine-year-old daughter had been stealing from her father and selling his things. A small part of her couldn't believe Lex was so well-known that kids wanted to buy items of his clothing. She was embarrassed that her parenting skills were being questioned by the headmaster and that Lex was exonerated because he hadn't been involved. She could admit that she felt she deserved most of the blame, but it still burned her up that he got to be the good guy.

She glanced back at him, but his eyes were downcast, so she avoided direct contact. Even through the haze of anger, she could appreciate his beauty. His hair was much longer than at the funeral. Even though it looked like it needed to be cut, it worked for him. No surprise there. Everything worked for Lex Pellitteri. She could tell he'd just come from practice because his fresh, clean scent had bombarded her senses in the office. He hadn't shaved yet today. Dressed in worn jeans, sneakers, and a sweatshirt, he oozed sex appeal. That she could be checking him out at this most inappropriate time seemed to send her anger to another level.

She finally found herself in front of Nina. Careful to maintain her daughter's dignity, even though she wanted to grab her by the ear and pull her out of the school, she merely said, "Let's go."

Her clipped voice and stern tone were not lost on her daughter. Looking up, Nina stood to precede them out of the main office. When they reached the parking lot, their division as a family seemed to hit each of them. Suddenly they all stopped, not sure how to move from this place to the next. More than any event in the last several months, this pause in their movement stood out to Lu as the epitome of their lives. Three people. One man, one woman, one child—intimately connected without a tie to hold them together. How could Lu have thought that Nina could handle this when she herself had been avoiding it?

"See you at the house?" she said, not wanting to issue an invitation but not willing to let him get out of this either.

Lex continued to look anywhere but at her.

"Sure," he answered. Turning away from them, he walked toward his car.

"I don't want to take the train," Nina whined.

"I don't really care what you want," snapped Lu.

Lu knew the moment Lex remembered that she didn't have a car. Turning, he walked back toward them. "Sorry. My car's over here."

Lu really didn't want to be in the car with him. The proximity would be stifling, but the quicker they got home to figure all this out, the better. The car ride was as bad as Lu thought it would be. No one spoke, each wrapped up in their own thoughts. As they traversed the London streets, Lu felt the anger from earlier in the day continue to beat at her. While she knew that they needed to deal with this specific issue, she also saw this for the opportunity that it was. Lex needed to step up and she intended to tell him that. When they pulled up to her building, Lex stopped the car to let them out.

"I'll park and be up," he told her.

Without responding, she grabbed Nina's hand and crossed the street. When they entered the apartment, Lu, who could only deal with one thing at a time, walked Nina to her room.

"You are to stay here until I tell you to come out."

"Time-out is for babies," Nina replied defiantly.

Lu glared at her, but kept her voice calm and level. "The only activity you are allowed to engage in for now is to read. If I come back and you are doing anything else, it will be reflected in your punishment."

"I'll just go live with Dad!" Nina yelled as tears pooled in her eyes.

Great, thought Lu. This is a threat I'll have to live with for the rest of my life. Maturity and maternal wisdom flew out the window as Lu responded, "You do that. I'm sure that will work out very well. You can learn how to be a good daughter and he can learn how to be a dad!"

Horror dawned on Nina's face and she crumbled to her bed as she yelled, "I hate you!"

Lu slammed her door. She moved down the hall and stopped, leaning on the wall. Real mature, she thought. She lightly banged her head against the wall. "Fuck," she whispered. What kind of haze had she been living in? How did she not see that Nina was struggling with all of this? "Mother of the year candidate I'm not," she muttered.

At the knock on her door, she heaved herself away from the wall. Depositing her purse, which she hadn't released when they walked in, she moved slowly toward the door. Complete-bitch mode took over. Pulling open the door, she glared at Lex. For the first time since the Sunday-school room, blue eyes met green. What Lu saw surprised her. The green eyes, which were usually so full of merriment, were lifeless and dull. Empathy filled her. Then out of nowhere, the anger that had been absent over the last several months blossomed into a prickly thorn that burst the bubble of empathy. "Ready to start acting like a father?" she snapped.

26

"Yeah right, Lu. I'll get right on that. Although somehow I think you'd be just as pissed if I knew exactly what I was doing."

"What's that supposed to mean?" she fired back as she stepped away from the door so that he could come in.

"Exactly what I said. I'm not mincing words. How am I supposed to be a father to a child whose existence I didn't even know about? She's nine years old. I'm supposed to just barge into her life and start acting like her father? How do I do that?"

"I didn't know how to do it either. But I've figured it out!" Lex continued to stand on the other side of the threshold, as if he couldn't decide whether or not to come in her home. Lu noticed his reticence. "Are you coming in or not?"

"I haven't decided yet," he hurled at her.

"Let me make the decision for you," she said as she attempted to shut the door.

"Well, you seem to be good at making decisions for me, don't you?"

Horrified, Lu stopped. The push and pull of her emotions made her feel like a ping-pong ball being volleyed back and forth. She wanted to get away from him, but she knew she needed to do something so that they could be parents to Nina. If she let him or pushed him away now, any hope of an amicable association would be lost.

Pulling the door wider, Lu signaled him that she wanted him to enter. When he still stood in the doorway, she buckled, "Please come in, Lex." When he entered, she murmured, "What are you, a fucking vampire that needs to be invited in?"

Despite himself, he smiled slightly, but as he was entering the apartment, she didn't see it. Taking quick note of the surroundings, he could feel Lu's influence all around him. They'd only been here for four months, but it seemed like a home. Lex walked over toward the kitchen and sat on a bar stool. Lu strolled into the kitchen, attempting to disguise her nervousness. She stood on the other side of the bar, leaning against the kitchen counter, facing him. As she looked at him, she was struck by his stillness, in his body and especially in his eyes. No sparkling mischief lurked in the beautiful green depths, and it made her sad.

"So, I am assuming Nina's never really gotten into trouble before," he said, seeking confirmation.

"No."

"It was bloody brilliant, wasn't it?" he asked with a sad smile.

She smiled back. "Yes, it was. Completely diabolical. What nine-year-old comes up with a plan like that?"

"One with your brains."

"And your mischievous nature."

"Ha. I couldn't have come up with that. Where did she even think of that?"

"We won't know until we talk to her."

He nodded. Then, in a totally Lex move, he rubbed his hands over his face, got up from the chair and started to move.

"There are a couple of issues we need to discuss with her and I think we need to be on the same page before we have this conversation."

"Makes sense." He looked around, "Where is she?"

"In her room. I sent her there when we got home. Right before she told me she hated me and that she'd just go live with you."

Nodding his head again in understanding, he asked, "Never had her say that to you before, huh?"

"True. Never had a father to compete with."

Taken aback, Lex stopped moving. "Is that what we're doing?"

Lu slowly shook her head. "No. We're not. I'm not really sure what you are doing with her."

He sighed. "Me either. I have no idea what to do. I am lost here, Lu. I don't feel like I have any right to correct her or give her advice. She hasn't done anything blatant, but there are things that I want to be able to say and I don't feel comfortable saying it. I feel like her uncle, not her father."

For some reason, the thought that Lex might struggle had never even entered her mind. He was Lex. Everything came easy for him. He could charm anyone. And she'd seen Nina after her visits. He'd charmed her too. So what was the problem?

"The best thing for you to do right now is to continue to spend time getting to know her. Once you're more comfortable with each other, it will come naturally."

"I hope you're right, because after my last couple of visits with her, I'm thinking it's too late to be her father."

"Lex, it's never too late."

"If you were in my position, you might think otherwise."

"This is the first time in your life that you've had to work at something," Lu nipped at him, some parts sympathetic, some part pissed.

"Oh, yeah, I didn't have to work at soccer," he replied, frustration building.

"Exactly. Think about how much time you've spent playing soccer. And multiply it. You have to go through this process if you want to be her father."

"Easy for you to say. You've been there since day one."

"Right. And where were you? Oh, yes, you were playing soccer." Sarcasm laced through her tone.

"Maybe I'd have been right there with you if I knew you didn't have an abortion. Don't try to throw the blame on me. You didn't give me a chance to be a father."

Finally, thought Lu. Maybe now she could apologize for everything and they could move forward. "Lex, I am so sorry. It shouldn't have happened the way it happened. I—"

"Lu, I can forgive that part. I can't forgive the eight years after that. I'm paying for it right now. She may enjoy being around me, but I'm making it as entertaining as possible. What I want is normal, and I can't get that. How can she really trust me when I wasn't part of her life for so long? She hasn't asked me, but I know she wants to. And I don't blame her."

Lex began pacing again. Lu didn't know what to say without seeming like she was defending herself. It didn't seem appropriate to do so when she knew she'd been wrong.

"Look what happened today. If she was OK with everything that was going on, she wouldn't have stolen things from me to sell to her friends. As entrepreneurial as it was, it was wrong."

"Correct. We have a number of issues that we need to discuss with her." Lu began ticking them off on her fingers and Lex couldn't help thinking about his first meeting with Nina. "Number one, stealing. Number two, selling the stuff to other students at school. Number three, being suspended. We have to talk to her about all of it, and we need to come up with a punishment for her. I was thinking that maybe she shouldn't go on the trip with you."

This statement brought Lex up short. "Are you trying to punish her or me?"

"Lex, she's been looking forward to that trip for two months. It's a good punishment."

"Why doesn't she miss your trip to the States tomorrow? It's more timely than our trip in three weeks. It's immediate and effective," he argued.

"I'm receiving my degree. She's going to see the family and visit her friends. It would devastate her."

"Lu, I need for her to come on this trip with me. I need a span of time where I can be the parent. Only having her on alternate weekends and once during the week doesn't allow us to establish a relationship. I'm taking her on this trip. We need to come up with an alternative punishment."

"No. I'm not leaving her here when I go home. She needs this trip."

"Well, she needs mine too, so we need to come up with an alternative," Lex yelled, temper finally taking hold.

Lu jumped, not used to seeing temper on Lex. It didn't suit him. He looked different, more dangerous, with his eyes glinting like shards of green glass and a scowl pulling his eyebrows together. The woman in her said sex, the mom in her said, shit. She wasn't up for a battle tonight, but she knew it had been coming for seven months, like a great storm cloud chasing across a summer sky.

Nina came out of her room, obviously summoned by Lex's voice booming through the cavernous flat. "What are you yelling for?"

Both Lex and Lu were caught off guard, so engaged in a silent battle of wills that neither of them heard her approach.

"We're just trying to figure out some stuff," Lu said reassuringly.

Nina walked over to Lex. "I'm sorry I stole stuff from you."

Lex wanted to tell her it was OK and that they were OK, but he knew that he couldn't do that. Dropping down to one knee, he said, "You know that if you had asked me for something, I would give it to you to show your friends. But taking it from me and selling it was wrong." He said it matter-of-factly, not directing his anger at Lu toward Nina. "I'm disappointed that you did that."

Nina burst into tears. Lu watched, fascinated. "No one believed me that you were my dad. They said you didn't have any kids. The papers never said that you did. They thought I was making it up," she hiccupped as the sobs broke through. Lex took her in his arms, but he didn't tell her it was OK, which made Lu smile inwardly.

"Why does it matter so much to you that they know?" he asked.

She shrugged. "Because I've never had a dad before."

Lu had to hold back tears. Her crying wouldn't make it any better. She turned away, trying to get ahold of the persistent tears.

"You've always had a dad. I'm just part of your life now." He pulled her in close to him.

"But where have you been?" Nina asked, tears still coursing down her cheeks.

Lex, thankful that Nina couldn't see the look of horror on his face, wanted to groan out loud. How the hell was he supposed to answer that? Did he tell her that he didn't know about her? He watched as Lu slowly turned back to the scene and met his eyes. He could see his mortification reflected there. So who did he implicate—himself or Lu? She seemed to be asking the same question. He didn't want to take the blame, but he didn't have the heart to place all of the blame on Lu either.

"I know it's hard to understand, but decisions were made for your mom and me that we didn't have much control over. We're trying to fix it now." He held Lu's gaze and felt like he'd done the right thing when she offered a tremulous smile.

He knew they needed to have this discussion, but he felt as though he was learning something about his daughter. She was diverting the attention from the issue. She'd had plenty of time to ask these questions and she hadn't. Shit, he thought, I'm always going to have to out-think her.

He pulled away from her and stood up. Grabbing her hand, he led her over to the couch and sat down in the chair across from it, allowing Lu to sit next to Nina.

"We have other issues to talk about, Short Stuff," Lex said, pinning her with the death glare he'd learned from his mother.

"I know," Nina admitted, and Lex could tell that she knew he was calling her on it. "I really am sorry that I stole stuff from you."

"You have to return all of the money," Lex said, gently. He leaned forward in his chair and rested his elbows on his knee, mostly to give himself time to figure out what to say next. Although he resented

Lu for putting this ball so firmly in his court, he knew that this time was overdue.

Nina's eyes bulged. "No one wants to give any stuff back."

"I realize that. They can keep the stuff."

Relieved, she sat back. "OK," she said, thinking that as a punishment, that hadn't been so bad.

"Your mom and I are trying to figure out an appropriate punishment. You have two big trips planned, one with each of us. We kinda think that you should have to give one of them up." Briefly, he thought he probably shouldn't have used the word *kinda*. It just didn't sound parental.

"What do you mean? I have to pick one?"

For the first time, Lu looked fully engaged. "No," she said, "we're going to discuss a punishment. When we figure it out, we'll let you know."

Lex raised his eyebrow. All of a sudden he was back to being pissed. One of the trips was the perfect punishment. Why was she fighting him on this?

"Your father and I need some time to talk, Nina. We'll let you know when we've reached a decision."

Knowing she'd been dismissed, Nina got up. She walked over to Lex and hugged him, whispering in his ear, "I'm really sorry," before she stomped down the hall, letting both of them know that she was not happy.

27

"What the fuck, Lu?" Lex hissed as soon as Nina's door shut behind her.

"If we give her the choice, she's going to pick your trip. Of course she is. How's that fair to me?"

"You really think I'm interested in being fair right now?"

"Yes, a little. You didn't throw me under the bus when she asked about why you'd been absent."

"Trust me, I didn't do that for you," he lied. He didn't need her to have any advantage. "I said that because it was the truth. We weren't making decisions about her, were we?"

"No. Maybe if we'd had a conversation after you jumped on the plane, we wouldn't be in this position."

"And maybe if you hadn't sold me on the fact that you'd had an abortion, I would have called."

"Ugh," Lu groaned in frustration. "We could do this all day. Let's try to stay focused here."

"Fine!" Sick of sitting, Lex jumped up and began his prowl of the apartment.

"Look, Lex, I'm getting my doctorate degree this weekend. I didn't walk for undergrad, I didn't walk for my master's. And thinking about Nina is what got me through school most of the time. I want her to be there. I want her to see that I've been able to accomplish this even though—"

"Even though you had a child at seventeen?" he finished sarcastically.

Glaring at him, Lu tried a different tactic. "What if we let her go on both trips and we find an alternative punishment."

"Like what?" he asked, finding a place on the wall to lean, which to Lu looked like he was posing for some photo shoot.

"Maybe she should have to pay back all of the money to a charity or something," she suggested.

"Don't tell me you're one of these new-age parents that doesn't think punitive punishments are good for their children?"

"What's that supposed to mean?"

"She stole stuff from me and sold it to her classmates. She got suspended. If you or I had done something like that, we'd have had a real punishment. I probably wouldn't have been able to play soccer for a month. Your mom would have probably ripped every encyclopedia out of your room and made you watch TV for a month. She needs to feel the punishment. Not some pansy-assed 'Oh, let's make a donation to charity so I don't ever take responsibility for my actions' punishment."

Lu couldn't help it; she laughed.

"What's so funny?" he said, a grin threatening to dawn on his face.

"You. Pulling out the Dr. J. parenting philosophies."

Shrugging, he pulled away from the wall. "It worked," he said, defending himself.

"Yeah, I guess you turned out OK," she teased, her anger with him dissipating again. Why couldn't she hold on to it, she thought. "Look, Lex, I want her to come home with me. I think she needs it right now. And I want her to get to go on her trip with you. I think she needs that too. So we need an alternative. She's been hoarding her money for an iPad 2. She saved all of her birthday money. I think it would hurt her to have to part with it." Shaking her head, she said, "Trust me, I'm not some helicopter parent who thinks their kid can do no wrong. I yell and I make all sorts of mistakes. I don't know what I'm doing half the time."

"You've never been unsure of anything," Lex said.

"You don't know me anymore, Lex. Just like I don't know you." It was a simple statement, not made in anger or retaliation. But it seemed to hang in the air between them—a picture drawn with words that described who they were in that moment. And it hurt. Lu felt empty. All of the anger of the morning and the day had drained away, leaving this picture of reality that she really didn't like.

Lex broke the silence. "OK," he said.

"OK, what?"

"If you think that giving her iPad savings to a charity would be effective, let's do it. But she still needs to give the money back to the students she 'fleeced,'" he said, with air quotes around "*fleeced*" and the perfect Mr. Seddon English accent.

"All right," she agreed. "I think we should tell her together. Don't you?"

"Yes, that's fine," Lex concurred. Lu started to turn toward Nina's room when Lex stopped her. "Lu, I've been trying to keep her out of the press. I just thought it would be better for her. Do you want me to have Caroline release a statement about her?" he asked.

She was touched by his thoughtfulness. "I don't know, Lex. She seemed pretty upset that no one knew about her, but I don't think she really knows what that entails. If your first instinct was to protect her, I think that we continue to do that." She paused, then seemed to think of something. "You know, having her on this trip with you is going to pose questions and probably unearth her paternity anyway."

"Yeah, you're probably right. I just don't want her to think I'm ashamed of her."

"Lex . . .," she began, then stopped. "Forget it."

He laughed. "I know she was playing me, Lu. I got that."

"Yes," she smiled, "which is why I didn't feel I needed to point it out to you." Winking at him, she made her way to get Nina so they could hand down the verdict.

⌒

Lex went back to his post on the wall, waiting for these two new women in his life to emerge. Vaguely he wondered what would have happened if Lu had answered the phone earlier today. Would she have included him? He needed to ask her. Not to be a dickhead, although that did come quite naturally to him, but just to appease his curiosity. He assumed that she wouldn't have, but he felt he at least needed to give her a chance to explain herself. Damn, this was going to be painful. He knew it was hard enough when the parents were together. How would they do this apart? And what happened if one of them met someone and there was a third or fourth person in the mix?

Hearing the clatter of feet coming down the hall, Lex pushed himself away from the wall once more. Let's just get through this so I can get out of here, he thought. He needed to get away so he could think.

Nina sat back on the couch, and Lu took up the space next to her. Finding the chair again, Lex sat. Leaning forward, forearms on legs, he looked to Lu to start. Rolling her eyes, she began.

"Your father and I have discussed this and have come up with a reasonable punishment."

Nina didn't say anything, merely continued to look at her mother since she was talking.

"After you return the money to the students who you sold stuff to, you will take your iPad savings and donate it to an appropriate charity."

"What?" Nina cried, tears immediately filling her eyes. "That's not fair. I've been saving all my money this year."

"Yes, you have. But since it's not fair for either your father or me to give up our time with you, we felt this was more than fair."

As the tears continued to flow down her cheeks, she wiped furiously at them. "It's not fair."

"Well, you should have thought of that before you took my things and sold them," Lex said. God, Lex thought, did I just channel my father? Is this what happens? You just throw out phrases that were spoken at you as a child.

"This is a stupid punishment," Nina cried.

"Excuse me? What did you say?" Lu said calmly.

Nina, sheepishly shook her head.

"You know how I feel about that word," Lu said, even though it didn't need to be said.

"Stupid, stupid, stupid," Nina mumbled under her breath.

Lu jumped off of the couch and got right in Nina's face. "You will go back into your room and you will not come out until I tell you to come out. When you do, you better have all of your money sorted. The money that needs to be paid back and the money that you are donating. If you even mumble, murmur, or look like you are mouthing that word, I'll leave you here when I go home tomorrow. *Do you understand?*"

Nina couldn't even look her mother in the eye. She merely nodded her head and slinked back to her room. Lu, who was now standing, kept her back to Lex as she propelled Nina toward her room with a look of absolute disappointment and anger. Lex watched it all, fascinated. He could tell that Lu was about to lose her shit, and although he wasn't wringing his hands with glee, it helped him to see her flustered. No one spoke for a moment.

"Are you OK?" Lex asked her back, since she hadn't turned around to look at him.

"Just go, Lex," she said softly, reclaiming her sanity. "I'll make sure she calls you while we're gone."

"Lu," he said, as he stood up and walked toward her, placing his hands on her shoulders. "You OK?" he asked again.

She shrugged him off. "Please just leave. It's been enough today."

"Of course," he said flippantly. "One question though." When she didn't interrupt him or balk, he said, "Would you have called me today if Mr. Seddon hadn't contacted me?" The answer was important to him. He wasn't sure why but he needed to know.

"I'd like to say yes, but the truth is, probably not."

Without a backward glance, Lex made his way to the door and slammed it shut behind him.

28

Willa refilled the wine glasses and discarded the empty bottle.

"One down," she informed them.

Lu swirled the wine in her glass. "Already?" she asked, looking around the table at both Sky and Willa.

"Yup. Don't worry, we stocked up before you arrived," Sky assured her.

"I'm definitely going to need it."

"All right," Willa said, "continue the story. You get the call from the headmaster and you show up to find Lex there already. You must have almost shit your pants."

"That wasn't what she was doing in her pants," Sky said, winking at Willa.

"You are both disgusting. Do I really expose my nine-year-old daughter to you?" Lu said, with a slight smile on her face.

"Yes!" they both agreed.

"Apparently, Nina had been," Lu paused, trying to get ahold of herself. "I'm just a little embarrassed for her," she said, giggling. Sky and Willa exchanged glances. "She had stolen some of Lex's stuff and sold it to her schoolmates," Lu said in a rush. That part she actually found to be funny. The reason why sort of broke her heart. "She said they didn't believe that she was Lex Pellitteri's daughter, so she brought stuff in to prove it."

Willa and Sky had identical reactions. They both sat back in their chairs, obviously touched. Then, Willa being Willa, she said, "That's fucking brilliant. She could be the perfect criminal."

Although Sky had thought the exact same thing, she could tell that it was really bothering Lu, so she chose the high road. This time. Reaching out, she grabbed Lu's hand. "That must have been tough."

Willa's eyes widened. When Lu looked into the swirls of wine in her glass, Willa met Sky's eyes and gave her a questioning look. Sky merely shrugged.

"How did Lex take it?" Willa asked.

"Actually, he did pretty well." She met Willa's gaze. "I don't want you to think I'm being soft on him, OK?" she asked. At Willa's nod, she continued. "He came over and admitted that he was having a hard time finding his way with Nina. I think it's the first time Lex has had to work at a relationship with anyone. He doesn't know how to be her father. And he feels bad trying to when they barely know each other."

"Well, perhaps he should have thought of all of this before he forced you to move over there." Willa's anger over all things Pellitteri wrapped itself around her like a cloak.

"We both should have." Stopping to fortify herself with a sip of wine before bringing this up with Willa, she finally bit the bullet. "I can see now why you wanted me to fight."

Willa, not used to anyone conceding anything to her when it wasn't in a court of law, didn't quite know what to do. Her opinions were often so resolute that people couldn't even share the tones of gray in her black-and-white world.

"Look, I should have stood up for Nina and I. I should have fought him. Maybe if I had fought him she wouldn't be peddling his memorabilia for cash."

"Is he worth that much?" Sky asked, doubtful.

"Over there he is. It's like a different planet."

"You did what you thought was right," Sky said, supporting Lu again tonight with her sister.

"You should have fought him," Willa concurred, "but it's too late now. At this point, you have to find a way to make it work. Over there."

"Yeah. I'm kind of locked in right now. Tentatively, if things don't improve or she fails to thrive, we'll move back here for the start of middle school. That will be two years which I think is an honest attempt."

"Have you discussed that with Lex?" Sky asked.

"Well, are you Miss Sympathetic tonight," Willa said snidely.

Sky merely smiled at her and rubbed Lu's arm, sarcastically bestowing her support.

"No. Our one and only conversation with each other happened on Thursday, during the Nina brouhaha."

"That must have been fun."

"Oh my Jesus," Willa erupted. "Will you can it?"

Lu laughed, Sky feigned innocence, and Willa continued to stew.

"You really need to get laid," Sky said to Willa. "You are severely uptight."

"Good segue. What are you going to do when Pete arrives this weekend?" Lu asked sweetly.

"Ignore him like the plague," Willa said.

Lu, who thought she had gotten through to Willa during Thanksgiving, felt her face fall. "Really?" she asked.

"I don't know, Lu. I'm going to keep an open mind."

"Really?" Lu said again, happy that Willa might let Pete make headway with her.

"I'm not promising anything, but I heard you last time we talked. I'm mulling it all over." Annoyed that she felt she needed to let Lu know that she wasn't completely anti-Pete, she stood up to get another bottle of wine.

"Drink up, ladies. We have some celebrating to do."

They should have stayed home. There was little doubt, as they paid the cab fare and made their way into the bar, that they were doing the big-girl responsible thing. But their voice of reason, Lu, had pulled on her big-girl panties this evening and allowed the three drunken girls to make their way to the strip. In Lu's mind—her drunken haze, really—Pete and Willa loomed large. If she could just get them together, drunk or sober, she felt certain that they could find their way to each other. Making their way into the bar, Lu spotted Pete waiting for them.

Flinging herself into his arms, she hugged him hard. "It's so good to see you," she said. "Did Lex tell you what Nina did? She's on her way to being a criminal mastermind." She rambled all of this into his ear as he hugged her back.

Laughing, Pete said, "It's good to see you too. How drunk are you?"

"I've got the big-girl panties on tonight, Petey. We're celebrating."

Meeting Sky's gaze over Lu's head, she shrugged. Willa wasn't ready to make eye contact yet, so she sat at the table and asked, "What are we drinking?"

Pete, who had been hanging out with a friend of his, stole a chair from another table to accommodate the new arrivals. After he introduced everyone to Andy, he left to get a pitcher of beer. Lu watched him go and noted Willa's eyes following him across the bar. All inhibitions drowned at this point, Lu kicked her under the table. When Willa looked up, Lu said, "He's by himself."

Willa wanted to roll her eyes at Lu's antics, but she was just drunk enough that the edge on her mad was dull. Standing up from the table, Willa made her way to Pete.

Lu, smiling stupidly, pumped her fist. Shit, she thought, I'm drunk.

Sky took the empty seat next to her and said, "Don't think we'll see much of Pete and Willa tonight."

"Hopefully not," Lu said. Feeling bad for excluding Andy, she leaned toward him and asked him how he knew Pete. Engaging him in conversation, Lu lost track of Pete and Willa, which, she decided, was probably best. Andy and Sky started talking business and Lu, suddenly bored, took out her phone. Without thinking about it, she pulled up Lex's contact.

We have to stop fighting. She'd texted because she knew it was safe. He'd be sleeping; he'd see it tomorrow and by that time, this impulse would be gone.

So when her phone buzzed, she pulled it down, under the table so Sky couldn't see it.

Is that what we're doing?

Puzzled, Lu thought, Of course it is. Knowing drinking and texting was surely not a good thing, she responded.

Of course it is. What would you call it?

She was smiling. She could feel it on her face. She and Lex were talking and it made her happy. Looking at the beer in front of her, she took another sip.

Are you drunk?

She laughed. Didn't take him long to figure that out.

Maybe.

No maybe about it. Ur drunk.

Smiling again, Lu felt his pull. She saw him leaning against the wall in her apartment. At the time, she was pissed. He'd looked like he was posing for some *Vanity Fair* cover. Long lean lines, relaxed pose, scruffy appearance. Enough to make any woman want him. Even her. Again.

You never answered my question.

Which one?? Lex responded quickly, as if there weren't an ocean between them.

What would you call it, AJ?

There she was pulling out all the stops. Wanting him to remember who they were to each other.

Foreplay. Lol!

She laughed, sidesplitting laughter. She couldn't believe he remembered. He'd made fun of her all the time. Lu wasn't frivolous or girlie or into girlie stuff. But her favorite movie had been *The Cutting Edge* growing up and he'd always ribbed her about it. Saying that the dialogue wasn't smart enough for her big brain. And that she didn't even know what that meant. And then he showed her what it meant. That he'd remembered, made everything inside her turn to mush.

That time, she caused Sky to stop talking to Andy.

"Whatcha doing over there?" Sky asked.

"Nothing," Lu responded, reaching again for her beer.

"I don't believe you. Who are you texting?"

"No one."

"Louisa May, are you lying to me?" Sky said, as she made a grab for Lu's phone.

Lu tried to hold on to it but her reflexes were slow. Sky grabbed on and looked at the text conversation.

Smiling a smile full of I-told-you-so's, Sky handed the phone back to her. "Oh, Lu," she singsonged, "you are going to regret that in the morning."

"Regret what?" Willa and Pete said, simultaneously as they picked that moment to reappear.

"Just being drunk the night before I graduate," Lu covered sweetly.

Buying it, Pete suggested that they head out. "Speaking of, it's late. We should probably get you home."

Pete pulled his phone out of his pocket and looked down at it, reading an incoming text.

Make sure she gets home safely.

Shaking his head, Pete walked over to Lu and helped her stand. "Let's go, lover girl," he said, close enough so that no one heard him. "I have orders to make sure you get home safely."

29

Pete was curious but weary of going down the Lex-and-Lu slope. His mission tonight had nothing to do with the two of them. The moment Willa walked with him to the bar, his whole focus shifted. Originally, he had planned to talk to Lu about her relationship with Lex. He'd tried the opposite approach and had taken too many knocks from his brother for comfort. Right now, Lex needed him more than anyone else. He could see Lex withdrawing from everything around him. He could even see it in his play—something he'd never seen diminish. He knew that Lex hardly talked to their mom, and with the death of their father, his knowledge of his brother's loneliness troubled him. So he'd decided to appeal to Lu—to beg her to reach out to him. The rarity of seeing Lu drunk weighed on his mind, though. And the text from Lex—where had that come from? His thoughts all scattered with one look into Willa's eyes. She actually smiled at him. So now, he needed to take care of Willa.

"Let's go, Sunshine," Pete said as the cab came to a stop outside of Sky's three-bedroom bungalow and he pulled Lu up from the seat. It had once been Lu and Nina's home too, so he was familiar with it and its layout.

Willa stepped out of his way and let him follow Sky into the house.

"Where's Bit?" he asked as he led Lu into her old room.

"At her friend's," Lu managed to get out before falling backward onto the bed. "I am so going to pay for this tomorrow," she murmured to the wall.

"I will leave this to you," Pete said, looking at Sky.

"I got her," she said, smiling at Pete. "Go take care of your business."

He turned to do just that, but stopped. "Was she texting with Lex?" he asked, his curiosity getting the best of him.

"Yup. She's going to regret that in the morning," Sky said ruefully.

"I didn't realize they were talking," he commented, more to himself than to Sky. But she caught it.

"Oh, so you haven't heard about your niece, huh?"

He cocked his head, a watered-down version of Lex.

Sky laughed. "Ask Willa," she said and nodded her head, trying to tell him to take advantage of his opportunity.

He smiled and left the room. No one had to tell him twice.

⌒

Pete thought about asking Willa to relay the tale of Nina, but he knew that would put them exactly where they didn't need to be—in the middle of his brother's family—and he needed them to be in the middle of their family. So he didn't say a word. He walked to the door of the room where Willa had disappeared and knocked softly.

"Come in," she said, just as softly, as if the tenuous spell between them would be shattered by any loud noise or sudden movement.

Pete slowly turned the knob, briefly resting his head on the door before pushing it gently open. He prayed silently, Don't let me fuck this up, before, he stepped over the threshold. He walked into the room, breathing a sigh of relief. He could hear the sink running. He sank into the decorative chair in the corner of the room, next to the table that held the TV. He tried to collect his thoughts, wondering what he might do to blow this. He couldn't help it. Suddenly with all of the turmoil of the last several months, he'd become a pessimist. He felt the bulk of everyone's expectations grinding his natural optimism into little smatterings of dirt that could hardly fill a dustpan. His father's death, his brother's withdrawal, Lu's departure to London, his mother's grief, Willa's rejection. It had all beaten him down.

Now, on the threshold of a breakthrough with Willa, he felt fear. And it pulled at the fabric of his confidence. How could he make it OK with her? Because he knew if he made it work with Willa, the rest of it would fade to the screensaver of his life, there but not forever present. Before he could form a plan or calculate what to say, the door to the bathroom opened.

Willa walked out, face scrubbed, shorts and tank top on. She knew he was there, so she took a few steps into the room and sat on the edge of the bed, perpendicular to him. Not facing him but not looking away.

"Lu OK?" she asked.

"I don't know. I left her in Sky's care."

She nodded her head, acknowledging that. "Can I be nosy?"

He glanced at her. "O . . . K," he said, slowly.

Willa didn't fluster — ever. So to see her seem nervous, even embarrassed, intrigued him.

"What was the text you got at the bar?"

Looking confused, Pete pulled his phone out his back pocket. Looking at his messages, he balked. He so didn't want to talk about this now. Knowing where this was going to go, he put his phone on the table next to him and got up to put himself directly in front of her.

"I don't want to talk about the text," he said, then he took her hands gently and pulled her up. With their hands interlocked, he stepped closer to her so that the tips of their toes were touching. Easing his hands out of hers, he placed them on her hip bones, fingers on her back and thumbs in front. He pulled her closer. "I don't want to talk about the text, Will, because I've been waiting virtually my whole life to be with you." He kissed her briefly but hard, so she'd know he'd been there. Then he released her hips and brought both of his hands up to her face. Her blue eyes stared at him, the inner battle reflected there. Ugh, he thought, she wants to know.

Gently laying his forehead against hers, he closed his eyes. "It was Lex. He wanted me to make sure that Lu got home OK."

He felt her eyes fly open and her draw back, not away, but back. "How did Lex know that Lu needed to get home OK?"

Dropping his hands, Pete stepped all the way back. "Best guess? Lu was drunk texting him."

"What?!" she said, shattering the gentle din of the conversation.

Pete rubbed his hands over his face. "It's always going to be like this, isn't it?" he said, resigned.

⌒

Willa had never been a fairy-tale kind of girl. If she let herself remember, she'd note that Lu hadn't been one either. They'd both kind of scoffed at the princess-waiting-to-be-rescued-by-her-prince genre. And that attitude had everything to do with their mother. You'd have thought their mother was a radical lesbian rather than a married mother of two girls. Her views on feminism and women's roles didn't include mothers' sacrificing their careers for their children. As an adult, knowing Amber's views, Willa had to admit that she was sometimes surprised that she and her sister had been born. Standing in front of Pete, Willa thought of all of this and knew that she had been throwing Lex and Lu's situation in between her and Pete. Perhaps she could blame it on fear of giving up any piece of herself for a man. Or maybe, after twenty-eight years, she wasn't sure how to give up anything for anyone.

Willa had always been the eat-'em-up-and-spit-'em-out girl. She'd spent some time thinking about what Lu had said to her during her visit. She could admit that Lu's experience had dictated her course, because at nineteen Willa knew there was no way any man was going to leave her loving him more than he loved her. At the funeral, she'd imagined spending a couple of nights with Pete and moving forward. Maybe if she had simply explained that she just wanted to fuck him, this would have all been so much easier.

When Willa overheard his conversation with Lu, though, she felt herself fall. There was no other way to describe it. It was as if the earth all around her had crumbled away, but she managed to remain right where she was in this more amazing place. And that had scared the shit out of her.

Looking at Pete now, she could see the exasperation in his eyes. In all her memories of Pete, she didn't have any with him wearing the expression currently adhered to his face. He was all patience, understanding, and optimism. He saw the fertile ground under the dog shit she saw. For Pete, this wouldn't be quick and easy—it would be long, passionate, and easy. And although she didn't want to think about the consequences, she didn't think their families could handle any more trauma. But she was tired of thinking about things. His hands drifted to his side, and while he studied her he started to slowly shake his head as if he was trying to talk himself out of something. All Willa could think was Fuck it.

Her hands crossed in front of her. Grabbing the bottom of her tank top, she pulled it over her head. Pete tried—she could tell he was trying to keep his eyes glued to hers—but they slipped and took in the view. While he did that, she pushed her shorts down and let them pool at her ankles. Stepping over them, she walked over to Pete and placed her arms around his neck, clasping her hands in back. She left some space between them. She needed him to give.

"I don't think we have anything else to talk about," she said.

Pulling her to him, he smiled—one of those smiles that lit the room and she felt down to her toes. "I don't think I can do much talking with you naked," he quipped.

"Moaning?" she asked impishly.

"Hmm, yes, let's see about moaning," he said as he kissed his way down her neck and pulled her more snugly against him.

Her giggle quickly turned into a moan as he nipped at her neck.

"I think I won that round," he teased, pushing her back toward the bed until she hit it.

"You know you should never throw down the gauntlet with me, Petey Boy, and right now you have way too much clothing on," she said as she sat on the bed, and pulled him between her legs. She quickly unbuttoned his shirt, then moved to his belt and jeans.

When he stood naked in front of her, she paused, maybe for dramatic effect. Then she moved up the bed and he followed, coming down on top of her, between her legs. "I didn't think we'd ever get here," he remarked as he bent to kiss her. She wanted to respond to the comment, wanted to tell him that she never had any doubt that she'd get him into her bed, but she knew that wasn't what he meant. She tried to hold on to the thought, but his soul-searing kisses were making it difficult to sustain them. As his hands moved reverently over her body, Willa got lost in him. For the first time, she didn't dictate what happened. She surrendered completely. When she absorbed his body into hers, she came so quickly she almost laughed and he smiled, obviously proud of himself. It was at the moment when she gazed up at his smiling face in the aftermath of her climax that she realized there was nowhere else for her to go. Pete Pellitteri was home. Then she couldn't do much more than wrap herself around him as he quickly found his release.

30

Jo walked wearily toward the front door, dragging her suitcase behind her, wishing for a valet or porter—someone to lighten the load. The ride back from Tallahassee had been long and arduous, much like her weekend, much like the last eight months. She'd known that attending Lu's graduation would be difficult, but she couldn't pass on the opportunity to see Lu, Nina, and Pete. Even so, spending time with Chris and Amber now took a lot of effort on all of their parts. Gone was the easy friendship built over the lifetimes of their children, during those trying years. She'd never thought about what her life would be without Mike. But she'd imagined that she would draw upon the strength of their friends. Instead, she felt herself withdraw from all of them. It was easier for her to not participate in their rituals, allowing her the free reign to not draw upon memories of him. Perhaps in time, basking in those memories would bring her comfort, but for now they only brought pain and resentment.

Unlocking the front door, she turned back to lug her bag over the threshold. She felt rather than heard someone behind her. Slowly and as inconspicuously as possible, she reached into her purse for an old can of Mace that she had buried in the bottom of the main pocket. Getting her hand around it, she turned around, ready to do battle.

"Shit, Mom, you still have that Mace?" Lex said, a huge smile on his face, eyebrow raised, taking in the sight of his mother getting ready to spray him.

Jo, completely caught off guard, dropped the can and the luggage, both of which clattered to the floor. Her right hand landed on her heart, which had just about jumped out of her chest. "Alexander James!" she screeched. "What are you doing here?"

For a woman who rarely lost her composure, she presented quite the sight. Her purse askew, eyes wide, hand clutching her chest, she stared in disbelief at her son, whom she'd hardly spoken to since Mike died. She couldn't believe Lex was standing in her foyer.

He didn't answer her question, instead gave her a stiff, quick hug, grabbed her suitcase, bent to retrieve the Mace, and gently pushed her inside so that he could shut the door.

She watched him put everything right and waited for an explanation. When the door was shut, he walked out of the foyer toward her room with her suitcase in tow. Still flustered, she righted her purse and followed him. By the time she made it back to her room, he had finished his task and met her in the hall.

"How 'bout a glass of wine?" he asked, barely meeting her gaze.

"Something stronger, please," she said, moving with him toward the kitchen.

"Have you eaten?" he inquired as he led her, not looking back.

"No. You?" she asked, slightly frustrated. Lex had been home twice since he left almost ten years earlier. The first was for his father's funeral; the second was today. What was he doing here?

"No. We can order in," he offered, still not looking at her as he made his way to the bar off the kitchen. He poured a drink for her without needing to ask what she wanted.

"That's fine," she said, setting her purse on the counter and heading to the breakfast bar to sit down.

Lex delivered her drink. Surprisingly, he had one in his hand. Normally, he didn't drink during the season. She looked at him as he leaned against the counter, facing her. She took a moment to study him. He really didn't favor either Mike or her. He definitely had his own look. When he was a child they'd often wondered who he looked like. The blond hair was easily explained as there seemed to be a blond per generation in Mike's family. But his green eyes were a deeper green than Mike's, as if the dark brown from her had given sustenance to Mike's green. Used to the perpetual spirit of mischief that surrounded Lex, she experienced some surprise at his rather somber façade.

Taking a sip of her drink, she leaned forward, resting her arms on the counter and clasping her hands in front of her. "I hope you don't take this the wrong way, but why are you here?" she said.

Lex didn't answer right away. Rather, he studied his mother. She'd lost weight since his father's death. But she still looked formidable, even in her grief. The grief had left an imprint on her face. She didn't look bad, she hadn't aged, she just looked sad. He imagined that even when she smiled, she didn't look happy. He remained quiet, sipping his Scotch, thinking about what he wanted to say. It had been an impulsive trip, but he'd still been surprised that she was away.

"Where were you?" he asked, choosing to deflect rather than start down the road he needed to follow.

She paused, cocking her head, illustrating for him where he and Pete inherited the gesture. "Lu's graduation," she responded, as if he should have known she would be there.

But he couldn't help but be surprised. "You were at Lu's graduation?"

"Yes, of course."

Brow furrowed, he questioned her with his expression. She ignored him. "Of course?" he said. The question evident.

"I wouldn't miss her graduation," she responded.

It pissed him off. Taking a sip of his drink, he stalled. They were all together again and he'd been alone, here, waiting for her to get back. For not the first time since the death of his father, he thought of how disfranchised he felt. His family had this whole other world without him. While he'd made them the outer circle of his world, sharing all of his triumphs with them, he'd been left out in the cold, alone, excluded. He'd been trying to shrug it off for the last eight months. It was time that he had some explanations.

"I need to know what happened, Jo."

"What do you mean?" she said, obviously confused.

"I need to know why everyone thought it would be a good idea to lie to me."

Jo's head dropped, her expression hidden from him. "It's taken you eight months to ask the question," she observed.

"Well there's been a lot of shit going on." He was back to being resigned. It was so difficult for him to hold on to the anger.

Jo lifted her head and took a sip of her drink. Peering into the glass as though it held all the answers, she shuffled the ice slowly back and forth between her hands, as if it were a hockey puck. "When you left, Lu was convinced that your plan would work. You'd go over there but that you'd come back for her and your child. Her faith in you never wavered."

That made him smile. He and Lu had come to an understanding early in their lives that they would never lie to each other. Pete and Willa had been there too and some blood had been exchanged.

"It's hard to look back on this. I'm trying to be objective." She explained.

"Jo, just tell me your version. I'll draw my own conclusions," Lex said, the irritation clear in his voice.

"It was probably six weeks after you left that things got crazy. At the time, Lu was about to complete her first trimester. Amber began to pressure her to have an abortion. To be honest, I was very conflicted about everything. You know how I feel about abortion. I couldn't allow that to happen, but I wasn't ready for you to give up your dreams either. I imagine it won't be long before you'll understand what it's like to be a parent."

For some reason, her statement brought him right back to mad. "What's that supposed to mean?" he snapped.

"Just that you want things for your child. You want their dreams to be able to come true. You were on the brink. Coming home to be with Lu and the baby would have stalled your career. You wouldn't be Lex Pellitteri if you'd known about Nina."

"That's fucking bullshit!" he said, hostility laced through his words.

"The person you are right now, the one who's achieved so much, you wanted that from the time you could talk. Anything less would have chipped away at you. Anyway, Amber started to wear Lu down. She was sad, missing you, and she started to believe that she couldn't be a teenage mother and fulfill her dreams. They made the appointment. And so help me Lex, I was OK with it. I thought that both of you were so full of promise that this was the best thing to do. I was relieved."

That surprised him. His mother had always been pro-life.

"There I was, going against everything I believed so that you could get what you wanted." She stopped and finished her drink. "Your father was very quiet during this. Amber was here almost every night. We'd talk through everything. I understood where she was coming from because I knew what would happen to you. Then, the night before the procedure, Lu came over. She was pale, drawn, looking every single one of her seventeen years. She begged me to talk to Amber. Lu couldn't do it, she couldn't have an abortion. She knew that I could sway her. I wanted to help Lu. I loved her like she was one of my own. And I just couldn't, in the end, see that my soul could handle it if she had an abortion. But I still wanted to save you. So I convinced her that we should tell you that she had it."

Lex continued to lean against the counter, although he wanted to move. Even though he had known that his mother had to be behind all of this, it still shocked him to the core that she had managed to conceal this from him for so long. She'd outflanked a seventeen-year-old.

"Lu was so grateful that I would help her that it took nothing to get her to agree to the rest."

Lex nodded his head. Raising his eyebrow, he asked, "How'd you convince Dr. A.?"

"That was far more difficult."

"I bet."

"We pushed if off until it was no longer the first trimester."

"Sounds like it was quite a busy couple of weeks for you. You don't sound like you regret any of it."

"What would you like for me to regret, Lex? Should I regret the fact that we have Nina? Or perhaps that you've been so successful?"

"You've been lying to me for nine years. Do you regret that?"

"I regret that I had to do that, yes."

"You don't sound very sorry."

"I'm not sorry," she said, her voice becoming higher. "You were one of the first Americans to play in the English Premier League. You've just signed a multimillion-dollar contract to do what you love to do. I did what I had to do to help you make that happen. I. Do. Not. Regret. It."

"You may not regret it, but I do. I regret that I lost the only girl I've ever loved at nineteen. I regret that I didn't get to hold my newborn daughter in my arms. I regret that I didn't get an opportunity to see her first step, hear her first words, or put money under her pillow when she lost her first tooth. I regret that I stayed away for so long because the thought of Lu aborting our child kept me from crossing the Atlantic until my father died. I regret that you made that decision for me without even considering that you might be making a mistake. I regret that my mother didn't think I had it in me to achieve my goals while also being a good guy and a father. I'm sure you don't see it, but to me that's a reflection on you more than it is on me. What I'm not going to regret is walking away from you now and not looking back."

His flight didn't leave until the next day, so he took off in the direction of Long Boat Key, heading for the Ritz-Carlton that had not too long ago sprung up on the shore of the Intracoastal Waterway. But as he passed over the North Bridge, he knew he'd forgo the Ritz. He passed through the Village and pulled into the now familiar driveway. Grabbing his bag from the back of the rental, he made his way to the door. His knuckles wrapped succinctly on the door.

"Lex?"

"Will—I need a place to crash tonight."

Willa didn't say anything. She merely stepped aside and held the door open for him to come into her home.

31

Aside from the frosty reception from her mother and the tension between Amber and Jo, there had only been one moment of disappointment throughout her weekend home. Although she knew it was impossible, her heart had this overwhelming wish—hope, really—that somehow Lex would show up to see her walk across the stage and receive her diploma. It was like the hope that you'll wake up on your sixteenth birthday and there will be a car in your driveway. You already know, in your heart of hearts, that it can't happen and you convince yourself that it won't happen so that you can't possibly be disappointed. But part of you holds on to this infinitesimal particle of hope.

Partly because she was proud of herself and partly because of Willa and Pete, Lu let her disappointment dissipate, much like her hope that Lex would come to celebrate with them all. She could barely contain her excitement over Pete and Willa. She'd done her best to not high-five, chest bump, or drop to her knees while crossing herself, but truly she felt a rush of exhilaration she thought she could only feel if something amazing happened directly to her. All in all, the weekend had worked out quite well, Lu thought as a smile hovered permanently on her face, while she prepped for her meeting with Mr. Helms.

She'd had time to meet with her mentor, Dr. Zeigler, while she was there. He'd been most encouraging of this opportunity for her to work while she was in England. Even as he encouraged her to continue to work with her football teams via Skype, he saw this as a chance for her to expand on her work. And he was all about challenging her. He didn't know any of the personal struggles she would encounter by working with soccer players; however, his excitement about the prospect for her career captured her imagination and served to bolster her confidence in her decision to meet with him.

As she stepped out of her apartment on the way to her lunch, she almost knocked over two vases of flowers that had been left on her front step. A little stunned, she bent to retrieve them and bring them into her apartment. The first was an assortment of different flowers, the second, a beautiful bunch of Stargazer lilies. Pulling the card from the first, Lu smiled at the thoughtfulness and wooing power of Mr. Helms. Very strategic to send the congratulatory flowers right before their meeting, she conceded. She paused before pulling the card from the lilies. Her absolute favorite flower, she knew that they had to have been sent by someone who knew her well. Pulling the card from the holder, Lu froze, slightly dumbstruck.

So proud—

Lex

In too much of a rush to take the moment she needed, Lu clutched the card in her hand and hurried out the door.

Mr. Helms was a fit, slender man who epitomized, for Lu, everything European. She'd done her research and knew that he was a former soccer player turned coach turned front-office man. He was well respected throughout the world of soccer for his many accomplishments, and he enjoyed a modicum of celebrity throughout Europe. He wore the classic suit that screamed metrosexual to Lu with its slim lines, fully equipped with his own slightly effeminate lavender scarf. She knew that her own American sensibilities were at play. Sue her, she liked her men to look manly. Even fighting against the clothing, she could admit that he was hot. And of course, the accent!

"Thank you so much for the flowers. That was very thoughtful," Lu said as she was seated for lunch.

"Quite an accomplishment should not go unacknowledged," he demurred. From there, they enjoyed an easy conversation that had little to do with the reason they were there. He was easy to talk to, and Lu found herself caught up in his charm. It was at the end of lunch that they began talking in earnest about the job.

"I've followed your work fairly closely, Dr. Knight." He emphasized the *doctor* with a smile. "I know you have doubts about transitioning to our football, but I think it would be seamless."

"Mr. Helms . . .," she began.

"Malcolm," he corrected.

"If you are going to call me Dr. Knight, then I am going to call you Mr. Helms," she responded.

With a slight smile, he deferred.

"I realize that all athletes have some commonalities, but most of my research, as you know, has been with head injuries. While I also know that you deal with concussions in your sport, it is not the main issue. I am not opposed to bridging some of the gaps, but I do want to continue my work with rehab and injuries—not to be confused with mental conditioning and sport psychology."

"That's exactly what I was hoping. I think you can be a great resource for all of our clubs. But I'd like you to start with mine. I have seen the results you have published. You've managed to cut rehab time by approximately 25 percent in some cases."

Lu merely nodded. She had statistics upon statistics to support her research, and she knew they wouldn't be having this conversation if he didn't already have faith in what she did.

"So does this mean you will consider working for us as a consultant this season?"

Lu paused before answering. She felt a draw to move in this direction while at the same time she felt a hitch in her step. What would this mean for her career and, although Willa would have beaten her, she wondered what this would mean for Lex? Surely he would find out, and when he did, would he feel like she was stalking him?

"Do you have something pending right now or are you just trying to be prepared?" she asked.

"I want to be prepared. We'll have an injury, no doubt. I'd like to have you waiting in the wings."

"I do not travel," she said bluntly.

If he thought it peculiar, he hid it well. "That's not a problem. We tend to keep our injured players here rather than have them make trips with us."

"Perfect."

"Do you have any questions for me, Dr. Knight?"

"Do you have a space for me to come to you?"

"I figured you could come to us at our training grounds when needed."

"That's actually what I prefer."

"Have you been?" he asked.

Lu felt confused. "Have I been where?"

"Have you been to an English football game?"

Lu smiled. "No I haven't."

"Well, that's the first order of business, isn't it?"

"Ah, I don't know."

"We play tomorrow night. I insist that you come as my guest. It will give you a chance to see the facility and watch a game."

"Evenings are hard, Mr. Helms. I have a daughter." She watched him take a quick glance at her left hand.

"I would of course want you to bring your family."

"It's just my daughter and me."

"Come, please. It's actually a big game for us. I think the excitement will rival your football atmosphere." He was teasing her, and she found it quite endearing, really.

"OK, we'll come."

"How old is your daughter?"

"Nine," she answered.

"And does she like soccer?" he inquired.

"Yes, actually, she does," although Lu kept the reason for that to herself.

"I'll send a car for you prior to the game so we can tour and you can get a look around."

"Thank you. That's perfect."

He called for the check as they talked about inconsequential things. Once he paid, he waited for her to stand and then escorted her to the door at the front of the restaurant by way of his hand at the small of her back. His hand left his imprint as she felt the warmth of it through her sweater. Lu could feel people watching him, recognition quick to dawn on their faces. As they made their way forward, Lu thought that she must have a thing for soccer players as she felt herself drawn to him. Then, as quickly as it appeared, she reined it in because she was about to be employed by him.

As they exited the restaurant, Mr. Helms stopped and held out his hand. "Dr. Knight, I appreciate your time. And I look forward to seeing your tomorrow. You are in for a treat as we are playing our archrivals, so it should be a festive atmosphere."

Lu held out her hand and they shook. "I look forward to seeing my first in-person English Premier League game."

"Hopefully, it will captivate your imagination," he said, smiling. "We always enjoy this rivalry. Ah, our archrival features an American, but you can't root for them tomorrow."

Lu felt some of the color leach from her cheeks. "You're the first, so you'll lay claim to my loyalties."

"Yes, well, as much as I hate to play against him, Lex Pellitteri is always fun to watch."

It kept running through her mind like a mantra. Lex Pellitteri is always fun to watch. Lex Pellitteri is always fun to watch. Over and over again until she felt like she might be going a bit crazy. Dropping her head into her hands as she sat at her kitchen table, she thought frantically of a way to get out of going to the game tomorrow night. In all the years that they'd known each other, Lu had never seen him play in person—and had only watched a few plays on TV before her heart would turn in on itself and she would have to turn the channel. As kids, Lex and Pete were gone every Saturday to some sporting event. Soccer for Lex, while Pete mixed it up and played a variety of sports. But going to watch Lex and Pete play wasn't what they did. They were girls. They didn't want to go sit at some park during the weekends. Not that the boys would have even thought to invite them.

When Lex started playing more competitively, all of his events were out of town. At first, he would leave for weekends. Depending on Pete's schedule, usually Mr. P. would take Lex and Dr. J. would stay in town with Pete. By the time they were together, Lex was playing at such a competitive level that he never played in Sarasota. Oh, she'd seen him with his soccer ball, she'd seen him do his dance, she'd seen him practice. The upshot of it was she had never actually seen him play soccer live, in the flesh. While she felt the irony of going to see him play the first time as the guest of his opponent, she could only lay the blame for that at his feet, as she wouldn't have been there, in this predicament, if it weren't for his high-handedness.

Then the flowers caught her eye. Pushing her hand in her pocket, she took out the card and reread it, a smile on her face. She needed to thank him. She struggled to decide if she should tell him that she would be at the game. Grabbing her phone, she shot him a quick text.

Thanks for the flowers. My favorite.

She glanced at the time and realized that if she called Willa now, she might catch her before she went to work. Selecting her name, she opted for FaceTime.

"Hey," Willa said, a big smile on her face.

Lu had to admit, it threw her a bit. "Hey yourself. You seem awfully chipper."

"You got chipper from one word?"

"No, from the big-ass smile on your face. Did I tell you how much I love FaceTime?" she smirked.

"Ha. Yes, it does remove some of the mystery, and actually freedom, of talking on the phone."

"That's right. You can't roll your eyes at me without me knowing."

"I'm fairly certain that the tone of my voice, as you just pointed out, gave away my eye-rolling," Willa responded good-naturedly.

Lu looked at the phone. Turned it upside down, jiggled it a bit.

"What the hell are you doing? That's making me nauseous," Willa bitched.

"I was looking for my sullen big sister. Do you know where I can find her?"

"I think the sullen got fucked out of her," Willa quipped.

Lu laughed. "I bet it did."

"So how was the lunch?" Willa asked. "This time-difference thing still throws me, and I didn't know when to call."

Lu propped her phone up on some books on the table. "Lunch was good," and Lu couldn't help the big grin.

"Now who's looking like the cat that ate the canary?" Willa teased.

"I'm excited. I was nervous at first, but I think this is a great opportunity."

"I'm proud of you."

"Thanks, Will," Lu said, taking a moment to collect herself after the surprise of her sister's compliment. "So some interesting things have happened."

"And?"

"I received some congratulatory flowers."

"From who?"

"Whom."

"Yeah, yeah, whom."

"You'd never know your mother is an English professor."

"Thank God!"

"Ha. One set was from Malcolm Helms."

"By the way, Sky and I Googled him. Wow!"

"Yes, wow. The second set was from Lex."

Willa leaned back, away from the phone, as if she were trying to get out of someone's way. "Well, isn't he just full of surprises this week," she commented.

"What do you mean *surprises?* Were you going for plural?"

"He was here Sunday night."

Suddenly, it was Lu's turn to flinch. "What do you mean *here?*"

"I mean he showed up at my door Sunday night, needing a place to crash," Willa reported matter-of-factly.

"O . . . K," Lu said slowly, struggling to understand this turn of events. She didn't want to sound like a petulant middle-school girl with a crush who nagged for information about the guy she liked. "Did you talk?"

Willa paused. "Yes and no."

Again, Lu restrained herself. Willa could take secrets to the grave. Her vault of gossip and facts that had been handed to her over the years overflowed with both trivial and important secrets. If Lex told Willa something in confidence, Lu would never be able to pry it out of her. A tiny fissure of jealousy snaked through her. Willa and Lex had a good number of confidences that Lu had never been privy to. It hurt her that when he needed someone, he'd shown up on Willa's doorstep.

"Did you make up?" Lu asked, thinking that perhaps Willa would feel that she could answer that question.

"To be honest, Lu, we didn't talk much. He showed up saying he needed a place to crash. And I could never turn him away. Not you, or him, or Pete. Too much history."

"It's not like he couldn't have stayed at a hotel," Lu remarked snidely.

"No doubt. But I think he needed to be some place familiar."

Again, Lu reined in her hurt. Seeking solace from the loneliness creeping into her, Lu told Willa her other news. "Mr. Helms invited me to a soccer game tomorrow night."

"Well that ought to be interesting and fun. Will you actually be with him? Because that could be promising," she said, winking at Lu.

"I'm not sure about with him. As his guest. But here's the rub . . ."

"Come on, spit it out, Lu."

"His club is playing Lex's. Tomorrow night I'm going to watch Lex play soccer."

Willa's head dropped to the table. Banging it lightly a couple of times, she picked it up, blue eyes dancing and peering into the phone as if she could get into Lu's face. "I give up. Just be careful."

Lu pulled back from the phone again. "What? Who are you?"

Willa shook her head. "Lu, I can tell you what to do. I can tell you what to not do. I can keep trying to control the universe. Unfortunately, I keep getting outmaneuvered. I tell you not to have sex with him. You do it anyway. I tell you not to go to England. You do it anyway. You were drunk texting with him the other night. What the fuck was that about? I mean, shit, Lu." Running her hand through her short hair in frustration, Willa looked at her sister. "Then he shows up here—Lex but not Lex. Not our mischievous, laughing boy, and he kinda breaks my ever-expanding heart."

Lu didn't say anything, just peered at her sister through the lens of her phone, vaguely wishing they weren't able to have this conversation face to face. She wanted to speak, but had nothing to say.

"Here's the thing," Willa continued, "when I slept with Pete this weekend, I cut the cord. I can't take on your burdens anymore—"

"I have never asked you to—"

"You didn't have to ask, Lu. I love you dearly, but I need to put my energy into Pete—not you and Lex. You two have to figure that out on your own."

"Point taken."

"Call me after the game, OK?"

"Yup," Lu said, detached. "Talk to you tomorrow." Lu was about to disconnect.

"Wait!" Willa cried.

"What?"

"I know I said I wouldn't interfere but—he's hurting. So go easy on him."

Lu almost fell out of her chair. "Seriously?"

"This is what sex has done to me. Turned me into a big ball of mush. Take advantage. You know this shit won't last." With a wink, she disconnected, leaving Lu feeling like she had stepped into an alternate universe.

32

"Big game tonight," remarked the guard as Lex made his way off the pitch, into the locker room.

"Yes, sir," Lex remarked, offering him his patented smile. He'd been on the field for a while. As was his habit, he arrived early in the day and conducted his own pregame warm-up prior to the team workout. Today was no different, even though he was suffering from a nasty case of jet lag. He wasn't quite sure what made him think to make that trip this past weekend. He'd been shocked that his mother had attended Lu's graduation, as he thought he'd find her at home, with the Knights' house empty beside theirs. Shaking it off, as he'd done since their conversation ended, he continued on his way.

He wasn't surprised to find Malcolm Helms waiting for him at the entrance of the locker room.

"Lex," he said as they grabbed hands and man hugged.

"Mal. Are you consorting with the enemy before the game?" Lex said, smiling. Malcolm Helms was one of Lex's favorite people. He'd been a brilliant player who left when he was at the top of his game. Although they'd never broached the subject, Lex was fairly certain that he'd wanted to leave while he was still on top. He'd been well into his coaching career when Lex arrived on the English soccer scene.

Even though Lex had been on a rival team, he'd taken him under his wing and given him a lot of solicited and unsolicited advice regarding his career.

"Walk with me," Malcolm said, placing his hand out as if to escort Lex where he wanted him to go.

"How are you?" Lex asked.

"Well. Your contract's coming up."

"Really?" Lex said, his face resounding with surprise, as if he didn't know.

"Still a smartass," Malcolm remarked.

Cocking his eyebrow and smiling, Lex responded, "Of course."

"I'd like to talk to you and Caroline. Give you some options."

Lex shrugged. "You know where to find Caroline."

"I do. But I've been having a difficult time tracking you down lately."

Lex nodded, the smile leaving his face. "Been an interesting couple of months."

"I am sorry about the loss of your father."

"Thanks. I appreciate the flowers you sent to my mother," Lex remarked, reaching out and touching his shoulder. "Really."

"You going to take it easy on my boys tonight?"

"Ha. I think I should be asking that question of you. I think last time we played I struggled with your defense." Lex knew that Malcolm had had a hand in coaching that game. "It had your name all over it."

"Let's see how that works tonight," his arrogance present, Malcolm smiled.

"Yes, let's," Lex said. Turning back to head toward the locker room, he looked back at Malcolm. "See you after the game."

Lex would have loved to play for Malcolm, but he had this thing about staying loyal. His club had picked him up when going after an American was not the thing to do. He'd been there his whole career. While the thought of playing for Malcolm Helms appealed to him, he didn't think he would make the jump. Most of it was loyalty, but some of it was his inability to take on any more change. Still trying to find his way with Nina, navigate his relationship with Lu, and deal with the death of his father, he refused to add learning a new system. Heading back into the locker room, Lex pulled out his iPod and his game face.

⌒

The sensory images that assailed Lu differed little from those she saw at the football games she had attended over the last couple of years. The laughter, the din of the crowd, flashes from cameras, the noise reverberating off of the walls around them, the smell. She couldn't deny that she enjoyed the feeling of being back in a stadium. She'd missed the adrenaline rush of watching people she knew compete for a victory that they'd trained for. She had to smile a little at the path her career had taken.

Lu could see the smug look on Malcolm's face as she smiled at the atmosphere. Even knowing that she was about to watch Lex play couldn't dim the feeling of excitement of being in the stadium. The fans, the chanting, the cheering all converged to create a bubbling anticipation. When the players entered the field, Lu attempted to keep her eyes off of Lex, but it was impossible. Even if he wasn't who he was to her, his personality and presence drew your eye. Watching him it felt as though she didn't know him. He was just as unknown to her as any of the players on the field. The disconcerting notion stayed with her.

She watched the game sitting on the edge of her seat, caught up in the excitement, cheering along with the rest of the crowd. Malcolm patiently explained everything to her and prompted her to watch as plays developed. He called it when Lex came off the left side, headed a ball that came into the center, and scored the only goal of the first half. Lu couldn't help but cheer and Malcolm even appreciated Lex's skill, saying as much to Lu.

"I hate playing against him and have been doing my best to get him to come to us when his contract expires," he commented.

"Will he do it?" she asked, feigning indifference when she wanted to drill him for information.

Malcolm laughed good-heartedly. "Probably not, but I'm going to do my damnedest. So how does this compare to your American football?"

She was thankful that she didn't hear any condescension in his voice, only curiosity. "I hate not knowing all of the rules."

"You'll pick it up as you watch more. I think I see a fan in the making."

Lu laughed. "You may be right."

Enjoying every minute of her night, Lu almost wished she wasn't planning on going to work for Malcolm Helms. She enjoyed his company, not to mention he was hot. She could totally see enjoying herself with him. But it wasn't something she'd pursue, knowing that their relationship would be professional. His attentiveness allowed her to forget that the Lex Pellitteri on the field had long ago stopped being the boy that she loved. Without realizing it, she got caught up in the excitement of watching him play and felt a pride that she knew she had no right to feel. Even those rooting against him appreciated his skill.

In the eighty-seventh minute, with the game tied, Lu felt rather than saw Malcolm's body tense. She focused in, trying to see what he was anticipating.

He leaned in. "Watch Pellitteri."

Like she needed to be told, she thought. She watched Lex come from the right. He received the ball but passed it quickly back, breaking to the middle. The ball came back to him. He trapped the ball and shot, sending it sailing past the goalie into the back left post, opposite from where he kicked. She wanted to jump in the air, but she contained herself out of respect, although the smile on her face gave her away. Lex looked heavenward and raised his left hand in the air, pointing his finger toward the sky. Then he brought his arm down and kissed the inside of his wrist. With three minutes added to the time, the last five minutes of the game seemed to fly by and before she knew it, the game was over. Lu's eyes stayed trained on Lex.

She saw him run toward the box where she was sitting and felt, rather than saw, something pass between him and someone in her vicinity. Glancing at Malcolm, she saw him nod his head, his eyes locked with Lex's and a rueful smile on his face.

"Smug bastard," he muttered.

Lu turned back toward the field and saw Lex see her. His whole body stopped, as if he had run smack into some invisible wall. He pinned her with his eyes, all the joy of his victory seemed to leach out of his body. As the rest of his team celebrated, Lex left the field.

Lu tried not to let his reaction affect her. She knew when she'd agreed to come to this game that she had gambled. But she convinced herself that surprise played the biggest role in his actions—not anger. She let Malcolm lead her from the box where they sat.

"I'm sorry your daughter was unable to come," he remarked as they walked down the steps into the bowels of the stadium.

Lu had made that decision. Nina still suffered from jet lag, as evidenced by her cranky mood over the last few days. Technically, she should have been grounded because of her stint as an extortionist at school. Leaving Nina at home had been a responsible parenting decision. One that she knew Nina felt as she had really wanted to see Lex play.

"With the trip this past weekend, I thought it best that she stay home."

"Are you able to stay for a bit or do I need to get you home?" he inquired.

"I'm at your disposal. I know you are working."

"I have someone I want you to meet."

Lu looked at him quizzically. "OK."

They continued past the home dressing room through the corridor. As they drew near the visitor area, Lu began to panic.

"Who is it that you want me to meet?" she asked, hoping what she was thinking was wrong.

He stopped and turned to face her. "I may be interfering but . . ." He paused. "Lex Pellitteri lost his father a number of months ago and I think he's having a hard time with it. I thought maybe he might be willing to talk to someone."

"That's not what I do," she said quickly, trying to find a way to avert this certain disaster. "I'm sure that there are qualified people that you could suggest."

"I know his club manager has made suggestions. He thought I may be able to help because of my relationship with him. And when I met you yesterday, I felt certain that you were the answer. You understand athletes and you work with them. I really think you could help him."

"Mr. Helms, I think you misunderstand what I do. This isn't what I do. I'm not comfortable with this," she said firmly. "And from what I saw tonight, he seems to be doing just fine."

"She's right, Mal. I'm just fine," Lex said from behind her. She felt every muscle in her body cringe, but she valiantly hid her reaction and didn't step away. "Oh, and we already know each other, don't we, Lu?"

The sarcasm dripping from his voice sounded sickly sweet in her ear. He'd moved toward her, she knew, because she could feel his body heat. Lu watched the impassive face of Malcolm Helms in front of her. He'd be good at poker, Lu thought, as she couldn't read anything in his expression.

"Lex, nice game. I could see that second goal when you crossed midfield."

"I figured. What the hell are you doing, Mal?"

"Favor for a friend," he responded.

"I think I told him to stay the hell out of my business."

Lu, sandwiched between the two men, shifted uncomfortably. Malcolm looked down at her as if he'd forgotten she was there. Grabbing her arm, he looked back at Lex.

"I'm going to see Dr. Knight home. Hopefully, we'll talk soon," Malcolm said, turning her back the way they had come.

"I'll take her," Lex said, surprising everyone.

"No, I brought her. I'll take her home," Malcolm said as he led her past Lex, whom she had avoided looking at thus far.

"Really, Mal, I want to take her."

Again, Malcolm showed no reaction. Lu felt the tension between the two of them and knew that she needed to do something to stop the showdown. She had a vague image of each man grabbing an arm and pulling her in two different directions.

Lu took her first look. Lex leaned against the wall, one leg propped up so that his leg bent. Straight from the shower, although the way he sweated, it could have been sweat, his hair slicked back, he smelled of soap and anger. He had on a pair of faded, worn jeans, a T-shirt, and warm-up jacket. On his feet was a pair of slides that Lu had always associated with soccer players. She took him in but didn't look at him.

"It's OK, Mr. Helms. Lex will get me home," she said.

"Don't worry, Malcolm. I'm not going to let anything happen to my baby mama." With that, he picked up his bag, reached for her arm, and led her away.

33

Seething and red with mortification, Lu followed Lex through the stadium and out into the night. Lex could feel the rage emitting from her pores, but he continued on, not stopping until he reached his car. Opening her door, he released her hand and tucked her safely inside. Walking around the back of the car, he opened the truck, placed his bag inside and lowered his forehead to lean against it. Taking a deep, steadying breath, he tried to get ahold of this incessant anger and pulsating jealousy that coursed through his veins. Looking up to Malcolm Helms and seeing Lu next to him had sent his exhilaration and adrenaline from the win spiraling into a vortex of emotion that he was unable to decipher. Thinking that he had everything tamped down, he closed the trunk and made his way to the driver's seat.

He sat down and put the key in the ignition. As he placed it in drive, Lu reached over and slammed the gearshift into park.

"What the hell is wrong with you? How could you say that to me?" Lu's face, flush with anger, bore into his.

"What? Calling you my baby mama?" He asked sarcastically.

"Yes!" she yelled.

"Isn't that what you are?"

"I don't appreciate you throwing colloquial phrases at me like that. For you to describe me as some typical cleat chaser who purposefully got pregnant degrades me and your daughter." Her indignation reverberated through the car.

Lex laughed. "Oh, I'm so sorry that you are offended that I compared you to some average girl. Did I offend the super-brain Lu?"

Lu leaned over the console, right in his face. "I am so much more than that and you know it. You want to be mad at me for what happened, *fine*. You want to pretend like I don't exist while you force me to move to a new country so you can have access to your daughter, *fine*. But don't you dare insult me in front of a colleague or degrade me and my daughter. That I will *not* stand for. Do you understand me?"

Lex pushed forward, moving directly toward her face so they were mere inches apart. "You stole nine years from me. You denied me my daughter. You don't get to make demands! Do you understand me?" He grabbed her around her arms and gently pushed her back into her seat. Reaching around her, he pulled the seat belt over and buckled her in. Throwing the car into drive, he pulled out of the lot and headed toward her house.

"Who's with Nina?" he asked, glancing at the clock on the dashboard.

"Mrs. Auberly," she mumbled as she looked out the car window, opposite his direction.

Shit swirled through Lex's mind. The issues bombarded him, and he had a hard time trying to figure out what to tackle first. This had been his burden since his father's funeral. He had no idea which problem needed his attention first. Right now, the problem he'd refused to deal with for eight months, the biggest issue, continued to pop up on his radar every moment of the last week. It was as if the dam of resentment and anger he'd built with the sticks of disappointment and hurt were cracking under the barrage that was Lu's presence. The why behind his refusal to talk to her was no mystery. Confronted with her again, he knew he couldn't continue to ignore her.

Still reeling from his conversation with his mother and his night at Willa's, he began to think that he couldn't take much more. Ironically, he began to see why his parents fought to keep all of this from him for so long. The constant controversy had strained his concentration and thrown him off his game. He knew he'd played well tonight, but the effort it had cost him was a price he'd never had to pay before. Between the loss of his father, the fight with his mother, and the effort to keep his mind off of Lu, he'd felt as though his nine years of markers were being collected.

He glanced over at her, caught up in the city racing by as he sped through the streets of London. Much like his decision on Sunday night, before he thought through what he was doing, he found himself pulling up to his apartment. Parking the car, he turned off the engine and pulled the keys from the ignition.

"Where are we?" Lu asked without turning toward him.

"My place. We need to talk." He said it matter-of-factly, without any of the heat of their earlier interaction. He anticipated an argument, but Lu merely opened her door and stepped out of the car. He grabbed his stuff and led her through the underground parking garage to the elevator. With the haze of his anger dissipating, he took in her appearance. In black slacks, boots, and a pea coat, the only dash of color a scarf of his rivals' wound around her neck, he tried not to think of her cheering against him tonight. Her hair was braided across the front and pulled to the side in a ponytail. He supposed it shouldn't have, but it looked sophisticated on her. Her eyes trained on the flashing numbers as the elevator rose. As he watched her, flashes of their bodies entwined scrolled across his mind. Trying to block the memories, he trained his mind to think of his game, the goal he'd shot wide, the give and go he'd missed, the corner he should have connected. Thankfully, the elevator made no stops and he soon found himself opening his door and allowing her to precede him into his apartment.

He walked directly to his room, leaving her to her own devices. He unpacked his bag, taking his time, getting control of his anger, then made his way back to the kitchen. He grabbed a wineglass from the rack above the counter.

"Red or white?" he asked.

"Red, please," Lu answered from where she sat on the couch. Walking over to the bar, he pulled a bottle out, opened it and poured. Walking back through the kitchen, Lex grabbed water from the refrigerator and headed over to where Lu sat with her legs curled under her. Handing her the glass of wine, he sat across from her in a chair.

"Do you not need something stronger?" Lu asked, without looking at him.

"I absolutely do. But I've already broken my no-alcohol-during-the-season rule once this week."

"You had a different occasion that warranted alcohol more strongly than this one?" she asked, again looking down into her wine.

Smiling ruefully, Lex said, "Yes. Jo trumps you in needing alcohol to handle."

Lu's head popped up and she met Lex's eyes for the first time since their yelling match in the car. "Well, that's something, I guess."

"This seems to be my week for cleaning up the messes in my life."

"Should I be offended?" Lu asked, holding his gaze.

"That I consider this a mess I have to clean up?" Shaking his head, he continued. "Nah. Save it. I'm pretty sure there's something that I will say that will be far more offensive than that."

"Hmph."

"Does that mean you need an example?" he asked, his temper feeling the stroke of her feigned indifference.

Lu looked away from him and took a sip of her wine. "What do you want to talk about, Lex?" she asked, throwing in the towel.

"What were you doing with Malcolm Helms?" It wasn't the most pressing issue, but it was bothering him, so he figured he'd get the easy one out of the way.

Lu eyes widened slightly, as if she couldn't believe that this was a point of contention. "He offered me a job."

Lex nodded. "Makes sense."

"What do you mean?"

"Your research is pretty convincing, Lu. I can see why he'd want you on his payroll." He saw the surprise flash across her face. He almost laughed that he could still read her so well sometimes. But then he remembered all that he couldn't read when they'd last been together and the desire to laugh vanished.

"What do you know about what I do?"

"Everything."

"Why?"

"We have a child together, Lu. I made it my business to know what you've been doing with the super brain." He saw her struggle to hold back the smile. "Look, sport psychology is a growing field. I know your angle is unique, but I also knew that it wouldn't take long for someone to want to exploit what you have to offer. I'm glad it was Malcolm."

"Oh" was all she could manage. "What else, Lex?"

"I have a list, don't you?" he said, his brows drawing together.

"Yes, but this is your show. And we don't have much more time."

Lex looked down at his watch. Getting up, he walked to the counter, where he'd dropped his phone. He picked it up and called Nina's nanny.

"Mrs. Auberly, it's Lex. Are you able to stay at Dr. Knight's tonight? Dr. Knight will be home, but it will be late. I figure this way you can get a good night's sleep. Thank you."

Walking back to where Lu sat, Lex said, "We don't need to worry about the time now."

Lu looked up at him, shook her head, and rolled her eyes.

"I need for you to tell me what happened." There were so many questions he had for her, but he needed to know it from the beginning. If he understood the sequence of events, maybe some of the answers to the other burning questions would be evident. He knew of one other question that he would absolutely have to ask, but he thought perhaps many would be answered when she told him the story.

"What do you mean?" Lu asked.

Lu wasn't one for acting, so he took the look of confusion on her face for what it was. Perhaps he did need to be more specific. Leaning forward in his chair, resting his forearms on his knees, he looked her directly in the blue depths of her eyes. "I got on the plane. Then, what happened?"

34

"I already told you what happened," Lu said wearily.

"I'm calling bullshit on that story you told me at the funeral, Lu. I'm sure parts of it are true, but I know you too well. You're not vindictive, and you'd never keep our daughter away from me on your own."

Lu bristled at his arrogance. They hadn't spoken in nine years and he was an expert on her and her motivations. "You don't know shit about me!"

Unfazed, Lex merely smiled. "OK, I don't know shit about you. But don't try to pawn that fairy tale of a story off on me."

Frustrated, Lu drank her wine and tried to figure out what she wanted to say. Having Lex five feet away from her drove her crazy. The smugness of his expression, as if he knew something she didn't, made her want to smack the smile off of his face.

"Look, I let you get away with the story at the funeral because I was angry and I'd just lost my father. It was easier to accept your story than try to weed through it. I've had a lot of time to think about it, and it doesn't add up. Come on, Harvard. Spill it."

This Lex, the one sitting in front of her, cajoling her, this was the one she couldn't resist. This Lex was the love of her life, the boy she'd fallen in love with when she was six.

"Let's play a little game. I'll start a sentence and you finish it."

"What are you talking about, Lex?" she said, exasperation apparent in her voice and her big blue eyes.

"You know. A little word association. Don't you psychologists use this stuff? First thing that comes to mind. So if I say, 'Jo is . . . ,' you would say?"

"My savior." Lu sat back, a little surprised that she'd tagged Jo with that moniker.

Lex's eyebrow crept up, surprise evident on his face. "Interesting. OK, so what do you think. Can we do this?"

Lu shook her head. "Fine," she conceded, knowing that he was determined to have this conversation.

"We'll start with my original question. Ready?" At her nod, he continued. "I got on the plane and you . . ."

"Cried for three weeks." Lu continued to look down at her glass, which was almost empty.

"Again, interesting. All right. This one's a little harder. My mother, and I mean Amber, not Jo, wanted . . ."

"For me to kill our child." She stopped thinking.

Lex took a deep breath as a surge of anger for Amber pulsed through him. "I was mad at Lex for . . ."

"Leaving me behind."

"But I went along with the plan because . . ."

"I didn't want you to end up resenting me and our child." Lu refused to look up. She didn't think she could take any reflection in his eyes. If she saw pity, sympathy, or confusion, she thought she'd scream. She didn't know what he needed, but she felt like she owed him an explanation. Her brilliant plan at the funeral seemed to serve him as she'd preserved his relationship with his mother and brother. She didn't want him to think of her as a sacrificial lamb. Lost in her own thoughts, she didn't realize that Lex had gotten up and refilled her wineglass. She merely saw the level of wine in her glass increase.

She took a sip that seemed more like a gulp and waited for the next sentence completion. This little game that Lex concocted was what made him so dangerous. You got drawn in by the good looks, the athletic body, the quick wit, but you just never counted on his intelligence. He called her super brain and Harvard, but he was no slouch in the smarts department. He calculated his moves. She knew an ulterior motive for all of this existed; she just couldn't figure out his game.

"You ready?" he asked as he returned to the chair.

Sighing and rolling her eyes, Lu looked up at him and wished she hadn't. "Fire away, AJ."

Chuckling, Lex sat back in his chair, thoroughly enjoying himself. "Jo is my savior because . . ."

"She saved Nina."

"Really?" he asked, forgetting the game.

"Absolutely."

"I didn't fight because . . ."

Lu jerked up, as though she'd been stuck with an electric prod. Her eyes locked with Lex's. "What did you say?" she whispered.

"I didn't fight because . . ."

Lu couldn't answer. Caught off guard by the question, she continued to stare at Lex. He didn't look like he was enjoying himself anymore. He looked deadly serious, his green eyes boring into her. Nervous about his motives and intentions, Lu couldn't figure out how to perceive the question.

"Fight what, Lex?"

"Any of it, all of it. Your mother, my mother. Why did you just fold? I left because I knew that when I came back you would be there with our child. I never doubted that. But you just crumpled. You let everyone else dictate the course of our lives. I just want to know why."

He didn't scream or yell. Leaning back in the chair with his legs stretched out in front of him, you could have mistaken his body language to mean that he was discussing the weather. No smile lingered on his face, but no anger lurked either. Without meaning to, Lu thought back to their exchange in the Sunday-school room. He'd been completely distant, as if some other man, one that she didn't know, had pinned her to the wall and invaded her. Now it appeared as though the answers mattered but didn't. As much as she'd hated what they had done to each other that day, she understood his passion and his anger. She wasn't sure she understood his seeming indifference.

"I was seventeen, for God's sake, Lex," she said, exasperation clear in her voice.

"You were never seventeen, babe. You were old the day you were born."

She didn't want to admit that her mother had worn her down. That as the days had gone by and there'd been no word from him, that she'd begun to lose faith. She couldn't tell him that Willa's looks of contempt for her blind faith had chipped away at her confidence in him. She'd never been a typical teenager, but she'd felt like one during that time. She felt insecure and silly for thinking that she could have found the person she would spend her life with at six. She didn't trust him to react in the way she needed him to react.

"Why Nina?" Lex asked suddenly.

Lu couldn't help it, she smiled. "Her name?"

"Yeah."

"You don't remember?"

He looked at her quizzically. "Remember what?"

"It's stupid, really. But I had no idea what to name her. And I was kind of shocked I had a girl. I thought for sure you'd produce a boy." They both smiled. "Anyway, in the aftermath of her birth, I couldn't think. I didn't know. She was a day old and they came by to do the birth certificate. For some reason I thought of us playing—" Lu stopped. "We've played this before."

Lex nodded. "A couple different versions," he agreed with a big, smug smile and a gleam in his eye.

"I thought of us playing this game where we'd pick things out of a group that we liked best. We did Columbus's ships for some reason and you chose the *Nina*. So in my morphine-induced high, I blurted, 'Nina Pellitteri Knight.' Later, Dr. J. asked me why I didn't name her Alexandra. I couldn't. It was too much. Even for her saving me, I couldn't give her your name. But I could live with the middle name."

"I like it."

She tried not to think of him exploring her body and asking about her tattoo. She'd lied to him and she wasn't ready to go there.

"Lex, we can amend her birth certificate if you want and change her last name."

He looked at her with gratitude. "Thanks, but I don't think that's my call. Nina can decide if and when she wants to change her name. She's had to deal with plenty and more change might not be in her best interest."

"OK," Lu said.

Lex looked down at his watch. "I should probably get you home," he said, standing.

Caught a little off guard, Lu stood, feeling both disappointed and relieved. Given a reprieve, she wondered if it would take another eight months for him to ask the rest of his questions or to push for the answers she'd held back. She watched him grab his keys and his phone. Walking toward the front door, he met her there and led her out to the elevator. She wished for the stairs. As they entered, Lex pressed the button. Leaning back against the wall, Lu prayed for a quick descent.

"Lu, just so you know, we're not done," he said softly, the words rippling over her like a caress.

She turned to look at him. "What do you mean?" she asked, not really wanting to know the answer.

"I have a lot more questions that I need answers to. And next time I'm not letting you off so easily."

He met her eyes then and what she saw scared her more than she'd considered. The man who stared back at her was all confidence and swagger. And Lu knew that whatever he was after, she'd have a hard time denying him.

35

Lex didn't go immediately home when he dropped Lu off at her apartment. Wired from his game and his discussion with Lu, he knew attempting to sleep would prove futile. For eight months he'd done nothing. His life had been in a holding pattern. Even forcing Lu and Nina to move here hadn't nudged him out of his grief and confusion. He'd ceased to function and thus let everything around him just happen. He hadn't checked on his investments, hadn't engaged in his contract negotiations. He'd barely shown up on the pitch for the first quarter of the season. He'd avoided all contact with Lu, pretending that she didn't even live here while he attempted to get to know Nina. He'd put some effort into his relationship with Nina, but even that had been hollow because he'd had so little to give.

Then came the call from Mr. Seddon. Lex couldn't, even now, pinpoint what had happened that day that woke him up. But his awakening pained him. When he returned home from Lu's he cracked open a bottle of Scotch and proceeded to get drunk. All alone. He followed every question he had with a shot as if it were an elixir for the wildfire of truth as it seared through him. For the first time in his life, he wallowed in sorrow. He raged at the unfairness of his father's death, the injustice of his daughter being kept from him, and the betrayal he felt. He wasn't pretty in the slop of his dismantled life.

As he came up for air from the worst hangover he'd ever experienced, he looked around and saw that he was alone. It was disconcerting. And that's when he decided that he needed to take action. He had a lot of issues that needed to be resolved. That's what had gotten him on the plane back to Sarasota. It was foolish, really. He didn't have the time and his body couldn't handle the punishment of the overseas flight, but he felt like his soul couldn't survive without it. His need to confront Jo had been overwhelming. He knew that Lu had exonerated her, but he couldn't come to terms with his mother's following Lu's lead. Deep down, he knew that she was the conductor of this orchestra. When he'd found her house empty and realized that she'd been at Lu's graduation, his soul took another knock. His whole family had been there with Lu—everyone except him. He'd been alone for so long that he'd never even noticed that he was lonely. He kind of hated his mother for allowing that to happen to him. Whether it was her fault or not, she'd pushed them all down this path.

The path that everyone had followed her down, even his dad and Pete. While he wasn't particularly surprised that his mother had attempted to convince everyone that her plan would benefit Lex, he felt astonished that his father had agreed with her and had lied to him for so long. His father's betrayal hurt almost as much as Pete's and Lu's. Mike had kept Lex centered. He'd been his biggest advocate, fan, critic. He'd carved out his own paths for Lex to follow. One of those paths had been to Caroline—another issue he needed to deal with.

Picking up his phone, Lex texted Caroline.

Need to talk contract negotiations. You up?

Caroline texted back almost immediately.

Of course.

Be there in 10.

Lex had always been the model client. He didn't ask for special treatment, even though he received it because of who he was. Smiling, he thought that was probably why he never felt the need to ask. But he wanted to know where they were with his contract. She could meet with him at midnight for the cut she received. As he pulled into the parking lot, he felt a brief moment of regret for the consequences of all of the deceit. But he reasoned he was merely playing the hand he'd been dealt.

Strolling through Caroline's door a few minutes later, he made himself comfortable at her dining room table. He needed formality for this conversation.

"Well, this is certainly a surprise," she remarked as he took the bottle of water she offered. Since it didn't warrant a response, he didn't offer one. "You had an amazing game tonight. Hal called to say that it seems like you're back."

Lex tilted his head. "Where had I been?"

"Lex, you know you haven't had the season that everyone anticipated, based on your performance last year," she explained, as if he were five and she were explaining why he needed to go to bed at a certain time. Taking a sip of her drink, vodka tonic, she continued. "It was fabulous timing as we'd had a pretty intense conversation this afternoon." She took another sip, eyeing Lex speculatively.

"Did the conversation include Malcolm Helms?" Lex inquired innocently.

Caroline almost spit out the sip she had taken.

Lex loved that she'd underestimated him. He looked at her, eyebrow raised, his face asking the question again. She really should know better, he thought.

"Lex, it's no secret that Hal's been disappointed with your performance. The conversation this afternoon was another in a string of conversations regarding everything you've been through over the last couple of months."

"So whose idea was it for me to talk to someone?" Lex saw Caroline reach into her bag of tricks and pull out the mask of innocence.

"What are you talking about?"

"I'm calling bullshit, Caroline. What I want to know is why you didn't tell me that Hal was reaching out to people to get me to talk to a therapist." Lex saw her accept that he was calling her out.

"What's the big deal, Lex? They send players to psychologists all the time."

"Perhaps. But they don't have a parent-teacher conference without the student present. What the fuck, Caroline? If you all were discussing my well-being, I'm enough of an adult that I should have been there. When have you ever gone into a contract negotiation without me present? Why would this be any different?"

Backpedaling, she tried to cover her ass. "That's not how it started out, Lex. Really. He'd mentioned a couple of times and I've blown it off, saying that you just need time. I don't think that he is trying to be an ass. He's concerned about you."

"Concerned. If he was concerned, he would have come to me. He's pissed I'm not scoring goals. He could give a shit that my father died. Which is his job. I don't hold him responsible for doing what he's paid to do. What I'm concerned about is that you're not doing what you're supposed to do, what I pay you to do."

For the first time, Lex saw Caroline contrite.

"You're right," she conceded. Which didn't surprise Lex. He paid her a lot of money to agree with him when he needed her to.

Lex sat back in his chair, looking at Caroline. She was a beautiful woman and she was good at her job. Her blonde hair was pulled back in a ponytail, and even scrubbed free of make-up, she looked good. But he saw a hint of the fear he wanted her to feel shimmering in the cracks of her smile.

"How long did you know about Nina?" he asked. He continued to watch her, reading every emotion she tried to hide behind her work mask.

"Soon after I signed you," she answered, not giving any more information than he'd asked, her lawyer instincts kicking in.

Nodding his head, acknowledging her intelligence, he continued. "Did you sign something with my father saying you wouldn't tell me?"

"No."

"Did he ask you not to tell me?"

Here she paused. "No. It was implied."

"Implied?" he asked, skeptical.

"Yes."

"So you could have told me at any time?"

"Yes."

"But you chose to keep my father's secret."

"Yes."

"What prompted you to tell me at the funeral?" This had been bothering him. She could have told him at any time. She could have told him when they found out that Mike had died. She could have taken him aside at any point and told him. But she didn't. So, why did she tell him when she did?

"I just thought you should know."

Again, Lex nodded his head, as if he understood what she was saying and agreed with her. He stood then and made his way around the table, until he was standing behind her.

Leaning down, he placed his hands on either side of her, resting on the arm rests and brought his head down next to hers. "I'm just confused about the timing. Because from what I understand, you told Lu that she could tell me and I think you even gave her a deadline. Perhaps *deadline* isn't the right word. I think *time line* would be more appropriate." He felt her tense in the chair. "So if you gave her a heads-up, why did you think the news would be better coming from you?"

He stood at that point and moved to lean on the wall across from her. He waited even though he didn't expect her to answer.

"Here's the way I've worked it out. You saw me and Lu together and you thought that wouldn't necessarily be good for my career. So you put another obstacle in our way. How am I doing?"

Caroline stayed quiet and Lex had to admit a grudging respect for her. No self-implication on that front.

"Since you don't have a whole lot to add, let me tell you where I am. I don't trust you anymore. And I can't have someone handling me if I can't trust them. So, you're fired." She flinched almost imperceptibly, but he was watching her so close that he could see the slight movement. "You don't have to worry. I'll make sure that my publicist handles the split amicably. I won't trash-talk—as you know. But I have to say, when I sign my new contract, I imagine it will hurt a bit. You were going to make a lot of money. I'll see myself out."

Lex walked to his car, a little lighter. The Caroline thing hadn't really been an issue until he'd talked to Willa. She told him what had happened—why he'd found out about Nina from Caroline instead of Lu. He'd have fired her just for that, but it was nice to have the other issue as part of the equation too. He didn't appreciate his agent acting on his behalf without his knowledge. Having that on the record books would make other agents hesitant to think they could get away with it.

He glanced at the clock on the dashboard. It was almost one o'clock in the morning, but that didn't stop him from making his next move. Putting his earplugs in, he picked up his phone and found the number of the person he needed to talk to.

He answered on the second ring.

"I didn't think I'd hear from you for a while."

"Yeah, that was a dick move," Lex said.

There was a sigh at the other end. "I was worried about you."

"Which is why I'm letting you get away with it."

"What's up, Lex?" Malcolm asked.

"I need a new agent. Can you help me out?"

"I'll have the names to you in the morning."

"Thanks," Lex said as he disconnected.

36

"Are you sure you have everything you need?" Lu asked. Nina took after Willa in her minimalist approach to clothing. Not that any of them could qualify as fashion plates but, Lu definitely had them beat when it came to packing.

"Yes. Dad said they'll have a washer and dryer wherever we stay, so we can do laundry."

Lu couldn't help it. Nina saying the word *dad* still threw her. She loved it, but it still seemed odd after so much time. Lu often wondered what Mr. P. had done to help Nina accept Lex so easily. She'd have paid untold amounts of money to be a fly on the wall during those conversations. She supposed it helped that Nina had always heard about Lex from the families. But still, she thanked Mr. P. daily for the foresight he'd had to prepare his granddaughter.

"Does your father actually do his own laundry?" she asked somewhat sarcastically.

Nina giggled. "I don't think so, Mommy."

"Well, then this should be interesting," Lu said with a smile. "Why don't you do a once-over to make sure you aren't leaving anything. They should be here any moment to pick you up." It had been three days since Lex had dropped Lu off at her apartment without a backward glance.

She tried to talk herself into believing that it didn't matter that they hadn't spoken since their conversation, but in the stillness of the night, when lying to yourself seemed foolish, she had to admit that her feelings were hurt. Although she could admit that she hadn't been completely forthcoming, sometimes even reticent with him, she felt that connection to him. Lex Pellitteri spelled danger for her. Any way she looked at it, she knew she would feel hurt. She could be noble and pretend that the only thing she cared about was Nina's relationship with her father, but she'd be a liar.

Sending Nina away with him for two weeks, including Christmas, scared the shit out of Lu. Even with all that had happened since May, she'd never been away from her daughter for that long and they'd never been apart at Christmas. While Willa continued to give her shit about her decision to allow Nina to go with him, there hadn't really been a decision to make. He'd never been able to spend Christmas with her and it didn't seem very charitable to deny him this request. She and Nina would celebrate Christmas when Nina returned from the trip. Willa had also reluctantly agreed to fly over to spend the holiday with Lu, although she'd conceded that point prior to giving in to her desire for Pete. But she hadn't tried to renege on the deal and Lu hadn't offered to let her out of it, which Lu supposed made her selfish, but she wasn't ready to spend Christmas alone.

Still lost in her thoughts as she rolled Nina's bag toward the door, Lu started when she heard the knock. Moving quickly to answer it, she was surprised to find Lex on the other side. He'd never picked Nina up before, as he always sent Mrs. Auberly.

"What are you doing here?" she said, perhaps a bit too zealousy. She felt awkward and then silly for her overly loud greeting.

"Hey," Lex said, with a crooked smile. "I came to get Nina," he told her as if this were a common occurrence. Closing the door behind himself, he leaned down to drop a kiss on top of her head. "How are you?"

Stuttering a bit from his presence and the familiarity of his greeting, Lu answered cautiously. "Um, I'm fine."

Nina must have heard Lex's voice, because she came bounding

into the room and slid to a stop right in front of him. "Daddy!" she exclaimed. Lex scooped her up for an off-the-ground hug.

"Hey, Bit," he said, borrowing Pete's nickname for her. "Are you ready?"

"Yes. Mommy helped me pack everything."

"Great." Setting her on the ground, he leaned down so his face was level with hers. "Can you give your mom and me a couple of minutes to talk?"

"Sure," she said and promptly bounded back toward her room.

"Runs everywhere, huh?" Lex commented.

"Yes." Lu looked at him, tilting her head. "Remind you of anyone?"

"Nah," he deadpanned.

"Yeah, right," Lu said, earning herself a Lex Pellitteri grin, which made her stomach do funny things. "Can I get you something to drink?" she offered as she made her way over to the kitchen and pulled open the refrigerator door.

"No, I'm good."

Closing the door, Lu leaned over and rested her elbows on the counter as Lex took a seat on the bar stool.

"I didn't mean to catch you off guard," he said, suddenly serious. "I've been kind of a dick."

Lu's brow furrowed. "What?"

"Sending someone else to get Nina for the past couple of months. That was a shit move and I apologize."

Lu had no idea how to respond. She wanted to tell him that it was OK and that she understood. Because part of her felt relief that she didn't have to see him on a twice-weekly basis. But the sincerity of his voice demanded a response.

"We're all adjusting," she said magnanimously.

He smirked. "Yes, we are. But I've chosen to make it more difficult."

Lu didn't say anything, just looked at him as the silence stretched between them. She didn't have any desire to condemn him for any of his reactions. She briefly pictured Willa, in a devil suit sitting on her shoulder, nudging her with a pitchfork. Make him pay, she would say.

LEX and LU

But how could she do that when he'd been reacting to the situation that the people he loved most had choreographed?

He raised his eyebrow.

"What do you want me to say, Lex?"

"I want you to call a spade a spade."

"What good does that do?"

"It might not do any good, but at least I'd know that you are being honest."

Lu felt like he'd slapped her. "What the hell does that mean?"

"It means that I can't read you and that pretty much sucks." He continued to hold her gaze, but all sense of play had dissipated in the air like a puddle in a desert.

Pushing up from the counter, Lu stepped back, leaning onto the counter opposite to have some distance. Crossing her arms over her chest, all of her defenses came up.

"Lex, are you trying to make me mad?"

Shaking his head, he said, "No. I'm not. Sorry. I wanted to apologize and somehow I think I've made it worse."

"It's fine. We're good."

Nodding his head, he got up from the stool and walked around the counter, seizing the space that she claimed. Standing in front of her, he asked, "Really? We're good?"

"Yes," she said, but she didn't relax her position. His proximity made all of the muscles in her body tense, while other parts of her loosened. She felt uncomfortable, but she could articulate why.

He leaned back on the counter, giving her much-needed space, as if he could read her mind and knew what she needed.

"I have a proposition," he said, as if she were stupid and he needed to talk slow.

Smirking and rolling her eyes, she said, "OK."

He smiled that smile over her actions. Jelly, her insides were jelly.

"This is my first Christmas with Nina."

"Yes, I know."

"And I want to spend it with her."

241

"And you are," she said, slowly.

"I know, but I've been doing a lot of thinking. I've haven't had a big Christmas since I left home. I have to concentrate really hard on my memories to bring back the excitement of them."

Lu smiled. Christmases had always been good when they were growing up. On Christmas Eve they had the Supper Club party. Every year was a different house, but the core people were always the same. As all the kids had grown, so had the party. Christmas morning they spent at home, but they'd always had lunch with the Pellitteris. The tradition never changed, even as Lex left, Lu had Nina, kids grew and moved on with their lives. The shared memory floated between Lex and Lu, a translucent bubble of commonality.

Lex returned her smile. Then he reached into his back pocket and pulled something out. He held it out to her. Hesitantly, Lu reached out and took it from him. Breaking eye contact with him, she looked down at the mystery object. She could tell that it was a plane ticket. She didn't study it, just looked back at him with questions in her eyes.

"What's this?"

"I am hoping you will join Nina and me in Malaga." At her startled expression, he continued quickly. "I rented a huge house, and I bought the ticket for the twenty-third through the twenty-sixth. You won't be with us the whole time. Just for Christmas. Nina and I will have to leave before everyone for my game."

She couldn't breathe, and she couldn't look at him. She stared at the ground, trying to get ahold of herself.

"Breathe, Lu," Lex whispered. He hadn't moved any closer, but his voice felt like he'd touched her intimately. Still holding his distance, he continued, "I know Willa's coming here so I bought a ticket for her too. And just so you know how much of a coldhearted bastard I can be, I bought a ticket for Pete too. I figure that will tip Willa's scale on my behalf. So that really just leaves you." He took a very small step toward her. "I want Nina's first Christmas with me to be special and I figure having all of her family there would make it that."

Lu's head came up. "You're not playing fair," she snapped.

"I rarely do when I want something," he retorted.

"I need time to think, Lex."

"I can appreciate that. It took me eight months."

Confusions clouded her face. "Eight months for what?"

"To think about everything." He laughed a kind of bitter bark. "Since you are going to think this through, you should probably have all of the information."

"There's more?" she questioned with a look of horror on her face.

Smiling, he said, "A little more, yeah."

Drawing a deep breath, she said, "Out with it."

"I invited Dr. A. and your dad . . ." He paused. "And my mom."

She couldn't have been more shocked. "Are they coming?"

"Yes. But I got them each suites at a resort down the road."

"Good thinking," she blurted.

"I also think it's only fair to tell you that I am planning to finish our conversation during this trip. There are questions I have and things I need to say. I need you to think about that really hard because if you agree to come, we are going to talk."

She merely nodded her head. Her mind refused to kick in. She just kept imagining the devil Willa perched on her shoulder shaking her head.

Without turning away from her, Lex yelled, "Nina, you ready?"

As Nina came flying out of her room, struggling to contain her excitement, Lu tried to pull herself out of her stupor.

"I'm ready," she said needlessly. Coming to stand in between Lu and Lex, oblivious to the tension between them, she leaned in to Lu, hugging her. "I'll miss you. But we can FaceTime, right?"

"Of course." Lu slid partially down the counter so that she and Nina were on the same level. "Remember: please and thank you. Listen to your father."

"And I get to open your presents when I get home, right?"

Lu smiled. "Absolutely. I love you, baby," she managed as she hugged Nina tight, keeping her eyes closed so she didn't have to look into the sun that was Lex.

Nina pulled away first, turned to Lex, and said, "Let's go."

Lex put his hand on the small of her back and ushered her to the door. As he was about to open it, Lu caught up with them. She reached out tentatively and touched his shoulder. When he turned to her, Lu asked, "Why now?"

He didn't even hesitate. "You graduated."

"What does that have to do with anything?" she asked, thoroughly confused.

"You graduated and everyone was there but me. It was like a cold bucket of water in my face. I can't really explain it other than it woke me up." With that he shrugged and opened the door. "We'll call you when we land."

Nodding, she watched her daughter walk out of her apartment on the arm of her father. Closing the door, she leaned against it and slid down to the floor. I guess I'm going to Malaga for Christmas, she thought. Then, banging her head against the door, she said, "Fuck!"

37

Lex, Pete, and Nina planned a day of sightseeing for Lu and Willa's arrival. They'd hit all of the major tourist attractions when they picked them up, ending the day at the Picasso Museum. By the time they had dinner and made their way back to the house, Nina had fallen asleep. Lu put her to bed, showered, and then joined the rest of the crew. She found Willa, Pete, and Lex sprawled on the couches in the living room, enjoying glasses of wine. When she sat down, Lex leaned over from the opposite couch and handed her a glass.

"Isn't this yours?" Lu asked.

"I don't drink during the season," he informed her, although he was fairly certain she knew.

"Oh, sorry, I keep forgetting."

"We were just discussing our plans for tomorrow," Willa offered.

"Are we going to take our parents all over the city so that they pass out by nine o'clock?" Lu quipped.

"That's not a bad idea," Pete chimed in.

"Have you spent every day like this?" Lu asked, not quite recovered from trekking through the city all day.

"Yup," Lex and Pete answered at the same time.

"No wonder Nina hasn't given you a hard time. You wear her out and put her to bed."

"Not a bad plan," Pete said. "She seems to be enjoying it."

Lu smiled, "I'm fairly certain that she is overjoyed that she's finally found someone who can keep up with her." Lu met Lex's gaze and smiled at him. "She's really enjoying herself."

"When it comes to energy levels, she is absolutely her father's daughter," Willa added. It was a comment that she'd had to refrain from making in the past, but now it just seemed natural to refer to Nina as Lex's daughter and she wondered when that had happened. Looking around, Willa attempted to keep her eyes off of Pete, but he looked so damn good, she just couldn't do it. She needed him alone, now. "I think I'm going to head to bed," she said, getting to her feet.

Lu looked at her skeptically. "You are so full of shit. If you want to be alone with Pete, just say so."

Willa, being Willa, turned to her sister, raising her eyebrows as if to say, are you serious? Then, just because Lu had thrown it out there, she said, "Lu, Lex, I am taking Pete. I'm going to fuck his brains out. Good night."

Pete choked on his wine, Lex threw back his head and laughed, and Lu shook her head, knowing that she alone had created that monster.

Pete jumped up, grabbed Willa's hand, and waved good-bye.

"Well done!" Lex managed to catcall through his laughter.

"Do you really need to encourage her?" Lu scolded.

"God, I've missed her," Lex said matter-of-factly, still chuckling.

Lu felt a hot streak of jealousy rip through her. Drinking her wine, she said nothing, bristling at Lex and Willa's renewed friendship.

Lex laid out on the couch, propping his feet on the opposite arm, completely relaxed. Turning his head to the side so that he could see Lu, he watched her for a couple of minutes, saying nothing. She seemed lost in her own thoughts. Finally, he said, "Nina is amazing, Lu. You've done a great job raising her. Thank you."

Lu raised her eyes and met his. "You know that whole nature-versus-nurture argument?" At his nod, she continued. "As a parent, I have to say that nature wins out hands down. It's like I've had no influence on her. She popped out at birth and was this being who existed as she saw fit to exist. While I appreciate the compliment, I'm not sure what I've had to do with her."

"Do you think our parents thought that of us?"

"Certainly exonerates them, doesn't it."

He laughed. "Yeah, I guess. And you are far more of an expert than me, but I can see you in her at almost every moment. She may have my pace, but she definitely has your brains and your ability to take everything in, evaluate it, and come to a decision about it. Half the time she's been with me I thought I was with you as a little girl. It was rather comforting. I thought, I can really suck at being a father and she is going to be OK."

"You're not going to suck at being a father, Lex. Just like everything you've ever done, it comes naturally to you."

He shrugged. "I hope." A comfortable silence descended between them. "Are you OK with being here?"

His question caught her off guard. "Yes, I am."

"Even with the grandparents showing up tomorrow?"

"Are you?" she shot back.

Laughing again, he said, "I don't know. The last time I saw Jo I essentially told her to fuck off. And I haven't seen Amber since you told me that she became mommy dearest when I left. I'm feeling a little put out by that. So, I'm not sure if I'm up for the next two days."

"Lex, why is all of this so important all of a sudden?"

Turning his head away from her and looking up at the ceiling, he seemed to contemplate his answer. "Are you sure you want me to answer that?"

She rolled her eyes. "I wouldn't have asked if I didn't want the answer."

"Does that mean you're ready to talk to me?"

"I thought I asked you a question, not the other way around," she retorted.

He turned his head again and pinned her with his eyes. "If we start this conversation, I'm going to be looking for answers too. I just want to know if you're ready for that."

"Yup," she responded as if he'd asked her if she wanted more wine. Without Nina, Willa, and Pete providing distractions, Lu's relaxed mood had fizzled into a nervous anticipation. If having this conversation would allow things to retire to some new normal for them, then she was more than ready.

Lex turned back to look at the ceiling, seemingly telling her it would be easier if he didn't have to look at her. Although she'd employed that method often during their exchanges, it hurt that he found more comfort in the ceiling than in her eyes.

"I told you that your graduation was almost a turning point for me. Up until that weekend, I'd been going through the motions. Not just in my personal relationships but with soccer too. That's why the whole scene with Malcolm," he reminded her. He turned to look at her to see her acknowledgement. When she nodded, he continued. "I think it was the drunk texts." He chuckled softly. "There you were, calling me out from across the pond. I texted Pete after that to make sure you got home OK. And when I did that I felt like it was all wrong. My brother was with you and my daughter, celebrating your graduation, and I was sitting alone in my home. I got mad and then I got drunk." He turned to look at Lu again. "I have never been that drunk. While I was drunk I needed to know." He paused. "You know, at the funeral, I knew you were feeding me a line of bullshit about the family not telling me. That's just not you, but I bought it because otherwise, I thought, everyone in my life had been lying to me for a very long time. It was one of those moments when I remembered how amazing you are."

He stopped, but Lu knew that it wasn't for her to make a comment.

"I jumped online and bought a ticket home. Which tells you how fucked up I was, because I had a game in four days and the last thing I needed was to miss practice for a transatlantic flight. Anyway, I get home and Jo's not there. She's at your graduation too. I couldn't believe it. Everyone was a part of my family except me. I don't know if I can describe the rage I felt."

He looked at her again. "You know it though, don't you?"

Lu stared at him questioningly.

"That day, in the Sunday-school room." He paused and let it sink in. "There is no description for the rage, Lu. And being mad just isn't part of who I am. I was out of control, unable to rein it in. Luckily Jo didn't come home for another twenty-four hours, and by then it had gone. I questioned her and she told me what happened—her version, which, by the way, fits with yours—except for the part where she's your savior. She didn't try to make herself look good, which I respect. But it all seemed so callous, and I couldn't take it. I left there after telling her to basically stay away. And then I found myself at Willa's."

He laughed again. "I wish you could have seen her face. You would have loved it. You know Willa is never caught off guard." More laughter. "Fucking classic."

"She didn't tell me anything other than you spent the night there."

He nodded his head and went back to looking at the ceiling. "Of course she didn't. That's Willa. If I ever need a lawyer again, I'm hiring her."

"Smart man," Lu said, grinning. "So are you going to tell me anything?"

"Probably not," he said.

Lu felt herself struggling with the mad again.

"I fired Caroline," Lex informed her.

"What?" Lu's surprise was evident in her voice.

He didn't elaborate. Lu guessed that was his way of telling her something, but she wasn't sure what she was supposed to get out of it.

"Mr. Helms wants you," she informed him, as though she knew anything about it.

"Yeah, I'm meeting with some potential replacements when we get back. My contract's coming up, but it's not happening right now, so I have some time to make a good decision." Lex sat up. Leaning forward, he said, "Our conversation that night, when you told me about my mother, that changed how I felt. I need to make it up to her. So that's why I want her here. I've also gathered that things between her and Dr.

A. have been pretty tense. I thought if I got them away from Sarasota, they could maybe see their way through."

Taking a deep breath, Lex shifted. "So, is that a good enough explanation?" he asked.

Lu looked at him and nodded her head. "Yes, it is."

"You feel satisfied? I explained myself."

Lu should have sensed a trap, but she didn't. She was caught up in his shared confidences and feeling as though they were forging some bond. "Yes. Thank you for telling me."

"Don't thank me, Lu. It comes with a price."

38

"A price?" she said, stupidly.

"Yes, a price."

"Well, don't keep me in suspense," she said flippantly, smiling at him like this was all normal banter.

Lex didn't say anything. He looked at her for a long while. Lu imagined she should have felt nervous, but something more like an adrenaline rush coursed through her. Like the anticipation of a first kiss. As he continued to study her, her stomach did flips. But his eyes never wavered from her face. There were no longing glances at her lips. He didn't look like a man in the throes of desire.

Lex knew that this conversation had to take place, but he felt caught between the desire to have it and the knowledge that it could snap the tenuous twig of their relationship. As much as he wanted to spare her any hurt, he needed for her to come clean. He had to know. He struggled to figure out if he should channel Willa's in-your-face approach or Pete's diplomatic one. What he needed from her had nothing to do with Nina or Jo or Dr. A. Bracing himself, he stepped to the edge of the precipice and prayed that he could have this conversation while preserving their fledgling truce.

He got up from the couch and sat on the coffee table directly in front of her, invading her space. His proximity took over the anticipation and turned it toward nervous. Bracing his arms on his legs, he leaned toward her.

"Why did you sleep with me?"

Lu shouldn't have been shocked, but the question threw her. Her hands shook, so she quickly put the wineglass down. She couldn't move away from him as he'd effectively trapped her between the couch, the coffee table, and himself. She wanted to look anywhere but at him, but the only way to avoid him would have been to close her eyes, and she wasn't that much of a wimp. But maybe she could bluff her way out of this conversation. She felt pretty confident that Lex didn't really want to know her reason.

She smiled what she hoped was a convincing smile. "Do I really need to explain basic chemistry to you, Lex?" She tried to keep her tone from flippant, knowing he'd sniff that out pretty quickly.

Raising his eyebrow, he attempted to model the death stare. Damn it, he thought, she's going to fight me on this. He knew then that she didn't trust him enough, but he'd already peered into Pandora's box and there wasn't anything he was going to do to try to fit the top back on.

"Sure, Lu. I get chemistry. Been doing it for a lot longer than you and have most assuredly mixed a lot more reactants together. That's what you want to chalk it up to? Just sex?"

Again with the jealously, thought Lu as his reference to his healthy sex life smacked her in the face. Part of her wanted to tell him, but she held tightly to her childhood dreams, not willing for them to be shattered by his adult reality. "Look, Lex, we were both in the same place at the same time for the first time in almost ten years. Of course we resorted back into the roles. It's completely natural that we ended up there."

"Completely natural, huh?" Lex studied her. He wasn't sure how far she would take the sophisticated-sexual-being routine, but for the moment he was content to let her continue.

"Yes." Lu leaned forward and put her hand on Lex's knee. The casualness of the effort took everything she had in her. "We are going to be raising a daughter together and I don't want things to be strange between us. I don't want to feel like I have to be ready for our interactions. We probably shouldn't have been together back in May, but we can't undo that now. Let's just chalk it up to a mistake and move forward."

"A mistake?"

"Yes. A pleasant mistake," she smiled, hoping that she was convincing him.

Annoyed with her, Lex got up, disengaging from her touch and putting some physical distance between them. "How many men have you slept with since I left?" he asked.

"That's none of your business, Lex," Lu responded, laughing, not rising to his bait while she prayed this would be over soon.

"I'm just trying to figure out if casual sex is your thing," he responded, a cutting edge to his voice.

"Lex. Why are you mad?" she asked innocently, but the act became harder.

Lex mentally threw up his hands. Talking to her wasn't working. He walked back to where she was sitting. Grabbing her by the arms, he pulled her off the couch and into his body. His left hand snaked around the back of her head drawing her mouth to his. Her eyes wide with surprise, he kissed her, hoping to knock the shroud of nonchalance from her. She resisted for half a second before her mouth opened to welcome his. He'd meant to jar her, but kissing her felt too good. He felt her arms move up around his neck, her fingers tangling in his hair. Pliant for the moment, he wished she would let him into her thoughts and not just into her body. Remembering May, he broke the kiss.

Lu felt him pull away from her. Part of her relieved, part disappointed. When he pushed her away from him, the look on his face didn't scream of passion and love as she'd hoped. Instead she saw his mad. Bracing herself, she stepped away from him.

"What the hell is wrong with you?" he snapped at her.

She hated her reaction to him. Her body betrayed her every time. Looking at his, she could see the tension radiating off of him, but she didn't understand why he wanted to push them down this path. What would come of it if she told him she'd waited for him for the last nine years? It would make every encounter difficult. They'd go back to communicating through his lawyer. She just wanted to be able to coexist with him. It was enough for now.

"What the fuck happened to you?" he said.

Startled by his anger and a little pissed that he was mad at her, she snapped back at him. "What is your problem?"

"My problem is you. Who are you? You're the fucking Ice Queen. Do you feel anything?" Lex was so frustrated he didn't know what to do with it. Was this really who she was? This woman who had no feeling, who could act like what happened between them was simple chemistry, not any emotion. Did she really think that the sex they had in the Sunday-school room was OK? He'd had nightmares about that encounter, had woken up in a cold sweat thinking he'd practically raped her. How was she OK with that? Why didn't she react? Had his desertion stunted her so much that she didn't, couldn't, wouldn't react to anything? He'd forced her to move to England and she hadn't even batted an eyelash.

Lu flinched.

He saw it and decided to hell with it; he was going for broke.

"I practically raped you that day, Lu. Can you sit there and tell me that it's OK?" he asked.

She flinched again. "You'd just lost your father and found out that you had an eight-year-old daughter—who I'd kept from you."

"Really? You're letting me off that easy?" He shook his head. "What happened to you? Why don't you defend yourself? Why are you letting everything happen to you rather than trying to have a say in it?"

Lu would never know what part of his tirade finally pushed her too far. She felt betrayed by him in that moment, as if everything she'd done for him and his daughter wasn't enough for him to allow her the existence that she knew she could handle. But suddenly, her mouth opened and her soul lay bare.

"Have a say in it? What have I had a say in for the last nine years? I certainly didn't have a say in you staying or going. Even though I believed you when you said you would come back and be with us, even knowing that, I knew you were leaving me. And you never looked back. I was alone and pregnant with my mother hounding me to have an abortion and my sister looking at me with pity because she knew you weren't coming back. For six weeks I lived in limbo. And then I had to turn to your mother. Yes, she saved our child, but the price I had to pay for that, the price of your absence from our child's life—that's a big price. I sold my fucking soul that day. And where were you? Oh, you were off pursuing your dream. The shit part of it, Lex, is that I loved you enough that I convinced myself that it was the right thing for you.

"When Mr. P. died, I couldn't stay away. I knew I should because I needed to stay away from you. But you wouldn't leave me alone. I begged you for distance. I tried to stay away, but you kept coming. I knew that I had to tell you about Nina and the only way to do that was to keep the distance between us. But you couldn't do that. You wore me down. Even then, fuck, even then I wanted to protect you. It was going to be hard enough telling you about Nina without having sex between us. You think I didn't know that? That's why I couldn't look at you. I couldn't have you inside of me and look into your eyes and lie to you. So don't you dare fucking come at me about not feeling and about not acting. I've been doing nothing but feeling for you for my entire life. And every goddamn sacrifice I've made in the last nine years has been for you."

Walking to him she got right in his face. "Is that what you needed to know, Lex? Did I stroke your ego enough? Does it make you feel better to know that I've loved you the whole time? That I never stopped? That my dreams, which I've buried but held on to, are filled with images of us being a family? Does that make you fucking happy, Lex?" Seething, with tears she couldn't feel coursing down her face, she held her ground. "Don't you dare call me the Ice Queen, you son of a bitch. You fucking left me. So any ice around my heart is on you."

He reached out for her, trying to pull her into his embrace, but she fought him, arms flailing as her strength was no match for his. He held her stiffly in his arms, with her still pushing him away.

"Lu, I'm so sorry."

Pushing against him with a force that surprised both of them, she flew back from his body. "Don't fucking touch me. I don't want your pity. I don't want anything from you." She turned and ran from the room.

⌒

He tried. She'd asked him to leave her alone and he did. For about fifteen minutes. Fifteen slow, agonizing minutes. Sitting heavily on the couch, his head resting in his hands, he fought the good fight. Then he followed her. Opening the door to her room, he found her standing at the window, arms wrapped tightly across her chest. He silently closed the door and walked to her. Engulfing her tiny frame, he slid his arms around her and pulled her against him. This time, she didn't fight.

He'd expected tears, but her silence spread through him, a chasm between them.

"I'm sorry," he whispered as he bent his head to her ear. Without meaning to or even being conscious of his actions, he kissed her below her ear, on the spot he'd claimed at seventeen.

Lu drew a long shuddering breath that rippled through both of them. "What are you sorry for?" she asked, no hint of her earlier anger present.

He didn't mean to, but he smiled against her neck. "A lot. Mostly for the funeral."

He felt her stiffen.

"What do you mean?" she asked.

Without relinquishing his hold on her, he tried to comfort her with his body, hoping to soften his words. "My relentless pursuit," he said simply.

"Of everything—that's what you are sorry for?"

He knew that if he'd been looking at her, her eyes would have been wide with questions. "Yeah. We'd be in a different place if I'd stayed away from you."

She shrugged. "Perhaps."

He lifted his head from her neck and rested it on hers. Standing together, they were quiet for a long time, both lost in their thoughts, not ready to share. Lex attempted to reconcile his part in the sequence of events that had brought them to this point. He'd been slowly maneuvering the pieces in his mind, trying to get a clear picture. He chalked up his laissez-faire reaction to Lu's supposed abortion and his subsequent radio silence to the category of immaturity. At nineteen, with his dream within his reach, he'd taken the out that was offered. Even with hindsight, blah, blah, blah, he thought the outcome would have been the same. What he could have changed, the thing he wished they could do over, was his relentless pursuit of her when they met at the funeral. He was so accustomed to sex without strings that he'd blown their chance. If he'd listened to her, her plea for him to give her time to talk to him after the funeral, maybe this outcome could have been different.

Or maybe not, he thought as his body began to react to her nearness. He wasn't sure when the embrace of comfort began to change. He'd wanted her then and he wanted her now. But that's exactly what had gotten them here—separated by their past. Kissing her on top of the head, he let her go.

39

Lex expected Lu to bail on their Christmas Eve activities. He'd expected it and almost welcomed it. After their fight, he'd been unable to sleep. He'd hoped that if he pushed her hard enough she'd let go of some of the tightly held control. Fairly certain that she'd held on to all of that anger and angst for the last nine years, he couldn't help but experience a myriad of emotions. She'd needed to say all of those things to him years ago. He'd robbed her of an outlet. Who did she have to talk to all of those years? Even Willa seemed to play some inadvertent role in their saga. While he felt sorry for all the pain he'd caused her, she'd admitted to him that she still hoped they could be together. He didn't know if she still held on to that dream, but he knew midway through their fight he wanted that.

He'd assumed that their coming together at the funeral had all been about familiarity and comfort. But being with her he experienced emotions he'd been unable to replicate during his years away from her. The night they'd spent together at his father's funeral haunted him—that and their last encounter. He didn't know if he would be able to convince her, but he wanted another chance. But he was stuck. He couldn't ask her to take another chance on him. He knew he could coerce her, but he didn't want to have to. So for the day, he left her to her own devices and did his best to provide her with the space she seemed to want.

They'd picked up their parents early and had strolled through the city without any agenda. Although Lu was present, Lu's reticence toward him was apparent—if not to everyone, then to Willa, Pete, and Lex. Her attentiveness to all the proceedings waned often, and she seemed to drop behind to take in something that everyone else had blown by. By three o'clock, they finished up with their touring and headed back to get ready for dinner. Lex had rented out a room at a seafood restaurant for their Christmas Eve dinner. It wasn't the traditional party, but the fare would be similar. Everyone had been on their best behavior, so he had high hopes that dinner would be a pleasant experience. He'd taken Nina shopping before everyone arrived and she'd picked out a very traditional Christmas dress that she'd kept hidden from Lu so she could surprise her.

Lex showered and got dressed. As he put on his suit jacket, images of him and Lu together in the Sunday-school room flashed through his mind. It was the last time he'd worn this suit and he hoped Lu didn't recognize it—a reminder of his darkest hour. He pushed his hands in the pocket and drew out an envelope. He saw his father's bold script. Feeling like the air had been sucked out of the room, Lex sank to his bed. In all of the chaos of that day, he'd completely forgotten about the letter. It took him ten minutes of internal debate to decide if he wanted to read it now or wait until after dinner. But having forgotten about it for so long, he pulled open the envelope and pulled it out.

Dear Lex,

Unfortunately when you read this letter, I will no longer be with you. It seems odd to write those words even though I've had a lot of time to get used to the idea. I've also included a letter for Pete in here figuring Caroline would safeguard both until it was time to hand them to you. Even though I know you will, allow Pete to decide if he'd like to share it with you. With the years and bond between you two, I imagine he'll do it on his own accord.

Being a parent to the two of you has been the greatest experience of my life. Had someone told me how hard it would be when I was younger, I was arrogant enough that I wouldn't have believed them but you will know soon what I mean. You hope every day that you are doing the right thing for your children and teaching them the right lessons. The men that you and Pete have become provide me with peace and pride as I know that your mother and I were able to get something right. Although I have to say that we were merely stewards as you were each your own people from birth.

We did make a mistake though—probably the biggest mistake of my life and every day I pay the price of that mistake. I'm not sure of the timeline of events but I hope that you have already met Nina when you read this. She is amazing and has given me untold joy over the last eight years. Two years ago, I told her about you. I feel bad for betraying Lu but I wanted you to have a chance with Nina—a chance that we denied you.

What I want you to know is that none of us gave Lu and you enough credit. She's never been able to get over you and I don't think you've ever really gotten over her. You've never let anyone else into your heart even though you have this amazing capacity to love. I know your first inclination will be to blame her, but we completely overruled, overpowered her. She had no chance. So as you two attempt to move forward, work to forgive her and help her to forgive you. In her mind, she's exonerated you of any wrongdoing, but I'm not sure her heart has had the time to understand that you left. Try to find your way back to her. And if it's not Lu who you want to be with, let someone in.

I wish I was going to get the opportunity to see you and Nina together. I know you will have to work at this parenting thing, as we ALL have to, but you will find that she is this amazing combination of all that is good in you and Lu with all of her own stamps of independence and personality. Enjoy her as I have enjoyed you and Pete. One more thing, try to forgive your mother too. She did everything she thought was right for you at the time. Her strength has fortified our family since its inception.

I am so proud, happy, overwhelmed that I was given the gift of being your father.

Dad

Lex sat for a long time, rereading the letter. Drops smearing the ink on the paper made him realize he had cried, finally feeling the grief of his father's death. He wondered if he'd read this letter back in May if things with himself and Lu would have played out differently. Funny that he was just starting to reach the same conclusions his father had reached some time ago. He'd met the love of his life at age eight. Who does that, he thought. He debated about giving Pete his letter before dinner since he'd withheld it for so long, it was time. He went to Pete's room, and knocked softly.

When Willa answered the door, he said "I need to speak to Pete."

Willa's eyes widened. "Of course."

"I look that bad?" he asked with a sad smile.

She pulled him into a hug. "Yes," she whispered. "You look like shit."

He chuckled. "Don't go far. Pete's probably going to need you," he said as he walked into the room and closed the door.

Pete walked out of the bathroom with a towel around his waist. He started at finding Lex standing there.

Lex smiled. "Sorry Bro. I'm sure you were expecting Will."

Pete laughed. "Good thing I didn't walk out here naked."

"Yeah, like I've never seen you naked before."

"But if I'm walking around naked with Willa around, it's a different look."

"Totally a visual I didn't need, Bro," Lex said laughing.

"Let me get some pants on, then we can talk?" Pete looked questioningly at Lex. At Lex's nod, he said, "OK, give me a sec."

Once he was dressed, Pete came out and sat on the bed, across from Lex, who had taken up residence in the chair opposite.

"What's up?" Pete asked.

"At the funeral, Caroline gave me a letter from Dad."

Pete's eyes got wide.

"With everything that happened that day, I forgot about it. But there is a letter for you also. I'm sorry I didn't get it to you sooner."

"Bro, don't worry about that." He took in Lex's appearance. "Are you OK?"

Lex didn't answer for a moment. "Yeah. Just . . ." he paused, ". . . most of the letter was fine. It's just one thing is bothering me. I'll let you read yours without me hovering, but I'm just curious if you have the same feeling."

Pete nodded. "OK. But stay. OK?"

Lex didn't move. Pete took the letter and began to read. He couldn't have read more than a couple of lines when he glanced up and met Lex's gaze. In that moment something passed between the two of them. Pete returned to his letter. When he was done, he looked up again.

"Was he dying?" Pete asked.

"That's what I want to know."

40

Dinner was a tense affair. The private room, set back in the restaurant, while cheery and light, seemed to cast a pall of irony over their assembly. Lu watched as Lex took in the uncomfortable atmosphere of the family gathering. She saw him decide that he needed to step in and try to make everyone comfortable. He turned his attention to the room at large. Before long, he'd turned the tide with his teasing, lighthearted banter. The effort cost him, she knew, but he'd brought it on himself. She found it interesting that he so clearly stepped right back into that role. She'd long ago decided that you couldn't escape the childhood role that you were destined to don the moment you returned to the fold. Thankfully—because by the time dessert appeared, everyone seemed to be relaxed. Eager to be done with the hellish torture, Lu almost choked on her wine when he suggested that everyone come to the villa for coffee.

Lu shot him a look of death. He'd been so caught up in working the room that she supposed he hardly noticed the tension radiating from her or he was so used to it by now that he couldn't tell her relaxed pose from her tension-filled rigidity.

"I apologize," he whispered.

She guessed he did notice as she shook him off. "It's OK," she muttered.

But it wasn't. As they all settled in the family room, sprawled on the couches that the night before had held just the four of them, the embers of tension began to ignite. Lu waited with Nina while she showered but brought her out so that she could bid everyone goodnight. Lex scooped her up and carried her off to bed, leaving Lu to find a seat in the viper's pit. Her parents were curled up together on the love seat. Next to them, Pete sat on the recliner, with Willa perched on the arm, never far from his side, which made Lu smile despite her desire for this night to be over. Jo, who had been sitting with Lex, looked at Lu, inviting her silently to sit with her. Lu declined by walking over and sitting in the other recliner, slightly away from the group, a party of one. The moment she sat down, Amber struck, a viper who'd been waiting for her prey.

"Louisa May, have you been able to find some gainful employment in London?" Dr. A. asked.

Lu tried desperately to hold the roll of her eyes. She supposed her mother had been put off for the twenty hours she'd been in Spain and the question had surely been burning a hole in her pocket. "I'm continuing to consult via Skype, but, yes, I've actually been offered a job that I'm contemplating."

Amber raked her with her eyes, and Lu had to wonder about all of this contempt that her mother seemed to harbor. "Why would you be contemplating a job? Don't you have to support yourself and Nina?"

Patience, Lu thought. "Yes, I do. And I will." She didn't elaborate, because she knew that any mention of working with English soccer would send her mother into a fit of apoplexy. When she dared to look at her father, she could see the brackets of stress around his mouth. She didn't know if this could be attributed to her or her mother.

"Well, don't keep us in suspense. What offer?"

This finally distracted Willa and Pete from their private conversation. Lu saw Willa's head pop up. Meeting her sister's inquiring look, Lu shrugged into a mute apology.

"English Premier League," she said simply.

For a split second, Lu imagined her mother's head spinning, which caused an inappropriate smile to leap to her lips. Looking helplessly at her father, she held his gaze, both of them hoping that the presence of the Pellitteris would help her mother hold her tongue.

With an ironic laugh, Amber shook her head. "A waste of talent," she muttered under her breath, but loud enough for everyone, including Lex, who was returning from Nina's room, to hear it.

Smiling widely, he leaped over the back of the couch, reclaiming his seat next to his mother, and commented. "Interesting," he noted, as if he had heard the conversation in its entirety. "Working for the most well-known sports league in the world—hardly a waste of talent, Dr. A."

"She always has been good at stroking your ego, Lex," she retorted.

Lu, Chris, and Willa looked horrified, but Lex just smiled. "Yes, well as long as I continue to invite you along, I'm going to need it." Then he flashed that smile with the raised eyebrow and dared her to continue.

Amber laughed like a schoolgirl. "Someone needs to keep you honest," she said, still smiling.

Just like that, the tension eased. And in that moment Lu both loved and hated Lex. She wanted to stay away from him, wanted to maintain their current situation, in which they parented their child together. But she knew they couldn't do a sequel. Sequels were never as good as the first story. *Electric Boogaloo* didn't even compete with *Breakin'*. But when he did shit like this, when he pulled on his cape and rode to her rescue, she found it hard to hold fast to distance. As she looked to him gratefully, she took note of the tension in his body. Before she knew how to react, he turned to Jo.

"Jo, did you think that maybe you should have told us that Dad was dying?" he asked to a stunned room.

Lu's intake of air was heard throughout the remaining silence.

Jo didn't look at Lex or Pete. She merely twisted her cordial glass in her hand, biding her time. Lu looked around and knew that she was the only one in the room who didn't know what was going on. So wrapped up in what had happened between herself and Lex the night before, she'd spent most of the day in an oblivion that seemed to accommodate her mood. She'd missed the tension in the boys at dinner; she'd missed the stress that Jo wore around her like a big, colorful scarf.

Lex didn't repeat his question or even look mildly disturbed. He continued to lean back on the couch, close to Jo, with his arms thrown over the back. "Dad left letters with Caroline. She'd given it to me at the funeral, but I completely forgot about it." He paused and looked over at Lu, their gazes locked. She knew she was the reason he forgot about the letter. She remembered seeing it in his hands in the Sunday-school room when she walked in—he'd stuffed it in his pocket, so his hands were free. "I found the letters today." He broke eye contact with Lu and turned to his mother. "Why didn't you guys tell us?"

Jo looked up. First at Pete, who had moved forward in his seat, but continued to hold on to Willa. Then at Lex, who still looked completely relaxed. There was no blame anywhere in his demeanor. Lu was hit with a wave of love for him that caught her completely off guard. Ten minutes earlier she'd wanted to hit him for his impromptu rescue.

"We found out two years ago, right before Christmas, as a matter of fact," Jo began. "He'd been having headaches and had experienced some slower reflexes. It was inoperable. . . . We could have tried to find a cure . . . tried radiation. But he wanted quality of life. He wanted to live like he'd been living, watching the two of you"—she looked at both Pete and Lex—"and Nina and Lu and Willa." She looked at the two of them. "He didn't want to give that up. We argued about it—over and over. But I couldn't change his mind."

"So the accident?" Pete asked.

"Exactly like I told you. It's possible that his reflexes played a part in the accident, but the medical examiner couldn't determine that one hundred percent." Jo didn't offer any other information and neither Lex nor Pete asked. Lu felt stunned, much as she imagined the boys feeling when they read their letters. How could she have missed this?

"Mom, why didn't you tell us when he died?" Pete looked forlorn, hurt. Willa moved closer to him, as though her presence could absorb the bad and leave him with nothing but the good. Lu watched the two of them, envy spurting out of her pores. She longed to comfort Lex.

"I probably should have, but he was dead. Not that I didn't think it mattered. That's not it. It wouldn't have changed anything." Jo continued to sit twirling her glass, looking off into a distance that no one else could see. Lu couldn't help her slight hero worship of Jo. She didn't apologize to the Lex and Pete, knowing that there wasn't much she could say to help them understand their father's motivations. They all knew Mr. P. well enough to know that Jo's version was dead-on. And while she probably should have told them when he died, she didn't try to convince them that her decision was right—it was merely her decision. She looked at both men. "Would it have made it easier?" she asked, wanting to know if she'd messed up.

Pete shrugged. "I don't know," he admitted.

Lex turned his head to face his mother. "There isn't anything that could have made Dad's death easier. But I would have liked to know that we didn't have all the time in the world." He stood and kissed his mother on her head. "I called the car service on my way in here. They should be here in five. We'll see you tomorrow." He left the room without another word. Chris, Amber, and Jo stood and gathered their stuff.

"I'll walk you out," Pete offered.

When it was just the two of them in the room, Willa turned to Lu. "Are you going to check on him?"

Lu leaned back heavily in the chair. Sighing, she said, "Yes."

"Are you going to be OK?"

Smiling wearily, Lu rolled her eyes to the ceiling. "My heart can't break twice, right?"

Willa merely smiled.

41

Lex stood on the balcony, staring out into the depths of the Alboran Sea. If one wanted to put the insignificance of their problems in perspective, they merely needed to look at the infiniteness of its sparkling depths. Bombarded by the events of the last eight months, Lex found himself smiling. The loss of his father would never leave him. He would feel it every day, but he also imagined that the sharpness would lessen so that the dull ebb would merely be a passing thought. Coupled with the discovery of his daughter, the scales seemed to somehow balance. What, he wondered, would it have been like to have them both at the same time? And Lu. What would it be like to have Lu?

As if he'd conjured her with his thoughts, he heard the door open and knew, without looking back, that she'd come to him. He turned and leaned back on the balcony railing, watching her stride purposefully toward him. She still wore her black slacks and forest green sweater, a testament to Christmas. She'd pulled her hair out of its ponytail so that it hung loosely around her shoulders. Last night, when he'd gone to her, her eyes had been red-rimmed and swollen, tiny red lines mixing with the white and blue, proclaiming her heart-wrenching trip to the past. Tonight, the cornflower blue sparkled, almost smiling, meeting his with a quiet determination that he'd always associated with her. He couldn't really imagine her broken and doubting like the seventeen-year-old girl she'd described. The woman walking toward him was the girl he'd loved, all grown up and magnificent. He wanted her—more than he'd wanted anything.

He smiled, his eyes mischievous, and her step faltered. Slight, a slighted stutter, as if she all of a sudden realized what she had walked into and his grin widened.

Suddenly, she laughed.

Raising his eyebrow, Lex copped the stare. "What's so funny?" he teased.

Not hesitating anymore, she stepped right between his parted legs, wrapped her arms around him and laid her forehead on his chest. She giggled. "Here I thought I was coming in here to check on you, but you don't seem to be very upset."

His arms snaked around her, and he pulled her close. He shrugged, causing her to lift her head and meet his eyes. "Seeing you makes me smile." Sincerity laced his words and made her draw a deep breath.

Lex's hands moved slowly, caressing Lu's back, mesmerizing her. When she looked away from him, he leaned back, trying to get her to look up at him again. She felt so good in his arms, but he didn't want to scare her away. She reminded him of a skittish colt, and the last thing he needed was to make her bolt. She finally met his gaze. He smiled again.

"I'm OK. I was surprised when I read the letter. And I felt bad that I hadn't read it sooner. But I think Jo was respecting his wishes and probably waiting for us to come to her. He's already gone, so it's not like I can change anything." It struck Lex as odd, right in the moment that he could be so accepting of this small deception, forgiving. There'd been so much. In comparison with the withholding of information about his daughter, it probably should have mattered more. He imagined Pete would feel this one more than he. He'd been gone for so long and, in retrospect, so focused on his life and his wants, that it had been so easy for his parents to keep things from him. He never asked. In all his desire to be who he was, he could now admit that he was selfish. There'd really been no room for anyone else's problems or ego in his life.

If Lu thought his explanation odd in any way, she didn't mention it.

"In the list of discoveries that I've uncovered in the last year, this is just part of it. But finding out about Nina and you, it's just what it is." Lex paused. "Am I an ass?"

"Sometimes," she said, smiling. When he pinched her, she jumped, laughing. "So hard to hear the truth," she teased.

He loved her like this. Relaxed, not tense, teasing him. He didn't want to turn the tide of the conversation, but he had to ask, because he couldn't operate in the dark anymore.

"What changed?"

She stopped smiling. "What do you mean?"

"Last night, you didn't want me anywhere near you. Now you've come to me. What's up?" He said it all as gently as he could. He could have let it go and maybe should have, but he wanted to have all the information this time.

Lu eyes flashed and he could see her assess him, see her make the same decision, and he wished she would let him in. She tried to step away from him, but he held on to her. A silent struggle ensued until Lex began to laugh and Lu followed.

"I'm stronger," he said matter-of-factly.

"Yeah, yeah, yeah," she responded, giving up the battle.

With the laughter lingering between them, Lex swooped in and kissed her. He intended it to be a quick, searing kiss. But once there, he didn't want to release her. She didn't fight him, merely opened up and let him in. Their arms tightening around each other, Lex pulled her closer and deepened the kiss, moving into her mouth. God, he loved kissing her. There was a tentative quality about her that made him feel all protective and worldly. He felt his smile against her mouth as he thought she would hate that he thought himself so much more sophisticated than she was. She pulled back.

"What's funny?" Lu asked, self-consciously.

Lex grinned. "Nothing. Just happy to be in your mouth again." A roguish lift of the side of his mouth preceded his sink back into the kiss. As he continued the onslaught, he began moving her toward the bed.

He wanted her so badly. He felt their destination as Lu halted abruptly, then he gently pushed her down onto the bed. She sat on the side, suddenly stiff and nervous.

"It's just me, Lu. We've been here before," he whispered as he lifted her under the shoulders and gently shoved her into the middle of the bed so he could have better access. Coming down on top of her, he went into coaxing mode because he could tell her nerves were getting the best of her. Moving her hands above her head and holding her wrists, he moved his right hand to her stomach, bared by her uplifted arms. Lightly tracing her navel, he grinned broadly at her when her muscles tensed. "Still ticklish here, huh?" he asked, teasing her. "Where else? Oh yeah, collarbone," he proclaimed as he moved his hand up, inside her sweater and traced her left collarbone, feeling her squirm against him, rubbing him in all the right places. When a reluctant giggle escaped from her lips, he moved in and swallowed it with his mouth.

He worked his way down her body, claiming his spot on her neck while leaving her collarbone in favor of her breast. Stopping, he moved his hands down and pulled her sweater up, over her head as she complied, helping him. In her most aggressive move yet, she removed his shirt at the same time, then watched him pull his undershirt over his head, baring his amazing body. He raised his eyebrow, as if saying, "Like what you see?"

Lu met his eyes. "I've had better," she said mischievously.

Lex laughed. "Oh really?" he teased before dropping his head and surrounding her still bra-clad nipple in his mouth and pulling. At her gasp, he merely smiled, his mouth still at her breast. "Guess I'll have to work really hard then, huh?" Then he removed her bra, pushed her back and gave all his attention over to her. As he licked and sucked his way down her body, she writhed and moaned, telling him what she liked and didn't. When he couldn't wait any longer, he got up and removed both sets of pants. When she was naked, he dropped between her legs and kissed her inner thigh, running his finger through her wetness. His tongue darted out, claiming her.

"Lex," she gasped, "you feel so good."

Driven on by her praise, he moved her legs farther apart and, with his fingers and tongue, pulled out a most magnificent orgasm whose breathy moans and groans he swallowed with his Lu-filled mouth. Standing, he left her. Lu's eyes popped open as she followed his movements to the bathroom, watching his amazing athlete's body, tatted up with artful works, lithely walk away, then turn back toward her. She tracked him and the heat of her gaze made him harder and more needy than he ever remembered being.

"Hey, beautiful," he murmured as he put on a condom and fitted his body to hers.

"Hey there, yourself," she said, smiling.

"I'm not quite done with you," he said, before he leaned down and kissed her. She laced her fingers in his hair and kept his head in place as she deepened his kiss. Then she let her hands appreciate his body, moving over his back and amazing ass before moving her legs around him, surrounding him with her heat. He entered her quickly and deeply, pulling yet another moan from her mouth. He broke the kiss and moved away from her so that he could watch her. This time, as he moved in and out of her, their eyes were locked. When the second orgasm claimed her, she didn't turn away. Instead she looked up at him and let go of every inhibition and doubt, riding the wave of pleasure while falling more deeply in love. He gazed at her, feeling her body milk his, seeing her let go, before he followed her.

Not wanting to leave her warmth, Lex stayed where he was, his weight still on her, while he came back to earth. Kissing her neck, he pulled out of her and rolled over, bringing her with him so that she was on top. He stroked her back, his hand gliding down and up her body, leaving a trail of heat wherever he touched. Kissing the top of her head, he said, "You are amazing, Lulu."

He felt her smile before she said, "You know I hate that."

"You do?"

She pinched his chest.

"Ouch. So vindictive," he laughed while grabbing and rubbing her ass, both punishing and worshipping her. "You know how competitive I am."

Moving her hand, she found his nipple and pulled it, then rubbed it between her thumb and index finger.

Groaning, he reciprocated. In his fastest recovery time ever, he was buried deep inside of her again, wringing responses from both of them he would have thought they were too tired to produce. They fell asleep, wrapped around each other, savoring their closeness and time.

⌒

Lex woke with a start and looked at the clock. Panicked, he shook Lu awake.

"Babe," he whispered near her ear, "wake up. We have to put presents out."

Bolting upright, Lu glanced at the clock. "Shit," she muttered before grabbing Lex's T-shirt and pulling it over her head.

They hurried to put Nina's presents under the tree, attempting to preserve the few remaining Christmases that equaled Santa. When they'd finished, giggling the whole time, they returned to Lex's room. He watched as Lu gathered her clothes and headed for his door.

He lightly grabbed her arm. "Where are you going?" he asked, even though he knew the answer. But he wanted her to tell him what she was doing.

"To my room." She walked toward him and planted a kiss on his cheek. "This," she said, moving her hand between them, "this is too complicated for Nina."

"We're her parents. How is that complicated?" he asked, trying to hold on to his irrational fear that this was it for them.

Lu looked at him, sadness in her blue depths. "Lex. We can't. She won't understand."

He returned her stare. "So, that's it?"

She sighed. "What is it you want, Lex?"

He hesitated. He wanted to tell her that he wanted her, them, a family. But she saw his hesitation and he could see her read it wrong. "I want you."

"But don't you see how bad that would be? What will happen to Nina when you don't want me anymore?"

Frustrated, he ran his hand through his hair. "What makes you think I won't want you?"

She rolled her eyes. "Come on, Lex, we need to be honest with each other. We can't pretend to be a family with Nina. She's already had to deal with too much this year." Lu paused, clutching her clothes more tightly in her hands, searching for a way to say what she needed to say. "She has to come first, Lex. I need to do what is right for her, even if it's at odds with what I want. I won't be my mother."

That last sentence summed it up for him. But he wasn't done fighting.

"I love you, Lu." He saw her eyes widen with a momentary spark of joy before she shut it down.

She offered him a sad smile. "Lex, you may love the idea of me, but I'm not sure you know what it means to love. I don't mean to be insulting. But the only person you've truly loved is yourself. It's only ever been about you. Please understand that I can't put Nina through my heartbreak. She was too young, but this time she'd remember. And I won't go back there—not even for you." She walked toward him and placed one hand on his cheek. "I'll always love you, Lex. But I can't love you more than I love her." She kissed his lips, lingering for a moment before she pulled away and walked out of his room.

Of all that had happened to him, that little speech hurt the most. He stood in the same spot for a long time, wondering what he could do to change their circumstance. Powerless, he walked back onto the balcony, gazing out into the vast sea, searching for perspective.

42

"I want to punch you!" Willa said to Lu, standing over her threateningly, while Lu sat patiently in front of her at the breakfast table following Christmas morning.

"You are one to talk," Lu retorted, rolling her eyes. "Seriously?"

"Why are you throwing this away? This is what you've dreamed of since you were eight. And in earnest since he left. Why are you fighting this?"

Lu picked up the mimosa glistening in front of her and took a delicate sip, trying to not look at Willa in her outraged glory. Slow always frustrated Willa, and right now Lu was all about that. She took another sip, pretending to contemplate Willa's questions. "Do we have any more champagne?" she asked innocently.

Sparks flew from Willa's eyes as she scoffed and headed to the kitchen. She came back with a bottle of champagne and a pitcher of orange juice. Without saying a word, she poured equal amounts into Lu's glass, then banged each onto the table, making the glass tilt precariously, forcing Lu to reach out and grab it.

"Temper, temper, Will."

Willa sat unceremoniously in front of Lu and leaned forward so she was right in her face. "He loves you, Lu. How can you not see that?"

Lu couldn't understand how they had ended up having the conversation. Christmas morning had actually been glorious. It may have been the alcohol as Lex had Bloody Marys waiting for everyone when they arrived. Who knew he was such a master host? Nina had buzzed around, acting as Santa's elf, passing out gifts, and tearing into hers. The only tension-filled moment came when Nina handed Lu a present from Lex—but she was fairly certain she was the only one who noticed it. And, OK, maybe Willa. Then Lex, Pete, and Nina rushed to get the parents to the airport, leaving Lu alone with her bitch of a sister.

"Who are you and what have you done with that bitch who used to hate Lex?" Lu asked again, drinking her mimosa, working her way toward drunk.

Willa's eyes gleamed hot. Grabbing Lu's wrist, she shook it in front of her face. Lu tried hard not to look at the bracelet he'd bought her. The bracelet suited her so well it made her head hurt. Fucking bastard had to be good at gift giving too. With disgust, Willa pushed Lu's arm away and sat back down, letting her head hit the table, telling the tale of her frustration.

"The question is who are you and what have you done with my fairy-tale believing, holding a torch for a man for nine years, pathetic brainiac of a sister."

Lu rolled her eyes again. "For real, Will, why are you championing him?"

"Championing? I hate when you use your SAT words." She looked away then back to Lu. "I don't know. Probably that night he stayed at my house."

"Oh, yes, the mystery night. The night neither one of you feels the need to talk to me about."

"Yes, that night. We spent a lot of time talking. About everything, Pete, Mr. P., Jo, Mom. We avoided talking about you for most of the night. Then we couldn't avoid it anymore. I told him how much I hated what he did to you that day—even though you never really came clean about what happened. The thing was, Lu, he hated it worse than I did. Once I knew that, the mad just melted away. He's alone and lonely.

Trying to be a good father to a child that's had nine years without him. He just wasn't who I thought he was. So, yes, I guess I am 'championing' with air quotes—him."

They were both quiet for a while, Lu working on her drunk and Willa nursing her mad.

Willa hated quiet in the middle of a fight. It was like being in a sprint but stopping to polish your nails, only to finish the sprint later. It wasn't how she played it. Lu smiled, thinking that she'd love to be there to see Pete and Willa fight. She thought it would be a damn trip.

"I just don't understand. This is what you've wanted. Why are you holding back now?" Willa's question was earnest and heartfelt, and as much as Lu enjoyed antagonizing her every once in a while, she couldn't block out sincere Willa.

"I don't know how to do it, Will. He's everything I remember, but so much more. Of course I love him, but I don't think I can control it. I feel like I would spiral into an abyss of Lex and lose myself in him. Even with Nina anchoring me, I don't think I can be with him and hold on to everything else. And what happens when he leaves me the next time? I don't know that I could face it. Imagine how interconnected we all are now. What would happen when we aren't together? It would affect everyone and everything I love. The only way I can manage is to stay away." Lu felt embarrassed admitting it to Willa, knowing Willa was more like their mother, scoffing in the face of romance.

"Why are you convinced he'd leave you?"

"He's Lex Pellitteri, for God's sake!"

"And?"

"And have you seen the women in his serial-dating list? They're these amazingly beautiful women. I'm just me."

Willa groaned. "You sound like an insecure sixteen-year-old. Get over yourself."

And she's back, Lu thought.

"Look, Lu, I'm not a mother. And I can see the concerns for Nina and her getting confused and the desire to protect her. Even though you didn't include that in your little pity party. You two were made for each other. When God was handing out soul mates, you two were in the front of the line. You with him is a much better version of Lu. So you need to get your shit together. Don't get on that plane in the morning without talking to him again. Don't let him walk away this time. Because this time, you won't have anyone to blame but yourself."

Willa got up from the table. Picking up the debris as she went, she headed back into the kitchen.

Lu dropped her head to the table wishing she'd never opened her mouth. She rolled her head to the side and lifted her wrist, studying the unexpected Christmas present from Lex. The bracelet wrapped around her wrist several times and finally joined at a clasp buried in its wrappings. The stones alternated blue and green, a testament, she knew, to the color of their eyes. It was beautiful and delicate. She could hardly acknowledge him when she'd opened it. But she'd put it on immediately, and now it was a constant reminder of him. Groaning, she stayed like that, so lost in thought that she didn't hear Willa approach her again.

"Just so we're clear," Willa said, startling Lu, who sat up to look at her sister, "the Lex I see, the one that I like so much, has everything to do with you. I know I said you are a better version with him around. But the only version of him I like is that one I see when he is basking in your presence. Just so we're clear." With that she left Lu alone again, head on table, attempting to figure out her life.

Nina and the boys returned late in the afternoon to a quiet house. Lu had long since succumbed to an alcohol-induced nap, and Willa had retired to her room to give Lu some space. Once home, though, a flurry of activity began as they had to start packing and cleaning up the house. The airport run the next day would be far more extensive as they all would be heading out. Lu and Willa to London; Pete back home; Lex and Nina, along with Nina's nanny, to a series of games. They reconvened for dinner, then headed off again to their own courts. Willa and Pete huddled together in his room. Lu and Nina spent their time packing and talking, because they wouldn't be reunited for a week. Lex sequestered himself in his room.

Once Lu put Nina to bed, she attempted to read. But with scenes from last night scrolling through her head and Willa's talk earlier in the day bouncing around, she was restless and frustrated. Throwing her book down on the bed, she literally kicked her feet, engaging in her own little temper tantrum. When a knock sounded at her door, she straightened up guiltily.

Another knock. "Lu, you awake," Lex whispered at her door.

Getting up, she went to let him in.

"Are you OK?" he asked, taking in her flushed cheeks.

So happy that X-ray vision wasn't a reality, she nodded, then opened the door more fully to allow him to come in.

He eyed her warily, knowing she was up to something. But when no explanation was forthcoming, he continued inside. He thrust some papers toward her.

"What's this?" she inquired, without taking the time to look at it.

"Itinerary for the next week. Cities, hotels we are scheduled to stay at, game schedule. Everything you should need to know where Nina is," he said proudly.

Lu smiled. "Thank you. But I'm not worried."

"I am," he admitted. "Almost ten days with her without any buffers."

"You'll have Mrs. Auberly," Lu reminded him.

"I know. But she won't have you."

He looked nervous and Lu fell just a little bit more. "You are familiar to her now," she said gently. "You'll be fine."

He took a deep breath, then nodded. "If you say so."

"I say so," she said.

"All right. See you in the morning," he said.

She nodded and let him walk to the door. As he left, she sat heavily on the bed, her head pounding from the mixture of a midafternoon nap and mimosas. She wanted to follow him, wanted to tackle him and take him inside of her, wanted to let go and love him with everything she had. Which is why she stayed in her room

By mutual agreement, they'd all decided to get up at six. With their flight times staggered slightly, they would all travel to the airport together—the last hurrah in Lex's Christmas surprise. He knew he'd set his iPhone to wake him up, but it had been one of the those nights when he'd woken every hour, flipped over, grabbed his phone, checked the time, groaned, and repeated. At five, he finally got up, did a final walk-through of his room and the rest of the house, turned on the coffee, and stood restlessly in the living room, waiting for everyone else to wake up. His restlessness had a name—Lu. While they would continue to see each other for Nina exchanges, he acknowledged that they wouldn't be in the same space again. It agitated him. He didn't feel comfortable in his skin. Pacing a hole in the floor, he turned and walked to her room.

Standing outside her door, he hesitated. He couldn't figure out what else he needed to do. He thought he understood the reasons she held back, but in the dark of night, they sounded like hollow excuses. Maybe he needed to be clearer. Resting his head on the door, he couldn't wait any longer. Decision made, he pushed open the door with a bit too much force and stumbled in as the door bumped and banged off the wall.

He'd expected Lu to jump or startle awake, but instead he met her blue eyes, illuminated by the light of the door. He stood awkwardly in the doorway, gazing uncomfortably at her.

"Couldn't sleep?" she quipped.

"You either?" he asked.

"Nah. Been up since about three." But it hadn't driven her out of her bed as his energy had. "Been laying here hoping I'd eventually fall asleep."

"Been up for a while," he offered. Lu continued to lie there, on her stomach, but she'd propped her head on her hands.

"I figured. You're showered and dressed and I smell coffee."

"Yeah." He didn't move, feeling more unsure of himself than he'd ever remembered feeling.

"Are you going to stand in the doorway or come in?" she asked.

"I'm deciding," he answered truthfully.

"What's going on, Lex?" she asked, pushing up on her bed so that she was sitting crisscross applesauce.

His hand found the door that'd run away from him and he shut it gently behind him. Walking to the bed, he sat down near her but without invading her space. He looked over at her and grinned. Without thinking anymore, he leaned over and kissed her hard. She kissed him back and dug her fingers in his too-long hair, holding him close. He pulled away from her but continued to hold her face in both hands.

"Look, I want us to have a chance. Can we take things slow and see what happens?" Lex said.

She reached up and pulled his hands away from her face. She jumped off the bed and ran into her bathroom. He heard the sink run and grinned.

"Really," he teased when she returned, "you had to brush your teeth?"

Looking slightly embarrassed she grinned shyly. "Yes. If we are going to be talking this close to one another."

He rolled his eyes. "Answer me."

"Ugh, Lex, why are you pushing this?" Her grin replaced by a look of dismay, she ran her hands nervously through her hair.

"Seriously, Lu? Since our parent-teacher conference, I haven't been able to think about anything else. I want to be part of your life and not just as a parent. I don't know how else to tell you. I love you. And I know you love me. I can feel it when you kiss me. I want a chance for us to be a family." He saw her eyes widen, and he knew she wanted to grab hold, but she continued to hold back.

"Lex, it's been a crazy year for you. You lost your dad. You said yourself you feel like you've missed out on something. There are too many reasons not to do it right now. I can't be a mistake that you regret later. We have too much between us. Please, just let this be."

If she'd tried to convince him that she didn't love him, he would have been able to fight her. He'd have kissed her into oblivion or held her until she capitulated. But her reasons, he could understand. He knew his feelings weren't going to change, but she didn't have that faith in him. While he wanted to be angry with her, he felt resigned.

"Look, I'm going to let this go for now. But it's not going away. And in one or two or three years, when I still feel the same way and I come back to you, you are going to regret that you let this time get away. We've already lost nine years. How much more are you willing to lose?"

He watched her, hoping it would sink in, wanting her to change her mind. But she didn't. She merely continued to stare at him before taking a deep breath and turning away from him.

"I need to shower." She got up from the bed and left him sitting there.

Lex waited until he heard the shower running. Then he left the room.

43

The last to leave the field, Lex entered the tunnel, the exhilaration of the win pounding through him, the adrenaline rush shaking its way out. He thought he saw her standing at the threshold of the tunnel waiting for him. Shaking his head to dispel the hopeful illusion, he made his way to the locker room. Thus had been his existence recently, since that painfully slow good-bye in the airport. His brain conjured her at odd moments. Not alone times; rather, in the midst of a game, in the crowd at the stadium, at a bar with his teammates—all places she would never appear. Wishful thinking, he knew. He thought his parting words would convince her, break through her scared. But somehow his abandonment of her at seventeen stood out greater in her mind than his love for her at twenty-six.

He accepted his teammates' congratulatory handshakes and pats on the back before he showered. Donning jeans, a long-sleeved T-shirt and slides, he grabbed his bag, heading back out into the now-empty tunnel. Except it wasn't empty. Standing directly in the spot he'd imagined her, Lu leaned against the wall. He often found himself startled by the woman who'd grown from the little girl with the serious blue eyes, the too-old soul, and the super-smart brain. Enveloped in a black midlength coat, a scarf that covered most of her neck and face and a pair of knee-length boots, she resembled an Alaskan bank robber. He almost blinked but knew that the vision wouldn't disappear this time.

He sauntered toward her, swag from the game making him cockier than normal. Only in the face of Lu did he feel any vulnerability.

"Everything OK?" he asked, eyebrow raised, grin in place.

She smiled because she found it hard not to smile in his presence. Nodding, she said, "Yes, Nina is good and all is well."

Although he knew the answer, he couldn't resist teasing her. "Here with Malcolm?"

He watched her eyes grow wide before she realized he was messing with her. "I thought I could treat you to a postgame meal. If memory serves, you are always ravenous after a game."

"You and your SAT words . . ." Shaking his head, he reached a hand out to her. "What'd you have in mind?"

"Steak?"

"God, I love you," he said, not in a serious, declaration sort of way but in a way that made Lu giggle as she took his hand.

They didn't say much on the ride. Of course they talked about and discussed Nina. Lex had recently disciplined her for the first time and had survived almost unscathed but admitted to Lu that he'd had a hard time resisting the tears. "I put my earbuds in and blasted Jack Johnson so that I wouldn't have to hear it."

Rolling her eyes, she assured him it would get easier.

After they plowed through dinner without any discussion of her unexpected appearance, Lex's patience began to wane, but he continued to wait. When the waiter brought them both coffee—he had never been able to get accustomed to tea—he sat back.

"What's up, Lu?"

Toying with her coffee cup, she remained silent.

Frustrated, Lex signaled the waiter, requesting their check. When he arrived, however, Lu aborted his attempt to place the check down.

"Can I have a Stoli and tonic with lemon? And then you can cash us out." She handed him her credit card and looked at Lex. "My invitation. My treat."

Lex didn't argue. Again he waited. The high from the game and the amazing meal worked against him and he started to get tired. Moving forward, he leaned his forearms on the table, taking away some of her space. "I'm getting tired and my patience is ebbing. I know you have something you want to talk about. It didn't used to be this hard to get you to tell me what you are thinking." There. Gauntlet thrown.

"What makes you think we can do this?" she asked, taking him by surprise.

"Do what?" he asked, teasing her. At her eye rolling, he continued. "I'm not going to make this easy, Louisa May."

"How utterly surprising," she murmured, smiling. "What makes you think we can make this work?" At his raised eyebrow, she added, "You and me, together."

"Ah, that wasn't so hard."

The waiter arrived with Lu's drink and the check. Signing the slip and putting her credit card away allowed her to avoid his gaze. But zipping up her purse, she stored it on the back of her chair and turned to face him. "We don't even know each other. You're suggesting we just pick up and do what, date? What happens when we decide we don't want to date anymore? It's not just you and me in this anymore. It would affect Nina."

Part of him was disappointed. This was the same argument they'd already had. He'd offered assurances, but she wasn't buying it, which meant that even though she showed up tonight, she wasn't any closer to capitulating.

"What do you want to know, Lu?"

Her eyebrows drew together. "What do you mean?"

"You said we don't even know each other. What don't you know?"

At her surprised expression, he sighed. "You want to know how much money I make?" he asked. He knew this would piss her off, but they had to start somewhere.

"*No!* I don't care about your money."

"I know. See, I know that about you because you haven't cashed one fucking check that I've sent for child support. But just so we're clear, and in the name of full disclosure, I make a lot of money. My last three-year contract was worth about twenty million dollars. I don't expect that my new one, which will be negotiated soon, will be any less. I also make some money for endorsements, but since I'm picky about that, I have only ever put my name on one product. I always felt that the more I endorsed, the cheaper the endorsement. I give approximately twenty percent of what I make to a secret trust"—he winked at her—"which you now know about. About thirty-five percent of it I give to charity—Doctors Without Borders is my favorite, but I also give to a number of schools for pregnant teenagers in the U.S." When her eyes welled up, he chased it away with his next statement. "I haven't been with another woman since I was with you in May. Absolutely no interest." On the heels of that statement, he continued. "I still love to play soccer and would play for free if they stopped paying me. When I'm done, though, or when my level of play starts to drop off, I will stop. I won't stick around. I definitely want to follow in Malcolm Helms's footsteps, because he's done everything right. Which means I'd like to stay here, but if it wasn't working for you or Nina, I'd go wherever we needed to go."

Lu sat stunned. Not really knowing what to say.

"Here's the other thing, Lu: I *do* know you. I know that you finished undergrad at twenty, even with a break for childbirth. You did a joint master's and doctorate program, which you finished in record time. You wrote a proposal to the athletic department regarding your research, and they allowed you to work with their football team. During that time, you also approached the NFL with your results at the collegiate level, and they requested that you work with their teams. So by the time you were twenty-five, you were making money consulting, which you used to support you and Nina, so you could stop taking money from your parents. I know that you still embarrass rather easily, which is a fucking blast for me, and that when I see you mothering Nina, it stops my heart. I've loved you since I was eight. It's never waned. It was buried for a while, but when you walked back into my life, it all was there, waiting for you. Now we can keep arguing and you can keep running away from me, but when you finally start to trust me you will have wasted more time."

Sitting back in his chair, Lex studied her. She didn't say anything while she finished her drink. Then she stood up and held out her hand.

He eyed her warily, raising his eyebrow, expecting something.

"Let's go."

He stayed in his chair. "Where are we going?"

"Home," she said, matter-of-factly, as if he hadn't just monologued for her.

"That's it?" he asked. "You have nothing for me?"

She smiled tentatively. "I hope I wasn't too presumptuous, but I asked Mrs. Auberly to watch Nina tonight."

He shot her the death glare, at which she laughed, the Lu laugh, which made his heart clench.

"You've got nothing on Dr. J.," she said. She must have realized that his calm façade was really just that—a façade. "So Mrs. Auberly and Nina are at your house."

He almost smiled. "My house?"

"Yeah. I figured I wouldn't want to leave you in the middle of the night, so it seemed the best solution."

Standing, he took her hand and pulled her in to him. "Awfully presumptuous of you."

She raised both her eyebrows, "You think?" she said, smiling.

"Yeah. It was. You have something to say to me?"

Her smile faded. "I love you, AJ."

"That's my girl," he said, right before he kissed her.

Acknowledgments

I've been writing stories all of my life. I even have a first novel, still sitting on my desk, with all sorts of editing left to be done. But, then I got married and had children. Finding time to write became difficult. A really good friend of mine told me about National Novel Writing Month. I missed it in 2011, but marked my calendar for November of 2012. Lex and Lu had already taken up residence in my brain—but forcing myself to sit down everyday and meet a quota gave me the extra push I needed to write this book. I loved meeting my word requirement and watching my characters come to life. I liked it so much that I did it again in November 2013. I can honestly say that without the National Novel Writing Month, I may never have taken the time to write this story.

They say that writing it is the hardest part. And maybe that's true, but for me everything that comes after it is overwhelming and intimidating. I may never have taken the next step if it wasn't for my friend Ken. When I sent him the file, I was extremely nervous. He's definitely not a romance novel guy. But he read it and liked it and pushed me to do something with it. His belief in me, and what I could do, made me feel like I could actually get it published. As soon as he finished it, he was on the phone reaching out to Lee Gordon. Before I knew it, I was calling someone I didn't know, asking him to point me in the right direction. When I asked Ken what I was supposed to say to Lee, his response was, "I wrote this awesome book and I want to get it published." Thanks to Ken and Lee, I was submitting my book for consideration the next week. Ken, I feel some sort of way about what you did for me.

The idea for Lex and Lu came about during a gathering of our neighborhood supper club and our families. Watching all of the kids run around and interact, it seems natural that somewhere along the way some of these children, who have known each other most of their lives, will fall in love. Suddenly, Lex and Lu were born. Thank you to the amazing women who took me in: Cathy, Leah, Heidi, Evette, Cori, Stephanie, Janice, Shelly, Chris, Stephani. Without your acceptance of our family into yours, this story would never have made it to the page.

I have to give my most heartfelt shout out to my GIRLS. It's not the traditional beta group—but it totally worked for me. They received my work every Monday, which made Tuesday my favorite day because they were always quick to respond—for better or worse. Brandi, Patti, Jen and Gwen, I love you all dearly. There's no way this happens without love, support, critique, and praise. And to my more-than-best friend Nhatle, thank you for always being there for me and my children.

Thank you to my team at Greenleaf Book Group, LLC. Hobbs, who brought me in; Bryan, who managed my project; Kim, my cover designer; and Amber, Elizabeth, and Don, who had the task of editing. I appreciate all of the help and guidance throughout the process.

I've watched my parents support us in whatever endeavors we've embarked on. I've always stayed on the straight and narrow, but I realize now that without their ever-present belief in our ability to do whatever we think we can do, I wouldn't have taken this leap of faith. I hope that I can be the same for my children so that they have the courage to be who they are.

Finally to my non-reading husband, Fatty. You are the perfect partner, an amazing father, the love of my life. Thanks for helping me find the time to do what I do.